MURDER'S SNARE

Also by Paul Doherty

The Margaret Beaufort mysteries

DARK QUEEN RISING *
DARK QUEEN WAITING *
DARK QUEEN WATCHING *
DARK QUEEN WARY *

The Brother Athelstan mysteries

THE ANGER OF GOD
BY MURDER'S BRIGHT LIGHT
THE HOUSE OF CROWS
THE ASSASSIN'S RIDDLE
THE DEVIL'S DOMAIN
THE FIELD OF BLOOD
THE HOUSE OF SHADOWS
BLOODSTONE *
THE STRAW MEN *
CANDLE FLAME *
THE BOOK OF FIRES *
THE HERALD OF HELL *
THE GREAT REVOLT *
A PILGRIMAGE TO MURDER *
THE MANSIONS OF MURDER *
THE GODLESS *
THE STONE OF DESTINY *
THE HANGING TREE *
MURDER MOST TREASONABLE *

The Canterbury Tales mysteries

AN ANCIENT EVIL
A TAPESTRY OF MURDERS
A TOURNAMENT OF MURDERS
GHOSTLY MURDERS
THE HANGMAN'S HYMN
A HAUNT OF MURDER
THE MIDNIGHT MAN *

* *available from Severn House*

MURDER'S SNARE

Paul Doherty

SEVERN
HOUSE

First world edition published in Great Britain and the USA in 2024
by Severn House, an imprint of Canongate Books Ltd,
14 High Street, Edinburgh EH1 1TE.

severnhouse.com

British Library Cataloguing-in-Publication Data
A CIP catalogue record for this title is available from the British Library.

ISBN-13: 978-1-4483-1310-5 (cased)
ISBN-13: 978-1-4483-1311-2 (e-book)

All Severn House titles are printed on acid-free paper.

MIX
Paper | Supporting
responsible forestry
FSC
www.fsc.org FSC® C013056

Typeset by Palimpsest Book Production Ltd., Falkirk,
Stirlingshire, Scotland.
Printed and bound in Great Britain by TJ Books,
Padstow, Cornwall.

Praise for the Brother Athelstan medieval mysteries

"This long-running series has yet to show signs of slowing down"
Publishers Weekly on *Murder Most Treasonable*

"Unsettling historical detail enhances a story of hate, revenge, and multiple murders"
Kirkus Reviews on *Murder Most Treasonable*

"Doherty doles out clues shrewdly and decorates the narrative with his characteristically sharp period details"
Publishers Weekly on *Murder Most Treasonable*

"Hair-raising descriptions of life in the Middle Ages enhance a challenging puzzle"
Kirkus Reviews on *The Hanging Tree*

"A tortuous, fascinating historical mystery"
Kirkus Reviews on *The Stone of Destiny*

"With consummate skill and pacing, Doherty answers the plot's mysteries in a series of startling revelations"
Publishers Weekly on *The Stone of Destiny*

"Outstanding . . . Doherty keeps the action brisk, the crimes baffling, and the deductions and solutions fair"
Publishers Weekly Starred Review of *The Godless*

"Doherty displays exceptional narrative flair as he brings the often-squalid sights, sounds, and smells of medieval London to life"
Booklist on *The Godless*

"Conjuring up medieval London in all its grime and glory, Doherty keeps readers guessing and the pages turning with another intricately plotted whodunit"
Booklist on *The Mansions of Murder*

About the author

The author of more than eighty highly acclaimed historical mysteries, **Paul Doherty** studied History at Liverpool and Oxford Universities, and is now headmaster of a school in Essex. He lives with his family in north-east London.

www.paulcdoherty.com

Dedicated to Luis Moniz of Chingford, a most fervent reader of my novels. Many thanks to him and his lovely wife Louise for their support and encouragement.

HISTORICAL NOTE

'Ancient sins must be confronted and absolved. Blood spilt in anger cries to Heaven for justice.' This warning from the Middle Ages was certainly true of France in the late 1380s. The kingdom had been wracked by war and suffered the hideous depredations of chevauchees organized by the English Crown.

Edward III and his son, the Black Prince, had truly destroyed the armies of France, greatly depleting the ranks of its nobles at battles such as Crecy and Poitiers. Many cities and towns in France had their fighting forces sorely depleted, which left them vulnerable to further English attacks. Free Companies were formed by English Milords and these rode across Normandy with one aim in mind: to seize as much booty as possible. Towns and villages, monasteries and abbeys, were pillaged and plundered. The lure of easy profit attracted men steeped in violence to join the stream of invaders into France. Massacres took place, yet, in the end, the English were checked and slowly but surely driven out of France. However, 'Ancient sins must be confronted and absolved. Blood spilt in anger cries to Heaven for justice!' And so we begin . . .

PROLOGUES

Avranches, Normandy 1358

'The snares of death surround me, the traps of Hell gape at me.'

Sir Edmund Lacey, Knight Banneret, reined in his great warhorse and stared around at the hideous scene he and his comrades had created. Avranches, a prosperous village close to the main road from Troyes to Paris, had been truly devastated. Lacey's comrades, who formed the Free Company of the 'Via Crucis – the Way of the Cross', had swept into Avranches like the riders from the Apocalypse. They had already sacked the manor a mile beyond the village – that raid had been a spectacular success. The merchant prince who lived there had been most cooperative after he had been lashed to a ceiling beam in his magnificent hall with a fire lit beneath his naked feet. He had confessed. A torrent of desperate words to ensure his wife and children did not suffer the same punishment. He had spoken the truth and the 'Via Crucis' squires, Gumblat and Henshaw, had broken into the secret place behind the tabernacle in the manor chapel. They had discovered a coffer brimming with gold pieces. Sir Oliver Ingham, Commander of the 'Via Crucis', had seized the coins as the spoils of war – they truly were. The coffer was broad and deep, the gold coined in the finest royal mint in Paris. Ingham had seized the treasure and ordered the manor lord to be released, then he and his company had galloped like the furies into the village.

Lacey fought to control his great warhorse. The animal was agitated. Iron-edged hooves scraping the cobbles. Head swinging to the left and right as the horse snorted its own agitation at the world crumbling around it. In a word, Avranches had burst into flames. Searing, scarring fire leapt up from buildings as if hungry to devastate more. The village was caught up in a ferocious red storm made even more terrifying by the gathering dusk. Death had set up camp, placed its standards and unfurled its banners in that village. Avranches would be totally destroyed. Corpses swung in the breeze. Fresh blood lapped across the cobbles to be nuzzled and drunk by wandering dogs and pigs. More dead hung from the open windows of different houses. The village had been transformed from a place of green calmness into a slaughter yard. Screams and cries pierced the hellish din of the roaring fires and the crashing collapse of timber and stone. Lacey was sick of it all. He had journeyed to France with his comrades to seize wealth and take hostages for ransom; he would then send them back to their families, if they paid the right price. He had not come for this: the wholesale slaughter and massacre of innocents.

'Sir Edmund, Sir Edmund!' Squire Gumblat cantered out of the smoke-riddled darkness. He pulled down the visor which covered the lower half of his face.

'Well, what is it, Gumblat?'

'Don't you know, Sir Edmund? Lord Ingham is calling us in.' Lacey strained his hearing. He was about to question Gumblat when the braying of a hunting horn cut through the clamour and din. It was repeated twice, the sign for the Company to muster. Lacey gathered the reins of his horse and followed Gumblat down the high street, turning into the parish church enclosure. This was no longer a place of prayer and peace. The brick curtain wall arounds God's Acre had, in places, been toppled over, along with gravestones, funeral plinths and memorial crosses. The front of the ancient wooden church was bathed in the light of torches. Ingham had ordered these to be lit and tossed on to the steps leading up to the main door of the church. The dancing flames brought to life the ugly gargoyle faces carved in the ancient wood around the door. Ingham had reined in just beyond bowshot from the church. He sat like a statue staring into the night with his comitatus spread in a line behind him. Lacey knew that Ingham had a well-deserved reputation for hating priests and churches. He had, according to rumour, once crucified a priest to his church door. He would burn any church he came across as he had here in Avranches.

'Sir Oliver,' Gumblat called out. 'Sir Edmund is now here.'

Ingham did not turn; he just took off his gauntlet, raised a hand and snapped his fingers.

'The Emperor has spoken,' Lacey whispered and pushed his horse through the comitatus to rein in beside Ingham. 'Sir Oliver?'

Ingham turned, his harsh face all blood-splattered. 'A good day's hunting, eh?' Ingham slurred, raising the wineskin to splash into his mouth. 'Fine Bordeaux,' he breathed. Ingham thrust the stopper back and retied the wineskin to his saddle horn. 'A very good day indeed,' he murmured. 'That merchant's treasure must be close to a king's ransom, a veritable fortune. I tell you this, Lacey, we will finish the business here and ride for Boulogne. We will feast by the quayside then secure passage on some war cog bound for Dover or the Thames.'

'So why are we here?' Lacey pointed to the church.

'To finish business. This is a strange place; been here for centuries, I reckon. There's the main door then there's the Devil's door in the west transept. Both are heavily blocked. There must be treasure inside.'

'If it's so secure, why don't we just leave it there? Surely, we are done here, Sir Oliver? We have inflicted damage and seized a fortune others would only dream of. Let us be gone.'

'No,' Ingham retorted. 'No,' he repeated. 'There must be treasure inside and we have to finish the business. We lost good men today. Two of our own knights. Roger Clipsham and Hubert Falken.'

'We lose men, Sir Oliver.'

'Yes, but not here, not those. I intend to storm that church, seize what treasure they have and deal out punishment for the killers of our brethren.' He broke off as Henshaw, Ingham's second squire, came hurrying out of the dark.

'Sir Oliver,' he gasped, 'I have been around the church.'

'And?'

'Something has gone wrong; I can smell smoke and I heard screams from within.'

Lacey stared at the front of the church. His gaze was caught by thin trails of smoke curling through a lancet window above the door.

'Sir Oliver, I will check to see what's happening.' Not waiting for an answer, Lacey turned his horse and rode down the north side of the church. He still felt as if he had entered the domain of demons, a pit which housed hideous nightmares. The noise from the sacked village still echoed: the screams, the curses, the crashing and clattering destruction. A sharp night breeze carried sparks and tendrils of smoke. Lacey tried to ignore these as he rode the boundary of the church. At first, he thought Henshaw was wrong, but abruptly, like a demon bursting out of the dark, fire and smoke began to escape from the church. Tongues of flame licked at the few lancet windows and along the gap beneath the Devil's door. Lacey's horse was now truly restless as plumes of smoke began to bother it.

'What is wrong?' Sir Edmund shouted at the church, speaking in French as he stood high in his stirrups. Lacey repeated his question. He listened for a reply, and one came. A man shouted that they had trapped themselves inside. Lacey could only guess at what had happened. The villagers had fled to their church, barricaded themselves in, blocking all doors and any gap in the walls of their wooden chapel. Agitated and fearful, the villagers had also lit torches and candles. One or more of these must have fallen and the fire would spread quickly, almost leaping from one place to another. The pillars, walls and roof beams, together with the floor and furnishings, were probably of old dry wood which would ignite swiftly and burn fiercely. The conflagration must have erupted so rapidly. The barricades the villagers had built had now become a trap of their own making, though Lacey suspected Ingham may have had a hand in all this destruction. The flames were turning the place into a furnace. Smoke was now billowing through the roof tiles; the cries and screams grew louder. Lacey spurred his horse around to the back of the church. The church had only one large window. This was now open, the shutters flung back. A woman stood there screaming for help. Behind her a wall of flame. Lacey dismounted and stared up. He realized that the woman must have climbed on to a narrow choir loft which stood at the back of the church. She was shouting in a Norman patois which Lacey could understand. She was begging for help for her twin boys. She held these up against the fiery glow. Lacey searched about. He found a siege ladder, a simple pole with rungs on either side. He placed this against the window and climbed up, mindful of his horse milling around close to the ladder. The animal wanted to flee but had been trained to stay close to its master. Lacey continued to climb. As he reached the top of the ladder, the woman thrust one of her son's out of the window. Lacey, seizing the boy, went down a few steps, lowered the child down and placed him on the ground. He then went up to collect the second boy, who joined his brother on the grassy patch. Both boys seemed unscathed. They stood clutching each other, staring fearfully at their rescuer. Lacey climbed back up the ladder. He reached the window. The woman came towards him, but the fire roared up through the wooden floor of the choir loft, which crashed down, taking the woman with it. Lacey screamed at the heat as a host of flame roared up. He felt the wall of the church give way, then he was falling. The ladder crashed down on to the horse, felling it to the ground. Lacey hit the hard path, screaming at the pain in his legs, trying to soothe the burning flame wound to his face. He stared up into the night. His world was falling, as was he, into the deepening darkness.

Walton on the Naze December 1382

Malroad Manor stood in its own grounds on the wild heathland overlooking the Northern Seas, a few miles from the village of Walton, close to the Orwell estuary. A lonely, haunted place, but it suited Lord Philip Kyne, Lord of the Manor, formerly a knight in the old king's household as well as a member of the Free Company, the 'Via Crucis', which had campaigned so ruthlessly against the power of France in its pursuit of wealth. They had launched chevauchee after chevauchee from their fortress on the Garonne. He and his comrades, under the command of Lord Oliver Ingham, had pillaged and plundered to their hearts' content. Now Lord Kyne feasted 'high on the hog', as he put it, here in his lavishly furnished hall of Malroad Manor. On that particular day, the Feast of St Stephen, the night after Christmas, Kyne was determined to revel. Once the holy season had passed, he would look forward to the Easter festivals. Kyne, a widower, had invited his son and daughter together with other friends and relatives to join him in this great festival. He was particularly pleased that Roberta Swinerton had accepted his invitation; she was a buxom widow-woman who now managed one of the manor farms.

'Oh yes,' Kyne whispered to himself, staring down the high table to where mistress Roberta, golden hair all gleaming, was cradling a bejewelled goblet brimming with the best wine of Alsace. Kyne hoped to catch her eye but then startled as the double doors of his banqueting hall crashed back. A gaggle of servitors streamed into the hall, followed by a comitatus of men, all buckled for war, their faces hidden beneath black visors. The musicians from the choir loft were also herded in. The sinister visitors pushed their prisoners towards the dais.

'What is this?' Kyne sprang to his feet.

'Shut up.' One of the black-garbed assailants stepped forwards. He raised his arbalest and released a bolt which whirled just above Kyne's head to smack into the tapestry-covered wall behind him.

'Sit down,' the leader of the intruders exclaimed. 'Sit down and remain still, all of you.'

'Who are you?' Kyne clawed at his grey hair then let his fingers touch the old ugly scar beneath his right eye.

'Sit down, Lord Kyne, and I will inform you.'

The manor lord slumped back in his chair. He rubbed his stomach beneath the costly houppelande. Kyne, a seasoned warrior, was genuinely frightened. Something about this abrupt, sudden ambuscade chilled his soul to the marrow. For some uncanny reason, Kyne wondered if his past, and the trail of destruction he and others had caused through France, were catching up with him. All that sinful destruction! Little wonder other men he'd fought alongside had experienced such fears about the vengeance of God hunting them down. Quite a few members of the different Free Companies had entered the religious life or committed themselves to good works. Kyne certainly had not.

'And so,' Kyne murmured to himself, 'my sins will catch me out. Oh Lord have mercy.' Kyne's fears were soon justified. First the intruders demanded the truth about all the manor people, including servants. They wanted to be certain that they were all in the hall. Both Kyne and his steward assured the intruders that they were.

'Good.' The leader pointed at Matilda the Milkmaid. 'If you are lying, she dies immediately. Now, Sir Philip.' He paused as Kyne, in his throne-like chair, leaned towards him. The leader immediately raised his arbalest, sliding another bolt into the groove. 'Come down here, Sir Philip. Come quickly! Remember the verse from scripture "in the midst of life, we are in death"? We now truly are, as you will soon find out. So come, come!'

Once the manor lord had left the dais, he was seized and made to kneel, his hands tied behind his back. Kyne now accepted that the horrors of the past, the furies unleashed so many years ago, had eventually caught up with him here in his own manor on a winter's evening shortly after Christmas. These intruders were not mere wolfsheads, outlaws intent on sacking the manor. They had seized none of his goods or raised a finger against any of his household.

'The manor chaplain?' the leader demanded in a carrying voice.

'The manor chaplain?' he repeated.

Father Hubert, an old white-haired priest who'd held the benefice at Malroad since time immemorial, raised a hand and stumbled forward.

'I am here,' the chaplain quavered. 'Sirs, what do you intend?'

'Like you, Father, God's business. So, I do not fear over what I do for the Lord is the stronghold of my life. I am here to do His will, to show that the wages of sin are death.' The leader pointed to those of his retinue guarding Kyne. 'Take him outside to a solitary place. Father, hear his sins, shrive his soul, then come back here.'

Kyne was dragged from the hall, his escort pinioning him close. The leader of the invaders glanced around, nodding his approval at how calm, albeit fearful, the manor people had become. The rest of the assailants stood silently, heavy arbalests at the ready. Their leader walked on to the dais. He sat down in Kyne's chair, filled the manor lord's goblet to the brim and raised it in toast to his terrified audience.

'I wish you well,' he declared. 'You are prisoners, but please, for the love of God, do not even think of doing something rash or impetuous. I have my sworn men here, elsewhere in this manor as well as on the roads leading to it. Soon we will be gone. Trust me, until then the snares of death will be close about you.' The leader turned as the door crashed open. Kyne was dragged back into the centre of the hall and made to kneel. Father Hubert re-joined the rest. The old priest sat down on a bench, put his face in his hands and quietly sobbed.

'Well, well, well.' The leader of the intruders came around the table. He stepped off the dais and walked to stand over Kyne, who threw him a look of pure hate. 'Now, now.' The leader patted Kyne on the shoulder. 'When you go to be shrived at the mercy pew, do you ever mention the small nunnery of St Sulpice which overlooked a tributary of the Dordogne? A lovely quiet place for a convent of Benedictine nuns. Ten in all, six fully professed, four were novices. You remember surely? You had left your main battle group, the "Via Crucis". Anyway, you plundered that convent, stole the treasures of the house, as well as the purses of the novices, who'd brought their dowry in preparation for entering the convent as fully consecrated nuns. Those who came after your visit found nothing but charred smoking ruins, every chest and coffer smashed to the point of utter destruction. Now . . .' The leader broke off as he walked back on to the dais. He collected the goblet and returned to stand over Kyne. 'At first, for weeks really, no trace of these poor nuns could be found. Now the ladies themselves came from great and noble families: these families petitioned the French Crown for help to find their womenfolk. A most thorough search was organized. The corpses were eventually discovered in a deep marsh close to the convent.' The intruder pulled down his visor, drank from the goblet, then let it slip from his hand to bounce along the floor. 'A terrible sight, Philip. Corruption had already set in, but it was obvious that all had been abused before their murder. So, Sir Philip, that's why I came here tonight. Judgement! Vengeance! Justice! To prove scripture right, for what does it profit a man if he gains the whole world but suffers the loss of his immortal soul?' He leaned down. 'Do you have anything to say in your defence?'

Kyne just groaned.

'Very well.' The intruder stepped away and, as he did, he drew his double-edged war sword. Bracing himself, he swung the blade back followed by a clean slicing cut which severed Kyne's head. The still erect torso spouted blood before collapsing to the ground, whilst the head pumped more blood as it rolled like a ball to rest against a pillar. For a few heartbeats, the execution imposed a chilling silence which then erupted into screams, yells and curses. Mothers seized their children, turning their faces away from the gruesome abomination they had just witnessed. Some of Kyne's family and household surged towards the intruders but then fell back as crossbow bolts sang just above their heads. The leader shouted at one of his retainers, who raised a hunting horn and blew three sharp piercing blasts which created an uneasy, tense stillness. The leader then took a leather sack from one of his company and placed the severed head carefully within it. He then turned and bowed elegantly at the manor folk standing either side of the hall.

'Rest assured,' he declared, 'our business is finished here, and we shall be gone. However,' he walked over to the hour candle fixed in its spigot on the left side of the dais, 'you must remain here,' he declared in a ringing voice, 'until the flame bites the next red circle. Only then do you leave this place.' He kicked Kyne's blood-soaked torso. 'What happens to this is up to you.'

'And the head?' someone shouted.

'Oh, it will be raised high so all can see it and it will take in all with its long dead gaze.'

Two days later, just before the lights in the steeples of London's many churches were extinguished, Robert Burdon, Keeper of London Bridge, Chief Headsman in charge of the gates on which he would spike the heads of executed felons, was disturbed from his sleep by a loud rapping. This dwarf of a man was summoned from his broad bed in the upper chamber of his house built close to the shrine dedicated to St Thomas à Becket. Robert moved carefully so as not to awaken his wife and their brood of children who lay either side of them, a long row of sleepy babies. Robert checked the capped braziers lined up along the window wall.

Again, the rapping. Burdon, cursing under his breath, grabbed a small lantern and left the chamber, going carefully down the steps of the small landing. He first checked what Burdon called his workshop with its row of severed heads. All of these had been soaked in salt and brine, the scrawny hair combed, their faces washed and ready to be poled above the gates either side of London Bridge. Again, the insistent rapping on the door.

'By God's good grace,' Burdon breathed. 'I suspect who you are. I mean it's so early.'

Again, the rapping. Murmuring a prayer to St Thomas, Burdon drew back the bolts on the heavy door, turned the key and pulled open what he called 'The Gate of Glory'. A river mist had boiled up, and this now swirled around Burdon, dampening the sweat on his fat face.

'Who's there?' Burdon called. 'For the love of God.'

'My friend, we have met before.'

Burdon could just about make out the shape of his 'midnight visitor' as he called him.

'Oh, you have another head?'

'Oh yes, justice has certainly been visited on this felon. I now bring his head so you can pole it on the spikes above the gates of this magnificent bridge.'

'And the name?'

'Justice.'

'No, I mean the name of your victim?'

'No victim, Master Burdon, but a criminal. Sir Philip Kyne. Lord of Malroad Manor in Essex.'

'His crimes?'

'Rape and murder!'

The midnight caller stepped closer, and Burdon had no choice but to take the small iron-hooped barrel his visitor thrust at him.

'And this is for you and your troubles, Master Burdon.' The midnight caller, hooded and visored, handed across a small clinking purse. Burdon eagerly grasped this.

'By the morrow, Master Burdon,' the sinister visitor grated. 'Have this head poled. I bid you adieu. Do not delay,' he urged. The midnight caller then stepped back as if waiting for the mist to cloak him further, then he was gone. Burdon went inside. He slammed the door shut, pulling across bolts and turning the key. He slipped the purse into a pocket on his robe before unlocking the door to his workroom.

Three severed heads rested in bowls along the bench. Burdon took another bowl down from the shelf just inside the door. He opened the barrel and quickly seized a pomander to cover his nose and mouth against the stink which even the salted water could not hide. Burdon grasped the head by the hair and moved it on to the bowl before pulling his stool across to stare at this latest offering, who gazed sightlessly back.

'Good morning to you, Lord Philip Kyne,' Burdon murmured. He noticed the small scrap of parchment nailed to the dead man's forehead. He pulled this free and read the scrawled words. 'Justitia Fiat.' 'Let justice be done,' Burdon whispered. 'And God knows what that means.' He studied the dead, weather-beaten face with its healed scars and cuts.

'A warrior,' Burdon whispered. 'But not the gentle, perfect knight. Oh no. Nevertheless, as with the others I shall wash your ugly face and comb your hair. Oh yes, you'll be well set to be perched on a spike to gaze blindly across the Thames.'

PART ONE

'God chases away the wrinkled enemy.'

ater that same week after Kyne's head had been spiked, Sir John Cranston, Lord High Coroner of London, sat in his judgement chamber at the Guildhall: that splendid, magnificently built mansion of many rooms, a veritable palace overlooking Cheapside, the great market area of London. The noise and clamour from outside was constant: the braying of pack ponies, the crashing of cartwheels, the crack of whips, the shouts of traders, the neighing of horses and the incessant barking of the dogs who roamed its alleyways.

'I should come here at night,' Cranston whispered. 'Perhaps I'll find peace then.' He rose to his feet and stared around the chamber, now empty except for Cranston's clerk and scrivener, Oswald and Osbert, deep in hushed conversation in a far corner of the chamber. They sat close by the dangling skeleton of one Richard Craven, a professional assassin despatched by a riffler chief some years ago to murder Cranston here in his own judgement chamber. Instead, Cranston had taken Craven's life with a piercing slash which opened the assassin's throat. The young king had heard about this and so had Thibault, Master of Secrets to the self-styled regent, the King's uncle John of Gaunt. All three expressed their anger at what had happened. All three insisted that Richard Craven's corpse be boiled until the flesh dropped off. The skeleton was then hung in Cranston's judgement chamber above a small plaque proclaiming this to be the fate of any who attacked or ill-treated the Crown's officers, especially Sir John Cranston, Knight of the Garter, who rejoiced in the King's deep love for him.

The Coroner, as he often did, patted the bony right foot of the skeleton as he walked over to the window. He lifted the bar and pulled back the shutters. Cranston flinched at the biting cold as he stared down at the crowds teeming below. A sea of colour: merchants of the Staple in their gorgeous gowns, throats and wrists bedecked with jewels. These rubbed shoulders with the dark-dwellers who emerged from their slums for another day's mischief. Cheapside was the place where everyone mingled and mixed.

'God and Mammon,' Cranston whispered to himself. 'Cheapside is a shrine to both.'

'What is that, Sir John?'

'Nothing, Oswald.' Cranston grinned over his shoulder at his two clerks. 'Just meditating.'

Cranston went back to watching the crowds and the different threads of frenetic activity. A group of jesters, jackanapes, all dressed in garish rags, danced around a line of prisoners being taken up to the stocks. Sewer-squires, street-swallows, jongleurs and minstrels wandered aimlessly, looking for any opportunity to better themselves, be it a dangling purse or something fallen off one of the many barrows, carts and stalls. Friars of the Sack led different processions, be it a coffin bobbing on the shoulders of mourners or a wedding party all garlanded and festooned with ribbons and streamers. Despite the harsh cold, the crowds were certainly out and about. The smells and mixture of the bitter sweet air mingled with the stench from the open sewers and the different jakes closets built along the alleyways. Cranston craned his neck and stared down Cheapside studying the labyrinth of evil-smelling rutted lanes where the dark-dwellers teemed as they swarmed across the approaches to London Bridge. Soon he would have to go there.

Cranston breathed in noisily. He'd already met Robert Burdon, Keeper of the Gates, who had reported how another head had been poled. Its owner, Sir Philip Kyne of Malroad in Essex, had been executed, and this had been confirmed by a messenger from Kyne's son and heir.

'God help us,' Cranston murmured. 'What does all this mean?'

The Coroner returned to his judgement table. So far, he'd had little work to deal with. It was too early in the season. St Stephen's Day had come and gone, and they were now approaching

Epiphany, the climax of the twelve days of Christmas. Once they had celebrated that, the yuletide season was over and both the wicked and the weak would emerge from the shadows. Nevertheless, there was business enough; six members of the lock-pick coven had been paraded in front of him that morning. They had been caught 'infrangtheof, red-handed'. Cranston had ordered all their goods to be seized.

'When I say that,' the Coroner had thundered, 'I really mean everything they own, which is probably other peoples' goods anyway.'

Cranston had rapped his knuckles on the judgement table as he glared at all six felons.

'You'll also do a turn in the stocks,' he bellowed. 'So your victims can have a good look at you as well as hurl anything which comes to hand, be it manure or rotten fruit. You'll stand there until the market horn sounds and the bell rings for the belfry fires to be lit.'

Cranston was about to pull out from the chancery desk his miraculous wineskin when there was a sharp rap on the door and a royal scurrier, wearing the gorgeous tabard of Lord John of Gaunt, strode into the chamber as if he was God Almighty's messenger. He stopped before Cranston, bowed and offered the Coroner the scroll holder.

'Sir John, I give this with Master Thibault's compliments.'

'And I return them,' Cranston replied.

He lifted the cap on the leather holder and shook out the roll of parchment. He broke the red seal and paused halfway through as his chief bailiff, Henry Flaxwith, entered the chamber. Flaxwith was, as always, accompanied by his mastiff Samson, whom Cranston and Athelstan, his secretarius, considered to be the ugliest dog south of the Trent. Irrespective of this, Samson adored Cranston and, as usual, had to be restrained by Flaxwith pulling hard on the leash. If Samson escaped, he would launch his powerful, muscular body at the Coroner. Once he was assured the dog would not break free, Cranston continued reading.

'Oh dear.' The Coroner lifted his head and stared at his chief bailiff.

'Sir John?'

'Hideous murder, Henry, hideous murder.'

'So we are bound for Southwark, Sir John?'

'We are indeed, Henry. I need Brother Athelstan. I have to take him away from that horde of mischief he calls his parishioners. You, Sir,' Cranston pointed at the royal courier, 'tell your masters I shall soon be with them. Henry, let us meet our good brother.'

Cranston swiftly changed his soft shoes for high-heeled riding boots fashioned out of the best Cordovan leather. He tied up his houppelande and strapped on his war belt. He made sure the miraculous wineskin was hanging ready beneath his robe and, satisfied, he waved Flaxwith to the door. Both coroner and henchman went down into the great courtyard. Once he'd handed over Samson, Flaxwith summoned six of his comitatus to accompany them and they strode through the magnificent gateway, along Cheapside and down to London Bridge. Cranston of course was soon recognized and was greeted with catcalls and filthy insults. However, when Flaxwith and his bailiffs moved to confront and apprehend the abusers, the insults and catcalls swiftly died away.

Two well-known characters made their usual appearance. Leif, the one-legged beggar, together with his henchman Rawbum, a former cook who, in a drunken fit, had sat down on a bowl of boiling oil. Both these characters spotted Cranston and hobbled across, calling down benediction after benediction on the Coroner's head. How they blessed his heart, his innards and even Cranston's codpiece and everything within it. How they would escort him to his favourite tavern, 'The Lamb of God'. They would then hasten to inform the honourable coroner's wife, the Lady Maude, on the whereabouts of her beloved husband, should she wish to join him. It was the usual attempt at petty blackmail for the Coroner did not want Lady Maude to know too much about his secret abode. Cranston spun them a coin then whispered a prayer of thanks that, at least on this occasion, he was not about to frequent his most favoured hostelry. Cranston, with Flaxwith's bailiffs either side, turned on to the approaches to London Bridge. The Coroner glanced up at row upon row of severed heads poled and spiked there. He watched the ravens

and crows pecking at the soft flesh, particularly the eyes. Scraps
of flesh floated down. As he watched, Cranston wondered what
was the reason for those night-time visits to Robert Burdon? The
stranger who brought the severed heads of manor lords to be
impaled over the bridge? Who was responsible for that? Why
had these manor lords been singled out for such gruesome treat-
ment? News of the deaths had reached the Commons at
Westminster and they had petitioned Gaunt to order Master
Thibault to investigate. But when would that take place? Cranston,
deep in thought, chewed the corner of his lip. He had already
begun his own superficial investigation and . . .

'Sir John?'

Cranston, startled from his reverie, glanced around at his
retinue of bailiffs. They were now on the great concourse before
the North Gate leading on to London Bridge.

'Sir John,' Flaxwith repeated. 'Are we to go by barge or shall
we cross the bridge?'

Cranston shook his head and walked on a little further. He
stopped where he could catch a glimpse of the river. Cranston
hastily stepped back.

'It's black, swollen and angry,' he declared. 'We will certainly
not go by barge on this journey. We will walk the bridge.'

Cranston and his comitatus carefully followed the ribbon path
which cut between the houses and other dwellings built either
side of the bridge. They passed the small chapel dedicated to
London's greatest saint, Thomas à Becket. Cranston crossed
himself and murmured a prayer for the saint to protect him and
all those he loved. Crossing the bridge, which Cranston believed
actually shifted under the constant battering from the wind, was
an experience in itself. The Coroner pulled his hood closer against
the cold. He tried to ignore the constant clacking of the mills on
Southwark side, the ever-pervasive stench of rotting fish and the
fury of the river as it hurled itself against the starlings supporting
the bridge. At last they were across on to the Southwark enclosure, a place both Cranston and Athelstan regarded as the ante-
chamber of Hell. The great common waste, which stretched either
side of the path, housed the gallows, gibbets, pillories and stocks
where the felons of the City could be punished. Baskets heaped

full with chains, gyves and manacles stood on a great battered table along with the knives, cleavers, axes and whips which the executioners would use to inflict this punishment or that, be it the loss of a hand or a branding to the face. All of London's grim macabre underworld gathered here for whatever profits they could find, the very place where such crimes were punished from morning till night. Today was no different, even though they were still in Christmastime. Felons screamed as their ears were cropped whilst other lawbreakers, who had narrowly escaped execution, were tied to a gallows post where a bailiff would smack their heads against the wood as a warning that next time they would hang!

Such a place always had a spectacle, and this morning was no different. A crude compound, a small paddock, had been roughly set up. In it five blind men, armed with sharpened poles, fought each other over who should kill the pig which rushed and squealed around. The noise and screech of the poor animal, the curses of the contestants and the roars of mocking laughter from the spectators dinned the air. Cranston rubbed his eyes against the acrid smoke pouring form the makeshift ovens hastily set up to feed the crowds bustling about. Cranston, bellowing above the noise, ordered his comitatus to move swiftly, so they pushed and shoved their way through the crowds, ignoring the catcalls and jeers they provoked. At last, they arrived at Southwark quayside with its busy stalls, shabby shops, bathhouses, windmills and stews. Flaxwith led them along the broad trackway leading up to St Erconwald's. They approached 'The Piebald Tavern', what Athelstan called his parishioners' second parish church.

'A true chapel,' Athelstan had blithely remarked. 'I just wish more would attend mine.'

This morning the tavern lay strangely quiet though. As they passed, Cranston caught sight of Scoresby, Bardolph's henchman, one of the principal tax collectors in Southwark. Bardolph was a man fiercely resented by those he fleeced both for the Crown and himself. Scoresby appeared deep in heated conversation with Bleakborn, the eldest son of Joscelyn, the one-armed former river pirate who owned 'The Piebald Tavern'. They hardly looked up when Cranston and his comitatus walked by and the Coroner

wondered what was happening between the two. He would, he
promised himself, ask Athelstan if he could cast light on that
precious pair . . .

Athelstan, the Dominican parish priest of St Erconwald's
Church in Southwark, as well as the secretarius of Sir John
Cranston, was also talking about light, that of the glory of Heaven
as well as the lurid glow of Hell. The Friar was determined to
deliver his sermon. He had risen early, recited the divine office
and looked at his homily before shaving and washing himself
at the lavarium. Once done, he had built up the fire, heaping the
logs on to the hungry flames. He then hurriedly checked on
Philomel, the old warhorse, snoring in his stable. Hubert the
Hedgehog was in his nest which Crispin the Carpenter had
especially fashioned for him whilst Bonaventure, the great one-
eyed tomcat, sprawled like an emperor in front of the strength-
ening fire. Athelstan had finished his preparations, grabbed his
cloak and hurried down to his parish church for the Jesus Mass.
Despite the harmony of the ritual, as the Mass swept toward the
climax of the consecration and eucharist, Athelstan sensed that
his parishioners, gathered just within the rood screen, were
deeply unsettled. Something had disturbed their humours, and
he became distracted, wondering what that could be. Once he
had sung the 'Ita Missa Est ~ the Mass is over', Athelstan went
across to the lectern and stared hard at his faithful, and sometimes not so faithful, flock. They were all there, wrapped in their
fustian garb, shifting their booted feet as they sat on the benches
staring expectantly at their little parish priest, a Dominican friar
devoted to saving their souls. Athelstan drew a deep breath as
he crossed himself and began his homily, a plea for love and
compassion, kindness and tolerance as they prepared for the
great Feast of the Epiphany and their journey to the Babe of
Bethlehem. He wanted his parishioners to realize that God loved
them and wanted to invite them into Heaven to enjoy his
paradise.

'Remember,' Athelstan raised a hand, 'no one is in Hell who
wants to be in Heaven and no one in Heaven wants to be in Hell.
God,' Athelstan continued, 'wants to seize you and keep you in
his love. He will do everything in his power to achieve that.'

Athelstan warmed to his theme. 'Let me explain. Let me tell you a story which proves this. There was once a wandering jongleur, uncouth, unwashed and ill-kempt.'

'Just like Watkin here!' someone shouted.

The dung collector sprang to his feet. He glared around, fists clenched, and the laughter died. Athelstan kept his peace, staring fixedly at his congregation. Pike the Ditcher, Crispin the Carpenter, Ranulf the Ratcatcher, Mauger the Parish Bell Clerk, Moleskin the Boatman. All of these, and the rest of the mischievous crew, which kept Athelstan so busy, were present. He waited until Watkin unclenched his fists and returned to his seat.

'Now,' Athelstan continued, 'the jongleur was filthy, his hair all a greasy tangle, his skin scabrous.'

'Just like Watkin,' someone murmured.

Athelstan took a step forward, gesturing at Watkin to keep his seat.

'No more interruptions,' the Friar declared, 'or I cancel the festivities of the Epiphany. Now back to my story.' Athelstan took a breath. 'This barefoot jongleur, this tramp, divided his life between the tavern and the brothel where he spent all he earned. At the end of his stupid life, he went straight to Hell. Now the Devil did not care for his songs, so they employed him to keep the fires going under the cauldrons where the damned were boiled. One fine day.' Athelstan paused. He knew his parishioners loved a story, especially one about Hell. 'One fine day,' he continued, 'St Peter passed that way. He played dice with our jongleur, who managed to lose all the souls he was supposed to be guarding. The devils were so furious they kicked the jongleur out of Hell and St Peter gleefully opened the gates of Heaven for him. Don't you see,' Athelstan smiled at his parishioners, 'God and the Court of Heaven will do anything to save our souls. So, remember that . . .' Athelstan was about to continue when the corpse door crashed open and Cranston strode into the nave, beckoning at Athelstan to join him. The arrival of Cranston made the parishioners scatter like pigeons before the hawk. Only Benedicta, the widow-woman, her raven-black hair and lovely face almost hidden by a nun-like coif, remained. She stayed until the church emptied. Once it had, she led Cranston into the sanctuary so she

could indulge in her favourite pastime – teasing Sir John as well
as asking him about his beautiful wife, the Lady Maude, and
their twin sons, the Poppets. Once Athelstan joined them beneath
the rood screen, Benedicta bade both men adieu and left,
processing like a princess out of the church.

Athelstan watched her go then plucked at Cranston's arm and
led him across to the chantry chapel of St Erconwald. A veritable
jewel. A small, enclosed house of prayer with its gleaming furniture, soft, thick turkey rugs and a beautiful stained-glass window
which coloured the light streaming through it. Cranston sat on
a wall bench beneath the window whilst Athelstan pushed across
a cushioned stool to sit opposite.

'Trouble, Sir John?'

'Trouble indeed, Little Monk.'

'Friar, Sir John.'

'Trouble indeed,' Cranston repeated. He pulled the miraculous
wineskin from beneath his cloak, took a generous gulp and offered
it to Athelstan, who just smiled and shook his head. Cranston
shrugged, drank another mouthful and hid it away. He got to his
feet and walked towards the door of the chantry. He stared down
to where Flaxwith and his bailiffs were warming their hands over
a brazier close to the baptismal font.

'Sir John, what is it? You are greatly out of humour?'

'It's the past!' Cranston replied, going back to his seat. 'The
past, Athelstan!'

'What past?'

'You fought in France?'

'You know I did, Sir John. I took my beloved brother with
me. He was killed and the news devastated my parents. They
both died of grief. I converted. I took the path of atonement,
which is why I became a Dominican priest and why I am now
waiting to hear from you what troubles you so much.'

'Murder, Brother, as well as evil deeds from former days. Like
the ancient furies, these have caught up with their quarry which
they've probably been hunting down the years.'

'Meaning?'

'Meaning, Brother, that the war in France may well be over.
Both kingdoms desperately want peace. John of Gaunt and others

of the royal council, including our mutual friend Master Thibault, have urged this on our noble king.'

'I understand that there are French envoys at Westminster.' Athelstan pulled a face. 'I have also heard the rumours. Moleskin, our bargeman, says that two magnificent French war cogs have berthed at Queenhithe. So, Sir John, I know the French are in London. Scraps of gossip. Is their visit important?'

'It certainly is, Brother. The delegation is led by Dom Antoine, Archdeacon of the Royal Chapel at St Denis. He is also reportedly the Magister, the Master of the French Secret Chancery, La Chambre Noir, the Black Chamber deep in the bowels of the Louvre Palace.' Cranston paused to take a more generous gulp of Bordeaux. 'Now,' he continued, 'Dom Antoine has brought the terms of a lasting peace.'

'Good.'

'Wait, Brother. One of their proposals is the extradition to France of individual members of an English Free Company, the Via Crucis, who fought their way across Normandy.'

'Fought!' Athelstan exclaimed. 'You really mean they pillaged, plundered, raped and killed. Sir John, I was a soldier, so were you. But we all know what these Free Companies truly were. Indeed, to call themselves the Via Crucis – the Way of the Cross – is an insult to both God and man.'

'Hush, Brother. I know that and now both God and man want to see justice done.'

'What do you mean?'

'As I have said, the French have included in their proposal for a peace treaty that all members of the Via Crucis, well, those still alive, be extradited to France: on this they are most insistent. They certainly want the leader of the Free Company, Sir Oliver Ingham.'

'And the English Crown's response?'

'Ah, there's the rub, Athelstan. The individuals they have named are extremely well protected by the Crown. After all, they are warriors. Veterans of England's so-called glorious war in Normandy. Faithful followers of the old king. Comrades of our dead noble hero, the Black Prince. Two of those named sit in the Commons where they nest with their own kind. Sir Oliver

Ingham is now the King's surveyor. Sir John Montague has become a peritus, an expert, on the origin of names. Sir Stephen Crossley has some malignant disease in his belly. Now, Athelstan, can you imagine that the Commons, the Kingdom, would allow such men to be handed over like trussed hogs for the French to slaughter.'

'They would be executed?'

'They would certainly stand trial in some French court. And, bearing in mind their crimes,' Cranston pulled a face, 'they could end up being torn apart at Montfaucon, Paris's human slaughter house.'

'So, the English Crown will refuse such a request?'

'They must do, but there again,' Cranston sighed, 'other problems have emerged.' He paused. 'Robert Burdon, you know him, Athelstan?'

'Keeper of the Bridge. He's also a headsman responsible for poling the severed heads of traitors.'

'Yes, that's him. Now, a few weeks ago, Burdon had a midnight visitor who brought him a rotting head to be impaled on a spike above London Bridge. Burdon believed he had no choice but to accept it. Now, he failed to recognize the head or the ravaged face, but Burdon did find a piece of dark blue cloth steeped in wax—'

'Corpse sheets are fashioned like that. They are washed and dried, then waxed before being wrapped around a corpse.'

'So it seems, Brother. Anyway, before he poled the head, Burdon placed it on his display table on the top step leading to his house in the hope that some passer-by would recognize it. Apparently, he does that quite often.'

'Yes, yes, I have seen his exhibits. A truly gruesome sight.'

'Be that as it may, Brother, someone did recognize the head and put a name to it: Roger Mortimer, a Knight Banneret, Lord of the Manor of St Giles, bordering on Epping Forest.' Cranston paused. 'Burdon informed me of his findings, and I made the short journey to St Giles Church. The parson there, an old venerable priest, took me out into the cemetery, a lonely, sprawling stretch of wasteland. He confidently asserted that Sir Roger lay buried deep in a cluster of yew trees. Well, believe me, he wasn't.

Sir Roger's corpse had been exhumed. The head was missing whilst the torso was wrapped in that blue waxen cloth. A scrap of parchment had been nailed to the skull of the severed head.' Cranston shrugged. 'I could make no sense of it, so I arranged for the decapitated head to be conveyed back to St Giles whilst I despatched a brief report to the Royal Chancery. I suggested that the desecration of Mortimer's corpse was an act of revenge by someone who wanted to settle a grudge. Oh,' Cranston lifted his hand, 'of course I reflected on discovering a motive for the desecration, be it vengeance or something else. Naturally I examined the message scrawled on that scrap of parchment, pinned to Mortimer's skull.'

'Pinned?'

'Well, rather nailed. A thin sharp needle which must have been hammered in as you would a spike.'

'And the message?'

'Justitia Fiat – let there be justice.'

'So, it probably was an act of revenge. Some soul demanding justice against the dead man.'

'Oh, but listen, Brother. Just about a week ago, Robert Burdon had another midnight visitor. He brought a freshly, or nearly so, severed head, once the property of Sir Philip Kyne, Lord of Malroad Manor, close to Walton on the Naze along the Essex Coast.' Cranston cleared his throat. 'This time Burdon's midnight caller named who it was, or rather had been.'

'And the same message?'

'Oh yes, Brother. Nailed to the dead man's skull. "Justitia Fiat – let there be justice". Our midnight visitor paid Burdon, who dressed the severed head, poled it then sent a report to me. I had hardly received that when a scurrier arrived from Malroad. He delivered a most macabre story. Shortly after Christmas a band of assassins entered Malroad. They terrified its occupants then their leader turned on Kyne, accusing him of dreadful crimes in France.'

'And was he guilty of such crimes?'

'For a while, Kyne served with Ingham and the Via Crucis before leaving them for pastures new. I suspect he relished slaughter, a true blood-drinker. Kyne certainly paid for his crimes on that evening out at his manor. In brief, these assassins decapitated Kyne, left his blood-spurting torso but brought the head into London for Burdon to spike.'

'And these assassins, could they be a cohort of killers despatched by the Chambre Noir?'

'Brother, according to witnesses, the assassins were definitely English. Well educated in their horn-book, the leader was quite a prolific quoter of scripture.'

'The Chambre Noir could have hired them surely?'

'I doubt that very much, Brother. Master Thibault keeps Dom Antoine and his entire escort under very close scrutiny. Even if he didn't, the Chambre Noir would find it very difficult to recruit professional assassins here in London. They would be fleeced of their money with nothing in return. Indeed, if they were approached, they would sell that information either to me or Master Thibault to secure a reward. No, I doubt if the French envoys are involved in this. The assassins spoke English. They were very well educated, or certainly their leader was, whilst the assassins seemed to know the lie of the land. How to thread the poacher runnels and coffin paths leading to Malroad.'

'Yet, Sir John, somebody must have told these assassins in great detail all about manor lords such as Kyne, where they reside, what they did as well as instruct them about the crimes they were supposed to have committed in France.'

'Brother, I agree. Moreover, the French demand is that the guilty individuals should be handed over to them for public trial and disgrace, not summary execution out on a lonely Essex manor.' He shrugged. 'I do wonder, however, if the French might settle for this!'

'So, what now?'

'You sound querulous, Little Friar.'

'No, Sir John, just tired, as well as being deeply curious and distracted by my parishioners. And you, Sir John? You have been commissioned to investigate Kyne's murder?'

'I will be. I will have to deal with Kyne's death, now there's more. The corpse of Sir Hugh Despencer, a Welsh lord, has been found murdered further down river on Southwark side.'

'This Despencer was a member of the Via Crucis?'

'He certainly was. Anyway, his corpse, greatly abused, was discovered very early this morning in a derelict warehouse close to an old mansion called "The House of Lonely Souls".'

'What was he doing there?'

'I don't know, Brother. Anyway, Thibault has demanded that I join him where the corpse was found, later today just after Nones. Until then, both the corpse and the warehouse are being guarded by Thibault's Spanish mercenaries. Now look . . .' Cranston broke off as the corpse door crashed back and Benedicta, all a fluster, hurried down the nave.

'What is it, Benedicta?' Athelstan demanded, leaving the chantry chapel.

'Father, Sir John, you must come! Murder at "The Piebald".'

'Who?'

'Bardolph the Tax Collector.'

'Oh sweet Lord,' Cranston exclaimed.

He and Athelstan collected their cloaks and followed Benedicta out of the church across the concourse and down to 'The Piebald Tavern'. Already a crowd thronged the entrance, shoving and pushing, craning their necks to peer into the tap room. Cranston rapped out an order to Flaxwith and his bailiffs to clear the doorway. Once they had, Cranston and Athelstan entered the tap room. As soon as those inside glimpsed the Coroner, most of them disappeared as swiftly as rabbits from a fox. Athelstan ordered the doors to the tavern to be closed and locked. Joscelyn, the one-armed taverner, arranged for more lamps and candles to be lit, whilst Athelstan stared around at those who remained under Cranston's hawk-like glare. All of them were members of Athelstan's parish council. One he did not recognize, though Cranston certainly did, was Scoresby, Bardolph's henchman, a weasel-faced, beanpole of a man. He jumped to his feet as Cranston walked into the centre of the tap room and called out his name.

'Sir John,' Scoresby screeched, 'Master Bardolph has been foully murdered.' He jabbed a finger at the ceiling. 'Upstairs in his chamber. He . . .'

'Upstairs in one of my chambers,' Joscelyn riposted, swaggering into the pools of light thrown by the lanterns, lamps and coarse wax candles. 'Nothing to do with us,' the taverner continued. 'We all went to Mass this morning. You saw us there.'

'I also see things,' the Coroner interjected. 'I saw you, Scoresby, arguing with Bleakborn, Joscelyn's son. What was all that about?'

'That, Sir John, was because I could not rouse my master. I was desperate to get into his chamber, but we had to wait for Joscelyn to arrive. I did, didn't I?' He looked at the others for affirmation.

Scoresby's question provoked strident shouts of agreement. Athelstan used this to check on who was actually here at the time. The usual merry band; Watkin, Pike, Crispin, Tab the Tinker and Ranulf the Ratcatcher. Two were missing. Athelstan clapped his hands for silence whilst Cranston roared for them to hold their tongues.

'Brother,' the Coroner demanded, 'what is it?'

'Where is Giles of Sempringham?'

'You mean the Hangman of Rochester?' Watkin demanded.

'The same. He's missing and so is Merrylegs. Why? As I came down here, I noticed he wasn't in his cook shop next door.'

'Both ill, Father,' Watkins sang out. 'An evil humour of the belly.'

'Sir John,' Scoresby wailed, 'Brother Athelstan, my master lies murdered upstairs.'

Cranston snapped his fingers at Joscelyn. 'Show me.'

'He's in the Avalon Chamber,' the taverner declared portentously.

Athelstan hid a smile. Joscelyn was so proud of his tavern he called it a second Avalon and named the chambers with titles taken from the legends of King Arthur.

'So, if it's the Avalon Chamber,' Cranston declared, 'or indeed anything else, just take us up there. No,' he held up a hand, 'no one else. The rest of you stay here until I am finished. Joscelyn, lead on.'

They left the tap room, going up the stairs on to a narrow, ill-lit gallery. The Avalon Chamber stood about halfway down. Its door had been forced and now rested against the wall outside. The room was poorly lit, so Joscelyn hastened to fire more lanterns and bring others in to brighten the chamber. In truth it was a tawdry room with its shabby four-poster bed, rickety table, chairs and stools with a crudely painted canvas of a knight on horseback which, Athelstan suspected, was a painting celebrating Lancelot, a knight of the Round Table. Athelstan turned and gasped as he glimpsed the figure slouched in a chair just inside the doorway, almost hidden by the shifting shadows. He and Cranston went over and crouched before the mortal remains of Bardolph, the chief tax collector.

'He was no beauty in life,' Cranston breathed, 'and death has not improved him.'

Athelstan had to agree. Bardolph's ill-shaven, liverish face was even more ugly in death with his popping eyes and half-open mouth which still dribbled blood down on to the dagger thrust deep into his chest. A direct blow to the heart. Athelstan rose and walked slowly around the chamber. He noticed that most of the candles on their spigots had spluttered down to a mess of hardened wax. The window was far too narrow for anyone to climb through whilst it was firmly shuttered from within. A wine jug with two goblets stood on a wall shelf. Athelstan sniffed at these carefully but could not detect any taint. At his request Cranston called Flaxwith up and had him take the wine and ensure that no other mixture had been added. Athelstan then resumed his scrutiny. The room smelt stale as if it hadn't been aired for weeks. The Friar went across and opened the shutters. The leather hinges creaked whilst the wood was covered in a mass of spider webs.

'No one could come through that window,' Athelstan declared, moving across to where the door lay propped against the wall. 'Bardolph liked this chamber?'

'The best this tavern could offer,' Joscelyn replied.

'And what happened last night?'

'Well, he adjourned to bed.'

'Was that late?'

'It was well after the chimes of midnight, Brother. We were all drinking with him before going off to bed.'

'So Bardolph came up here, yes? And Swithum?'

'He bedded down on a straw paillasse in the tap room.'

'And then, this morning?'

'Well, we all woke up. Swithum said his master wanted to break his fast on salted meat, fresh croutons and morning ale. I agreed and sent Swithum up to rouse Master Bardolph. He took his stoup of morning ale with him. We heard Swithum knock on the door and shout Bardolph's name, but there was no reply. Time passed. I wanted to attend the Jesus Mass, so I left the tavern in the care of my eldest son Bleakborn and joined you in church.'

'And afterwards?'

'Why, Brother, once Mass had finished and Sir John had arrived, we decided to force the door to Bardolph's chamber. Benedicta was here. She will attest to what we did.'

'And the door?'

'Locked from the inside, Brother, with the key hanging there and the bolts drawn both top and bottom.'

Athelstan scrutinized the door more closely. He could clearly see the ruptured bolts and damaged lock.

'Quite impossible,' Athelstan breathed. 'The door was locked and bolted. Three firm clasps on a door which sealed this chamber whilst there is no other viable entrance. No secret passageway, Joscelyn?' Athelstan demanded over his shoulder.

'None, Brother.'

'Well . . .'

'Brother Athelstan, Sir John?' Swithum yelled from the stairs. 'Have you found the monies? A pannier holding the taxes my master had collected?'

'He's asked that before,' Joscelyn murmured.

'And?' Athelstan demanded.

'Nothing, Brother. No sight of that pannier. We've searched this room as we have the entire tavern. We found nothing.'

'So, our assassin is also a thief,' Athelstan mused. 'Was that the reason for the murder, to seize the taxes? Joscelyn, please ask Benedicta to join us here.'

The taverner nodded and scurried down the stairs. He shouted at the others that he could not answer their questions and a short while later returned with Benedicta. Athelstan waved her to a cushioned stool and smiled at this beautiful woman who constantly played on the strings of his heart.

'Father?' Benedicta sat staring coquettishly. 'You want to question me?'

'No, no, not really. I need you to describe exactly what happened when the door to this chamber was forced.'

'Well, after the Jesus Mass we all adjourned here. Scoresby was still arguing with Bleakborn . . .'

'I stopped that,' Joscelyn declared.

'Yes, yes, you did,' Benedicta agreed. 'We gathered in the tap room where you ordered the door to be forced and so it was. Brother Athelstan, I was on the gallery outside when it happened. I saw that door, locked and bolted at the top and bottom, buckle, break and snap. Once it had fallen, I followed Watkin and Joscelyn into the room. Very much like it is now. Bardolph sat sagged in that chair, a knife thrust deep in his chest.'

'Whose knife?'

'From what I understand it was his own.'

'Good Lord,' Cranston exclaimed. 'So, we have Bardolph here in his chamber, the door locked and bolted. The assassin enters, stabs him, steals the taxes, then leaves, apparently through a sturdy door that is firmly locked and bolted. He does all this as silent as a ghost, a shadow across the wall. I wager Bardolph was a roaring boy; he wouldn't give up his life quietly.' Cranston turned to Joscelyn. 'There were no sounds of violence?'

'None, Sir John.'

'Perhaps,' Athelstan declared, 'Bardolph came up here deep in his cups. The assassin, whoever he is and however he did it, had concealed himself in the chamber beforehand. Bardolph takes off his belt and sits in that chair. He falls fast asleep. The assassin emerges from the shadows. He seizes Bardolph's dagger from its sheath and thrusts it deep into the tax collector's heart.' Athelstan shook his head. 'I admit it's possible, but the great mystery remains. How did the assassin leave a chamber locked and bolted from within?'

'And there's no other entrance?' Cranston asked.

'As I have said before, none whatsoever.'

'Master Joscelyn,' Athelstan smiled at the taverner who stood nursing his damaged shoulder, 'of your goodness go down to the tap room and entertain your comrades. We shall be with you shortly.'

Joscelyn left. Athelstan raised a finger to his lips, waiting to continue only when he was sure Joscelyn had truly left. Once he'd satisfied himself the taverner was gone, Athelstan turned back to Benedicta.

'You were definitely here when the door was forced?'

'Of course, Father.'

'Tell me. Did any of the gospel greeters downstairs disappear for any considerable period of time either last night or this morning?'

'No, Brother, apart from the Hangman and Merrylegs, who stayed in their own houses with a bad humour of the belly. I visited both men to see if I could help in any way. They informed me they were getting better. I didn't believe them, Father, both individuals look like death warmed up. They were too sick to join in the usual carousing. Why, Father?'

'And the rest? You are sure they were all here both yesterday evening and this morning. There wasn't one who went missing, maybe for several hours or so?'

'Father, not to my recollection. I would certainly have noticed that. Why? Do you suspect one of them below was lurking in this chamber when the door was forced?'

'A strong possibility,' Cranston declared, taking a slurp from the miraculous wineskin.

'Well, I can assure you, Sir John, no one was lurking in this chamber and, when the door was forced, nobody was absent or missing from the madcap crew downstairs.'

'Sir John, Brother Athelstan!' Flaxwith came into the chamber. 'I fed the wine to a rat Ranulf had captured and caged – the rodent was thirsty and soon lapped the wine.'

'And?'

'One drunken rat, Sir John, otherwise definitely no taint to the wine.'

Cranston thanked him and Flaxwith left.

'Ah well.' Athelstan slowly walked around the chamber, scrutinizing certain items. 'We are finished here,' he murmured.

'Good,' Cranston declared. 'Brother, the hour of Nones is fast

approaching. Moleskin is downstairs. Let's hire his barge and
make a journey along the river to meet our good friend Master
Thibault.'

Athelstan agreed. He thanked Benedicta, exchanged the kiss
of peace with her then both coroner and friar hurried down to
the tap room. Once there Athelstan asked Joscelyn to arrange for
Bardolph's corpse to be taken across river to the great mortuary
of St Mary atte Bowe. At the same time, he refused even to
acknowledge the spate of questions his parishioners were shouting
at him as he pushed his way through them. At the doorway
Athelstan turned. Such matters, he declared to his parishioners,
would have to wait. He then followed Cranston out into the mist-
hung street and down to where Moleskin had moored his barge
in a small enclave along the quayside.

Moleskin's oarsmen were in their hut breaking their fast on
freshly caught grilled fish. They finished their meal and swiftly
organized themselves. A short while later, with Cranston and
Athelstan sitting in the stern and Flaxwith and two of his bailiffs
in the prow, Moleskin cast off. Athelstan crossed himself as the
barge turned on the angry swell to go down to the House of
Lonely Souls. The river was most turbulent and the currents very
strong. Athelstan closed his eyes and prayed fervently to St
Erconwald that their journey would be swift and safe. The mist
swirled in, thick and freezing. Athelstan wondered if it hosted a
horde of demons sent to plague poor travellers such as himself.
Other craft were on the Thames, so there was a constant braying
of horns as they warned each other off either by horn or lantern.
Cranston, however, was more settled. He peered round the canvas
awning at the derelict dwellings and warehouses. This part of
Southwark side was a lonely, bleak place sorely blighted by the
great pestilence which had ravaged Southwark in particular almost
thirty years previous.

'There's nothing here,' Cranston declared. 'Nothing but shabby
whore houses, brothels and all the other sin shops.' He turned,
leaned forward and stared to starboard. 'Ah, there it is, Brother.'
Athelstan reluctantly leaned over and followed Cranston's direction. A great war barge, its title 'Thanatos' emblazoned on both
prow and stern, broke through the shifting mist. The hooded

oarsmen on board, four either side, furrowed the river, driving
the barge forward. On the raised stern stood an imposing figure.

'God bless the Fisher of Men,' Cranston breathed. 'He may
well be heading for the same place we are.'

'No.' Moleskin, sitting on the bench in front of them pointed
at the balding, near-naked figure on the prow of the 'Thanatos',
an eerie-looking individual.

'Ichthus,' Athelstan declared. 'They must be hunting for the
drowned.'

'Be that as it may,' Cranston retorted, sitting back under the
canopy, 'we should be having words with the Fisher very soon
but, for now . . .'

'The House of Lonely Souls,' Moleskin sang out. The barge
suddenly lurched to starboard as it turned, heading directly
towards the crumbling quayside dominated by a derelict
merchants' mansion, a two-storeyed building with a large warehouse beneath. Others had already assembled there and, as soon
as Moleskin berthed his barge, Cranston and Athelstan disembarked and walked towards the group of men gathered around
Thibault.

John of Gaunt's Master of Secrets looked as cherubic as ever
with his carefully crimped blonde hair, smooth shaven face and
delicate features. Athelstan knew this was only a pretence, a
covering to hide a most devious soul. As soon as they met,
Athelstan realized Thibault was not in the best of moods. Gaunt's
henchman stamped his booted feet against the ground, shivering
dramatically as he exchanged greetings with both Cranston and
Athelstan. Thibault glanced over his shoulder at his cohort of
Spanish mercenaries gathered around the doorway.

'Me and my beloveds,' he gestured at his escort, 'have been
waiting some time, Sir John, as have the others summoned here.'

'Well, we were delayed,' Cranston retorted. 'Now we are here.
So, let us see why we are here!'

Thibault immediately spun on his heel, snapping his fingers
at Cranston and Athelstan to follow him and his mercenaries into
the warehouse. This was a gloomy room which seemed to stretch
into a darkness broken only by a pool of light created by sconce
torches fastened high on a pillar. A group of men stood further

down the chamber warming their hands over braziers crammed with flaming charcoal. The smoke perfumed the air, but it could not conceal the horrid stench of blood, corruption and death. The two mercenaries guarding the pillar quickly stepped aside so Cranston and Athelstan could view the nightmare. A man stripped naked, his filthy hair falling down to cover his bruised face, his mouth cruelly gagged. There was no doubt the man was dead, his corpse fastened tight to a stout wooden pillar. He had been bound hard and sharp. The coarse rope used had buried deep into the soft flesh from the nape of his neck to his feet, almost hidden by the puddles of blood which had cascaded down. The dead man had apparently been scourged to death. The lash scars had opened up deep wounds from head to toe as the flesh ruptured, bubbled and popped.

'In God's name,' Athelstan breathed. 'Who could do this to another human being? Who is this poor soul? Or rather who was he?'

'Hugh Despencer.' One of the men warming his hands over the brazier walked across, followed by his comrades.

'And who are you, Sir?'

'Why, Brother, Sir Oliver Ingham, friend and close ally of Lord John of Gaunt. I am also the King's own surveyor in the City of London.'

Ingham was a squat man, his steel-grey hair cropped close, his face that of a drinker with his slobbery lips and deep-set, dark-ringed eyes. A man of blood, Athelstan wondered as he turned to accept the introduction from the others. John Montague and Stephen Crossley. Athelstan studied both knights quickly. Fighters, he concluded, their hands steeped in blood, souls full of harsh piercing memories. He had met the likes before, upright townsmen, prosperous merchants, members of this guild or that, on this council or another. They were men who had hacked a fortune in France and returned to revel in the wealth and privilege this brought. Tough men, formidable warriors, their faces scarred by countless affrays, battles and ambuscades. Hard, muscled men, their bellies beginning to sag as they sank deeper into a life of luxury and ease.

Eventually, they finished the introductions, Ingham adding that they knew Cranston of old. Thibault, sharp and peremptory, brought them back to the matters in hand.

'Lord Hugh Despencer,' he declared, pointing at the ghastly sight. 'A knight of the Court much favoured by my Lord of Gaunt. A former warrior,' he continued, 'a member of the Free Company, the Via Crucis.'

'And how was he found like this?'

'A mudlark, Sir John. One of those boys who scavenge along the river. He stumbled into here, saw this ghastly sight and went searching for someone, anyone, to report what he'd found. Eventually he met a port reeve.' Thibault shrugged. 'And so the alarm was raised. I heard about it and, when I could, sent messages to Sir John.'

Athelstan walked closer to the corpse. He placed a hand to the cold, sticky, dead flesh. 'Hard and frozen,' he declared. 'I suspect he was murdered yesterday morning. But why was the Lord Hugh here in the first place?'

'He came on behalf of us all,' Ingham spoke up. 'We are the surviving members of the Free Company – the Via Crucis. There's two more, Squires Gumblat and Henshaw. Over twenty years ago we fought under the banner of the Black Prince across Normandy. We returned wealthy men.'

'Very wealthy,' Cranston interjected.

'True, Sir John.' Ingham breathed in noisily, revelling in his own self-importance. 'The years have passed; life has been very good to us. We have decided, with the support of Master Thibault and my Lord of Gaunt, to fund the building of a great leper hospital. A hospice for those poor unfortunates ravaged by that malevolent infection. We plan for a dwelling to serve at least forty souls. This place here, with its old warehouse and mansion, is a most suitable location, standing as it does on Southwark side, well distanced from any other dwellings. We intend to repair the quayside and broaden the lanes which would serve the hospital. Of course, there will be gardens, kitchens, stables, granaries and other outhouses.' Ingham's voice trailed away.

Athelstan stared around and nodded in agreement. A leper house in such a location was logical. It would be self-sufficient and far from any other dwelling. Such charitable foundations were becoming quite common. Even his own order had benefited from similar bequests. Athelstan walked away lost in thought.

'Brother?' Ingham called out.

'Gentlemen.' Athelstan walked back to the group. He could now feel the cold seeping through his cloak and robe. 'Gentlemen, I suggest we adjourn and assemble in more comfortable quarters.'

'I agree,' Cranston declared then paused as Thibault raised a hand.

'Sir John, Brother Athelstan, whilst we are here, I would like you both to join Sir Oliver.'

'For what?' Cranston snapped. 'Master Thibault, I am cold, hungry and wish to be rid of this benighted place.' He paused. 'True, you did mention the possibility of meeting the Fisher of Men.'

'Sir Oliver,' Thibault continued remorselessly, 'is the King's surveyor in London. One of his principal tasks is to enforce the Crown's rights and privileges when it comes to the question of treasure trove.'

Ingham, his lower lip jutting out, nodded solemnly.

'Master Thibault is correct,' he declared sonorously. 'I am the King's surveyor and treasure has been found where the Fisher of Men has his church, the "Chapel of the Drowned Man". I must go there, you must follow. I understand you know the Fisher, so you can smooth our way in. Just as importantly you can be my official witnesses.'

'In sweet God's name,' Cranston murmured. He turned to hide his temper and walked back to stare at the nightmare fastened to that pillar. Athelstan joined him.

'Be careful, Sir John,' the Friar whispered, 'be prudent and let us leave this place of hideous sorrow. Ingham has exercised his authority to lord it over us. You can do the same. You are the King's High Coroner in London.'

'Clever, clever little friar.' Cranston clapped Athelstan on the shoulder. 'Lead on, my friend.'

They re-joined the others. Cranston threw his cloak back over his shoulder so all could see the gold medallion bearing the royal arms. 'I am also the King's officer,' he declared, imitating

Ingham's voice. 'I am Lord High Coroner of this city. So, Master Thibault, gentlemen, I would appreciate it if you could have the corpse removed to the death house at St Mary atte Bowe. Oh, and by the way, the dead man's possessions?'

Thibault called out to his mercenaries and one of these brought a large pouch already fastened and sealed. He gave this to Thibault, who passed it to Cranston, who pushed it back into Thibault's hands. 'Take that, my friend. The seal is not to be broken. Send it to my clerks at the Guildhall. Now listen, all of you, I summon you to a meeting in that same Guildhall in three days' time as the bells peal for Terce.'

'Does that include me, Sir John?'

'Master Thibault, it certainly does. All must attend or I will submit the King's own summons against you. That's all I have to say on the matter, well, for now anyway. Sir Oliver, let us cross the river and view this new-found treasure.'

They left the warehouse. Cranston informed Flaxwith and his comrades that he would meet them back at St Erconwald's. Crossley and Montague excused themselves whilst Thibault re-joined his Spanish mercenaries. They then walked along the quayside. Moleskin ushered them on to his barge. Once ready, he loosened the mooring ropes, and they were soon battling the sullen, swift-flowing river. The Thames was still boiling with anger. Ingham seemed nervous, even more so than Cranston and Athelstan. The Thames was certainly in a most turbulent mood, chopping waves and swirling currents, whilst a heavy river mist almost hid the shrieking calls of the gulls circling above them. As if to distract himself, Ingham questioned Athelstan about the Fisher of Men. The Friar, also eager to divert himself, described how the Fisher of Men was an officer of the Council. He held a commission to comb the Thames from London Bridge to the furthermost western boundary of the City. He was to collect the corpses of those who suffered any accident, been the victim of murder or committed suicide. He was to collect any such corpses from the Thames and prepare them for burial. However, this was not to take place until the corpses had been exhibited by the Fisher in the 'Chapel of the Drowned Man'. Here, relatives of the deceased could, if they so wished, retrieve the corpse of their kin, for a published fee, be it a pound sterling for a suicide, three pounds for a murder and so on.

Ingham listened attentively then startled as the barge abruptly turned to come alongside the quayside. Cranston ordered Moleskin to wait, then clambered out followed by Athelstan and Ingham. They were immediately welcomed by the Fisher of Men, accompanied by the eerie-looking Ichthus, the human fish who could swim the Thames as swift and as certain as any porpoise. Ichthus was dressed in a simple white shift which only accentuated his fish-like appearance. He was completely bald of any hair be it on his head, face, even his protuberant eyes and cod-like mouth. On the Fisher's left stood his gaggle of dwarves, all garbed in leather, their misshapen faces almost hidden by the deep hoods they wore, which were now pushed back as they recognized Athelstan. They screeched their welcome and promptly knelt, inviting Athelstan to bestow upon them his most singular blessing. The Friar did so, declaring their strange names: Grimdyke, Hackum, Soulsham, Brickface, Maggot and the others. Once the introductions were finished, the Fisher stepped forward, welcoming his three visitors. Nevertheless, Athelstan immediately sensed something was wrong. Ingham started forward but then thought better of it, swiftly stepping away, a look of surprise on his face. The Fisher also seemed startled. He pulled back his deep cowl to reveal his shaven head and face, the skin burned dark by the sun, eloquent proof that the Fisher had once served in Outremer. The Fisher drew himself up, hand going towards the dagger which hung in its sheath on his war belt. The ominous silence which had shrouded the meeting was abruptly broken by the Fisher's little henchmen bursting into song, their high-pitched voices chanting the opening verses of the Salve Regina. The tension eased. The Fisher nodded then smiled grimly at Athelstan and, when the high-pitched chanting had ceased, led his visitors off the quayside to the 'Chapel of the Drowned Man'.

Athelstan had visited this place before. It was a sturdy shed with a black tiled roof and shuttered windows either side of the doorway. Inside was gloomy, so they had to wait until the Fisher's little retainers had lit lamps, lanterns and candles. The chamber, despite the herb pots and scented braziers, still had the cold sour reek of death and the stench of corruption. The stone floor was scrubbed as were the white plastered walls adorned with nothing but stark black crucifixes. Whilst they were waiting, Ingham stood as far away as possible from the Fisher. Cranston tugged Athelstan by the sleeve and led him to the far side of the chapel.

'Did you see that, Friar?'

'You mean the tension between Ingham and the Fisher?'

'Of course, they know each other, don't they? They recognized one another. Some relationship from the past.'

'And?'

'God knows what the story truly is, but for the moment . . .' Cranston broke off as the Fisher lifted a gauntleted hand.

'Sir John,' he declared, 'Brother Athelstan and you, Master Ingham, follow me.'

The Fisher of Men led them down the Hall of Mourning to a corpse table covered by a thick linen cloth. He pulled this back to reveal a skeleton. Its bones were well preserved and white. The head, ribcage, legs and feet were all unbroken. However, what was even more remarkable were the precious items, heavy golden trinkets, which adorned the skeletal remains from head to toe. Bracelets, wrist clasps, necklaces and even a circlet for the head. Other precious jewellery lay scattered about where rings and other adornments had simply slipped from the skeleton. Cranston whistled under his breath. Athelstan stared in disbelief. Even with his limited experience, he could tell the gold was both heavy and precious.

'Where did you find it?' Ingham demanded.

'In a thick wooden casket floating on the river.'

'And where did it come from?'

'Sir John, we hope to build a well-furnished death house with adjoining chambers. We began our digging for this work then we came to a mound, a mass of slimy, slithering mud. However, we had to remove that mound so we could lay the foundations. We were digging deep. Carts full of mud were taken down to the river and dumped.'

'Oh yes!' Cranston intervened. 'As you may know,' he continued, 'I am writing a history of this city. I have come across references to funeral barrows. Yes, that's what they were called, funeral barrows, which ranged along the Thames to the sea. In ancient times, both river and sea were well-known symbols of eternity; that's why the corpses were buried there. The treasure buried with them indicates the dead person's wealth and status as well as providing gifts they can use in the afterlife. It's all wrapped up in symbolism. I must go back and study it again. However, the dead we are looking at are not the victims of murder but just deaths which occurred hundreds of years ago.'

'Congratulations, Sir John,' Athelstan exclaimed. 'A man of learning indeed.'

'True scholarship,' the Fisher added, gesturing at the gold. 'There must be more.'

'If there is,' Ingham retorted, 'it must be reported to me immediately and I mean immediately. I am, at this moment in time, along with my comrades, lodged at "The Golden Oriole".'

'A splendid tavern!' Cranston declared.

'Yes, it is. Our company bought it and share the profits. When we come to London, we lodge there, free of any cost, and enjoy the best in the City.'

'And who manages it?' Athelstan asked, his curiosity pricked by the apparent wealth of these manor lords.

'Two former serjeants. Mailed clerks who fought in our company, Squire Gumblat and Squire Henshaw. Gumblat is the taverner, Henshaw is skilled in wines. "The Golden Oriole" is most prosperous.'

'Yes, yes, it certainly is,' Cranston declared. 'Almost as comfortable as my own personal chapel.'

'Sir John?'

'Why, "The Lamb of God" not far from the Guildhall and within walking distance of "The Golden Oriole".'

'Sir John.' The Fisher pulled his cowl back over his head. 'Sir John,' he repeated, 'do you want refreshment?'

'No, no.' Athelstan swiftly intervened and glanced warningly at Cranston not to delay any further. 'My friend,' Athelstan gestured at the Fisher. 'Could you please see us back to the quayside? Sir Oliver, do you wish to accompany us?'

'No, I will stay and make an inventory. I must make sure the gold is safely sealed and despatched to the Clerks of the Exchequer.'

Cranston grunted his agreement, wrapped his cloak around him then followed Athelstan and the Fisher down to the quayside. Moleskin and his crew were patiently waiting, warming themselves over two braziers crackling with burning coal. Athelstan paused to bless the Fisher's retinue, who were waiting for their master.

'The most solemn blessing,' Hackum called out.

'The most solemn,' Athelstan agreed. 'And so it is.' He lifted his hand and sketched a cross in the air as he intoned the benediction. 'May the blessing of God the Father, God the Son and God the Holy Ghost and that of Our Lady, the most fragrantly beautiful Lady of Walsingham, come down and stay with us all for ever and a day.'

Hackum and his comrades sang out the 'Amen'. Cranston clambered into the barge. Athelstan went to follow then abruptly turned, plucking at the Fisher's sleeve.

'Tomorrow,' the Friar whispered. 'Be at my house about Terce, just after my Jesus Mass. You must come!'

The Fisher nodded his agreement. Athelstan climbed into the barge and took his seat next to Cranston in the canopied stern.

'What was that all about?' the Coroner whispered.

'Oh well, they definitely know each other, Sir John. They have a common story and I intend to discover what it is. I have told the Fisher to join me after Mass tomorrow morning. I can listen to both, but I wager I could get the truth out of the Fisher rather than our royal surveyor.'

'True, true,' Cranston agreed. 'Ingham is a pompous ass. Harmless enough but as arrogant as Lucifer. God knows what he'd say.'

'God knows who he really is,' Athelstan replied. 'Ingham may be a pompous ass, but I detect something else. There is a hardness about that man's soul. I suspect he is a killer to the very marrow. A blood-drinker. We all wear masks, Sir John. We put those masks on to face other masks and that's what we have here. So who is Ingham? What does he hide? As for the rest, well, your guess is as good as mine, Sir John. But we'll see. In the meantime . . .' Athelstan sat back in his seat half watching the other ships, cogs and barges struggling up and down the river, battling the angry swell. Eventually they reached Queenhithe where they gratefully disembarked. Cranston paid Moleskin. Athelstan blessed the crew and added that he would return to Southwark by crossing the bridge where he had other business.

Both friar and coroner made their way along the riverside till they reached the approaches to the bridge. Here, life bustled in all its richness, exuberance and, as Athelstan often remarked, hideous cruelty. Bears and bulls had been brought to the specially fashioned pit within a wooden enclosure. People scurried about, coins in hand, trying to get inside and rent a seat. The clamour of the would-be spectators was almost drowned by the roars of both bears and bulls whilst the air stank of the stable. The pillories and stocks near the bearpit were being busily prepared for a long line of malefactors. Makeshift street traders offered a range of cheap goods and rancid food filched from elsewhere. Two house breakers, caught red-handed, danced on the end of the hanging ropes, the scaffold creaking and snapping as the doomed men slowly strangled to death. Witches and warlocks flocked close; these kept a sharp eye on the hanged men. Once their corpses were cut down, their clothes could be used in the fashioning of philtres and magic potions. Such macabre items were already being touted. The noise dinned the air. Bagpipes wailed. A guild of minstrels and troubadours loudly offered to recite or sing their ballads and lays. Smoke curled from the makeshift ovens carrying the reeking stench of salted meat. The noise was, as Athelstan murmured, the merry tune of Hell. He quietly thanked God for Cranston. The Coroner soon cleared a way through the crowds and on to the narrow lane which cut between the buildings either side of the bridge. They passed the Chapel of St Thomas à Beckett. Pilgrims gathered on the steps outside holding votive candles capped against the strong breeze which constantly swept the bridge. Thankfully, Master Robert Burdon was at home. He was sitting in what he now described as his 'chancery closet', carefully combing the hair on a severed head, once the property of a river pirate caught and decapitated earlier in the day. Burdon got down from his high stool as one of his many sons ushered his visitors in.

'Sir John, Brother Athelstan.' Burdon waved them into a bench beneath the shelves where rows of what he called his 'trophies' stared sightlessly back at him. 'Do you want wine? Some food?'

Athelstan, whose stomach pitched at the sights and smells of this chancery closet, just smiled and shook his head. Cranston too, though he helped himself to a generous gulp from his miraculous wineskin.

'Well.' Burdon clambered back on his high stool. 'How can I help you?' He tapped the decapitated head on the table. 'Don't worry about him, he's still fresh. I like them that way. Just as they turn ripe, that's when I like to pole them. So,' he smiled at his two visitors, 'what do you want?'

'Robert, my friend,' Cranston retorted, 'your recent midnight visitor? Can you tell us any more about him?'

'I have reflected,' Burdon stammered, 'but all I can say is that my sinister visitor comes in the dead of night. On both occasions he brought a severed head, that of Sir Philip Kyne and the decaying limb of Sir Roger Mortimer.' Burdon spread his hands. 'Brother Athelstan, Sir John, men are being decapitated up and down this kingdom. I have little choice but to accept what the visitor brought on each occasion and pole it alongside my other lovely trophics. A reflection really of the bloodletting in this city and beyond. I mean, Sir John, where else could I put them but in a place where, as proven, they might be recognized?'

'And your visitor,' Cranston demanded. 'Any indication who he might be? Who he was working for? Why was he doing it?'

'Nothing, Sir John.'

'And his speech?'

'Oh, definitely English but with a slight burr. Perhaps a man from north of the Trent.'

'Is there anything else?'

'No, Brother Athelstan. What I have told you is all I know.'

Cranston and Athelstan left soon afterwards. They reached the Southwark side of the bridge without incident. The sprawling area just off the bridge, however, was a different matter. Many of the City's colourful characters had crept out from their mumpers castles, devil-haunted dungeons and putrid pits. They came ripe for mischief with a sharp eye for any profit. The unlicensed markets were doing a roaring trade as were the shabby, derelict sin shops where the ladies of the night thronged in the doorways looking for custom, hungry for a coin. Once against Cranston forced his way through, knocking aside the would-be sorcerers and magicians dressed, as usual, in black, their faces hidden behind nightmare masks. At last, they reached the trackway leading up to St Erconwald's. They paused and entered 'The Piebald' where Flaxwith's cohort of bailiffs were busy finishing their meal in the tap room. The other customers, in the main Athelstan's leading parishioners, sat quietly as if overawed by the presence of their visitors.

'It's time I departed. Come, Little Friar.'

Cranston gripped Athelstan by the shoulder and pulled him close. They exchanged the kiss of peace, Cranston promising that he would wait until Athelstan was safely housed.

The Friar bade them all good rest, sketched a hasty blessing, left the tap room and made his way up to the priest's house. He unlocked the door and found all in good order. Mauger and Benedicta had cleaned the floor and table. The hearth was swept, the fire banked, and a bowl of stew stood on top of a capped brazier. Athelstan climbed the ladder to the bed loft. He smiled and murmured a prayer of thanks. The bolster, blankets, sheets and coverlet had all been changed. He heard a scratching at the door; Bonaventure had returned! Athelstan went down, opened the door and the cat sped in as swift as a shot from a sling. Athelstan was about to follow him when he glimpsed the small scroll lying on the floor, slightly crushed where it had been pushed through the gap under the door.

'When did that happen?' Athelstan murmured to himself. 'Was it there when I first came or not?' He went back out into the cold and stared across God's Acre. He glimpsed the lights of 'The Piebald' and heard the sound of Flaxwith's bailiffs now crowding around Sir John for their journey back across the bridge. Athelstan returned to the house. He closed the door then sat down on his stool in front of the fire. He carefully unfolded the square of parchment. Its message was clear and stark: 'Bardolph's death. Resolve this riddle and you will deduce the truth of it all. The riddle is as follows: John is a prisoner held fast and under the constant careful vigilance of three jailors. Matthias, Bernard and

Conrad. At least one of these three men were to be on duty at all times. If Matthias was off duty and Bernard was off duty, Conrad would be on duty. However, any time Bernard was off duty Conrad would also be off duty. Quaestio? Could Matthias ever be off duty? Resolve this and you will resolve Bardolph's death.'

'Will I indeed?' Athelstan whispered. He became lost in thought for a while, letting the parchment drop from his hand, and he slipped into a deep reflection on what he had discovered.

PART TWO

'Light is honoured by the Dark.'

The following morning after checking all was well, Athelstan celebrated his Jesus Mass. Few parishioners made their way through the heavy curtain of icy river mist to join him. Benedicta, however, was one of the first to step inside the rood screen, one hand on the shoulder of the sleepy-eyed altar boy Crim, who then staggered to and from the sacristy as he helped Benedicta prepare the altar. Athelstan seized the opportunity to ask the widow-woman if she had reflected on what she had described the previous day about events at 'The Piebald'. She shook her head.

'Nothing, Father,' she murmured. 'Nothing at all.'

'Well, I have.' Athelstan passed her one of the three copies he had made of the riddle he'd found the previous evening. 'Read this,' he urged. 'And see what you make of it. Keep it close. Please don't show it to anyone else.' She promised she wouldn't. Athelstan smiled his thanks and then blessed himself. 'Come,' he declared, 'let us meet Christ under the great mysteries.'

After Mass, Athelstan announced that he would be confined to his house for the day; he would appreciate it if the parish would respect this. He also welcomed back into 'the land of the living', as he put it, the Hangman of Rochester or Giles of Sempringham, as Athelstan preferred to call him, together with Merrylegs. Both men looked as if they had been very ill as they came into the church just after Mass finished. However, they assured their priest that their humours had vastly improved. Athelstan gave them a special blessing and anointed their foreheads, a pledge that they would continue to return to good health. Athelstan then left, promising Benedicta he would eat the bowl of oatmeal and the other items she had brought across the previous afternoon.

Once back in his house, Athelstan broke his fast. He then laid out the contents of his chancery satchel: ink pot, sheath of quills, pens, sander and the rest. Once ready, the Friar unrolled the scroll of the riddle left under his door and slowly read it out. 'Bardolph's death. Resolve this riddle and you will deduce the truth of it all. The riddle is as follows: John is a prisoner held fast and under the constant careful vigilance of three jailors. Matthias, Bernard and Conrad. At least one of these three men were to be on duty at all times. If Matthias was off duty and Bernard was off duty, Conrad would be on duty. However, any time Bernard was off duty Conrad would also be off duty. Quaestio? Could Matthias ever be off duty? Resolve this and you will resolve Bardolph's death.'

For at least an hour Athelstan tried to draft a resolution to the mystery the riddle posed, but he found it nigh impossible. He studied the phrase about Bardolph's death. 'Death?' Athelstan whispered to himself. 'Death? It was murder! So why did the author of the riddle not state that rather than the bland statement "Bardolph's death"? True,' Athelstan continued, whispering to himself, 'people often prefer something innocuous rather than the dramatic word murder. Is that true here?' Athelstan sighed and put the scroll away. He rose and stretched, wondering if he should walk the stiffness out of himself when there was a rap on the door. Athelstan opened it and the Fisher of Men swept in followed by Ichthus. The human fish smiled at Athelstan and promptly sat down in front of the hearth, putting one arm around Bonaventure. The cat purred in pleasure and drew even closer to his new-found friend.

'Remarkable, isn't it?' The Fisher paused to take off his cloak and hood, which Athelstan put on a wall peg close to the fire. He greeted the Fisher then gestured at the tomcat.

'What is remarkable?'

'Ichthus, Brother. He loves cats and they in turn adore him.' The Fisher of Men took off his war belt and gratefully acknowledged the brimming goblet of hot posset which Athelstan thrust into his hands. The Fisher raised this in thanks and sat down on the room's second chair. 'I think,' he continued, 'indeed I am sure, that what attracts Ichthus to cats and cats to Ichthus is that

my friend constantly smells of fish. Anyway, Brother Athelstan,
I am here. Why?'

'You must suspect,' Athelstan replied. 'You and Ingham recognized each other yesterday. I could see that. Sir John realized
that. What was it, a memory from the past? If Ingham was
involved, I am sure it wasn't a pleasant one.'

The Fisher just stared across at Ichthus cuddling Bonaventure.

'I should tell you, shouldn't I, Brother?'

'Yes, my friend,' Athelstan answered. 'But please, the truth.'

'Very well.' The Fisher put the cup of posset on the table and
drew himself up. 'My true name is Sir Edmund Lacey or rather
that was my name when I was baptized in the great abbey church
at Tewkesbury. I was the apple of my parents' eye. I revelled
in the love and favour they lavished on me. I was their only
darling son. I suppose I was somewhat spoiled. I became wild,
impetuous.' He smiled thinly. 'The ladies thought I was very
handsome. Anyway, some twenty-five years ago, during the last
decade of the old king's reign, I joined a Free Company, a cohort
of knights and squires to fight the King's cause in Normandy.
Of course, that was just a pretence, a pretext for wholesale
plunder and pillage. Our leader, our captain . . .' Athelstan caught
the sarcasm in the man's voice, 'was Sir Oliver Ingham. Now,
during one of our forays across Normandy, we reached the
beautiful village of Avranches or rather,' he added bitterly, 'the
once beautiful village of Avranches. We plundered the manor
there, during which we found a coffer of gold coins, a veritable
fortune.'

'And the manor lord?'

'Died of his wounds after being tortured by Ingham and others,
including myself.' The Fisher paused, breathing noisily, eyes
blinking.

'What then, my friend?'

'What then, Brother? God be my witness, matters went from
bad to worse. We were overjoyed at finding such treasure. We
celebrated. We found wine casks in the manor lord's cellar. We
broached one after another. We all drank, though I admit I became
deeply concerned at the nasty twist in events. Finding that gold
and drinking that wine brought about a change. Our chevauchee

fast became a massacre. Men, women and children being cut
down and slaughtered in cold blood.'

'And you?'

'I did not take part in that. Buildings were torched, then the
real tragedy. Many of the villagers had fled to their parish church,
an ancient wooden structure on a stone base. They locked themselves in and barred all windows and doors, then they lit fires.'

'Why did they do that?'

'I don't really know. I suspect they planned to loose fire arrows
at us, frighten our horses and so drive us away. Anyway, someone
inside that church must have fumbled. It's easy to imagine. Those
poor villagers must have been terrified. God knows what truly
happened. I am still not sure about the true sequence of events.
Anyway, the fires broke out and the flames must have raced
around that wooden church. I am sure you've seen the likes
before? Fires which can run faster than a man. As I said, the
parishioners had barricaded themselves inside and this hindered
them in trying to escape.'

'And you had nothing to do with the fire?'

'Nothing at all, Brother.' The Fisher lifted a hand. 'I swear it
was a hellish scene. The flames roaring like a horde of demons
breaking free of the underworld. The cries of all those victims
were pitiful. The horrid sounds from elsewhere like the refrain
of some dire choir. I had broken free of our main group, but I
was summoned back by Ingham. By then it was too late, though
I did try to help. Somehow or other, a woman inside the church
had climbed up on to the choir loft and reached the church's one
and only large window. She dragged her two sons to that window,
screaming for help. I dismounted and climbed up. Oh yes.' The
Fisher paused, rubbing the side of his forehead as if he was trying
to purge some hideous memory.

'What happened?'

'Sometimes, Brother, I still hear those screams, I see the
dancing flames. I can hear the crash of wood and timber.'

'And the woman?'

'All was confusion.' The Fisher sighed noisily. 'I tried to reach
her. Some of the more sober members of our company came to
help me. In the melee below, my warhorse was sorely wounded,

screaming in pain. I had to ignore it. I grabbed both boys and dropped them to some of my company waiting below. I tried to rescue the woman, but a ball of fire engulfed her. I slipped and fell to the ground. I was aware of lying there, my body in pain from head to toe. My warhorse, which had fractured his leg, was put out of pain. I thought my comrades would then help me. However, one of our scouts came hastening in with news that a comitatus of French knights were fast approaching. In a word, Brother, I was left forsaken.'

'They abandoned you?'

'Yes, they did, Brother. Now we had sworn an oath over bread and wine, the materials of the eucharist, to live and die by each other. They certainly did not keep that oath. They thundered out of the village, leaving me injured and deserted. I knew I had to escape from Avranches. If the French took me prisoner, they would torture me. I crawled and hobbled. I staggered into the forest, and I hid. I had a sack with some food which I took from my saddlebags. I was young, my injuries healed fast, then one day, by sheer chance, I met a comitatus of horsemen, not the French, but Lazar Knights.'

'Lepers?'

'Yes, Brother, leper knights. They were making their way to the coast where a ship was waiting to take them to Outremer. They gave me a stark choice. Join with them, lepers or not, and serve under their banner for a certain number of years.'

'And you accepted?'

'Yes, I did, Brother. I sealed indentures with them. I joined their company, and I contracted their disease. A hideous contagion, but due to God's mercy, I survived. I was reconciled to what was happening. After all, what else could I do.'

'You had no choice, my friend.'

'Yes, Brother, I had no choice. I served in Outremer,' the Fisher continued. 'I helped defend our pilgrims. I also reflected on my life and the pain and suffering I had inflicted on others. The years passed; I served my indenture with the Lazars. Eventually, I left their company and decided to return home, not to Gloucestershire but London. I became a hermit, a recluse living out my life on an abandoned quayside. I studied the river. I glimpsed the occasional corpse drifting on the current and I

decided something should be done to give such corpses dignity.
Now when I left the Lazars, I had a pouch full of good coin. I
used this to buy provisions and of course showed hospitality to
all who asked for it: that's when the others joined me. Hackum,
Brickface, Soulsham and, above all, Ichthus.' The Fisher's
henchman, warming himself before the fire, turned and smiled
at the master, who took out a set of ave beads. The Fisher began
to thread these through his fingers, quietly murmuring the 'Ave
Maria'.

'My friend?'

'Sorry, Brother. My mind wanders. Out on that quayside I
reflected upon my life. I wanted to make some reparation for my
many sins, so I became what I am now. Sir John knows a little
about me. He and others supported my proposal to cull the
Thames for corpses. I was granted those desolate buildings on
that lonely quayside just past "La Reole". People offered to help.
My status and office were confirmed by the Council.' The Fisher
shrugged. 'And so it was and so it is.'

'But come,' Athelstan retorted. 'On your return to this kingdom
and this city in particular, you must have done careful search on
other members of the Via Crucis who had abandoned you so
callously?' The Friar got to his feet. 'Let us have some morning
ale.' He crossed to what he called his 'little buttery' and poured
three stoups. Ichthus smiled his thanks and offered his to
Bonaventure before drinking himself. The Fisher raised his cup
in silent toast to Athelstan then sat staring across the room whilst
continuing to sift the ave beads through his fingers. 'My friend,
time passes, the candle burns.' Athelstan pointed across to the
hour candle on its spigot in the corner.

'Yes, Brother, time is treacherous. Of course, I went searching.
I got to know all about my former comrades, their wealth and
power. Nevertheless, I decided that silence was part of my act
of reparation. "Video Atque Taceo" became my motto – "I watch
but I keep silent". As for my former comrades? Well, they did
not, and could not, guess that the grim figure of the Fisher of
Men was in truth the spoilt brat Sir Edmund Lacey. All that
changed today. Ingham recognized me and I had no choice but
to acknowledge him.'

'And you had no approach from any of them before today?'

'None, Brother, and I left them all, Ingham especially, well alone!'

'Who is left? I mean of the actual Free Company, the Via Crucis? Those members who swore an oath, signed articles and sealed indentures. Who is left, tell me?' Athelstan smoothed out a piece of parchment and prepared a quill pen. 'Sir Edmund, their names?'

'Myself,' the Fisher sighed, 'three others have been recently attacked, Lords Kyne, Mortimer and Despencer. Mortimer, I understand, was roughly exhumed, his corpse abused and his head severed. Kyne was executed in full sight of his family and household out at his Manor of Malroad. Hugh Despencer was whipped to death in that filthy warehouse, or so I understand.'

'And the other survivors, I mean apart from yourself and Ingham?'

'John Montague who styles himself a scholar, an expert, a peritus on the origin of names.' The Fisher waved a hand. 'A man who likes to journey and study the origin of things. Then there's Stephen Crossley, a would-be merchant, but I understand he has an evil humour of the belly. Finally, there's the two squires Gumblat and Henshaw. They manage "The Golden Oriole", that splendid tavern which the Via Crucis bought, invested in and now own. Both squires,' the Fisher continued wryly, 'are well regarded in the tavern trade, but they are also killers to the very bone.'

'The rest don't seem any better.'

'True, Brother, and I am not their judge.' The Fisher blessed himself. 'The names I've given you are all members of the Via Crucis who were present in Avranches when the treasure was discovered: those who'd left the Company before that or joined us afterwards were given no share. Of course. Time and Nature have culled many of those who were in Avranches, which,' he added, 'only increases the amount available to those still living.'

'And the twin boys you rescued?'

'Oh, I made enquiries and followed them from afar. Benjamin and Benedict Vaucort. They are identical twins, both very

capable. Once they returned to England, the Via Crucis did some
good. They made careful search, and the two boys were entrusted
to a merchant and his wife who lived along Cripplegate. They
were a childless couple and were absolutely delighted to have
two handsome boys in their care. From what I can gather, this
kind, generous couple lavished love and care on the boys. They
became scholars, attending St Paul's school held in the transept
of that cathedral. They proved to be clever, erudite, studious and
eager to learn. They graduated from St Paul's to Stapleton
College Oxford where, once again, they demonstrated their
considerable ability. Both young men left Oxford, "cum laude"
– indeed with deep praise for their skill and expertise. Little
wonder they were appointed as Clerks to the Chancery of Receipt
in the Royal Exchequer at Westminster. From what I gather they
are still there and live in the house they inherited from their
foster parents.'

'Good, very good,' Athelstan murmured. He pointed at the Fisher.
'According to what you say, my friend, you have forsaken the path
of revenge. I believe that. However, have the Vaucorts? After all,
they lost their mother in that horrid fire in the village where they
were born and raised. She was snatched away from them in the
most ghastly fashion, a memory which must sear them?'

'You mean they could be the killers of Kyne and Despencer
and the abusers of Mortimer's corpse?'

'Yes, that is exactly what I mean.'

The Fisher of men smiled to himself.

'Well, my friend?' Athelstan remarked.

'Brother Athelstan, both young men could be waging a war
of revenge, but there again, so could I whilst hiding behind a
mask of mock sorrow.' He shrugged. 'Brother, I agree it is
quite possible that the twins have turned to vengeance. But
why now, so many years later? Oh yes,' he added, 'it's feasible.
After all, both Benjamin and Benedict are mailed clerks who
have served in the royal array along the Scottish March.' He
paused. 'Brother Athelstan, I cannot really speak for them,
only myself.'

'In which case,' Athelstan retorted, 'you claim to be innocent
of any wrongdoing? There is nothing you need to confess?'

'Brother, my only recent sin, and I speak as if I knelt before you to be shrived. Yes, my most recent sin is that I was most tempted to keep that ancient gold.'

'I am glad you did not. The penalties for interfering with royal treasure trove are most painful. There again,' Athelstan smiled, 'you do have a claim to a portion of what you found. In the many rules about treasure trove, there is a clause which states that appropriate payment must be made to whoever found the treasure in the first place. I would have no objection to you taking what is legally yours.'

The Fisher leaned forward, his harsh face transformed by a smile.

'Of course,' the Fisher whispered, snapping his fingers. 'Now that, Brother, is a matter I will pursue. Do not worry, I am honest, but I don't trust Ingham. He is dangerous and cruel. If he caught me helping myself to what I shouldn't, he would certainly make his authority felt. A ruthless man, Brother, who has no fear of God nor man. Oh, he can hide it well, but he hates churches and priests. I do wonder about that fire in Avranches. Was it started by accident or did Ingham somehow cause the conflagration? He had no time for religion, and I wager still doesn't. Anyway,' the Fisher pushed back his chair, 'Brother, I have told you everything about my past and my present. Above all, please accept my assurance that I have not, and I will not, pursue vengeance against my former comrades.'

The Fisher rose and made himself ready. He murmured to his henchman to do the same. Ichthus patted Bonaventure on the head then rose to receive Athelstan's blessing. Both master and henchman left. Standing in the doorway, the Friar watched them go then returned inside, locking the door behind him. He crossed himself and knelt on his prie-dieu before the Cross of San Damiano nailed to the wall beside the steps leading up to his bed loft. Once he had finished reciting the psalm, he got to his feet and stood listening as Mauger the Bell Clerk sounded the Angelus. Athelstan waited until the constant pealing finished. 'Very good,' he whispered to himself, 'my beloveds will be gathering to break their fast and I shall join them.'

Athelstan found the tap room of 'The Piebald' busy enough.

Most of his flock had gathered, including Benedicta. They sat
on stools or overturned barrels placed around battered tables.
When Athelstan strode through the door, they all roared their
approval, Watkin and Pike raising their tankards in toast. Athelstan
stared around, surprised at the jollity and festive atmosphere. The
Friar raised his hand for silence.

'My beloveds,' he declared, 'I rejoice that you rejoice, but
what's the cause?'

'Tell him.' Thomas the Toad, Keeper of the House of Abode,
the mortuary Athelstan had built in the centre of St Erconwald's
cemetery, clambered on to a stool. 'Tell him,' he screeched.

'Oh shut up and get down,' Watkin bellowed.

'You shut up,' Thomas yelled. 'My toads have more sense than
you, Watkin. Now I am here, can I offer those same toads to clear
your dwellings of flies, spiders and other such vermin . . .'

Thomas's attempt to promote his business provoked howls of
derision. The toad keeper climbed down. Athelstan clapped his
hands and kept doing so until he had silence.

'Now, Benedicta,' Athelstan invited the widow-woman over
to join him in the centre of the tap room. She did so, smiling
from ear to ear. She swiftly winked at Athelstan but schooled
her face.

'Father,' she began, 'I am here to do your bidding.' Benedicta's
smile faded as Pike murmured some salacious witticism. She
glared at him until the ditcher bowed his head and mumbled an
apology.

'Right,' Athelstan proclaimed, 'the rest of you keep silent.
Benedicta, tell me what has happened?'

'Early this morning, Father, long before prime, Horace the
Housebreaker was caught red-handed breaking into a shop near
the Great Conduit in Cheapside. You know Horace, surely,
Father?'

'I have heard the name more than once, but I don't think he's
a gospel greeter. And, if my memory serves me right, nor is his
lady wife Helga?'

'That's me, Father.' A woman sitting deep in the shadows
rose and shuffled forward. A bony, rough-faced woman garbed
in a patched gown, her iron-grey hair pulled back and tied with

a piece of string at the back of her head. She was watery-eyed, lower lip trembling. She stretched out a bony hand, pointing at the Friar. 'You speak the truth, Father,' she grated, 'Horace and I did not pay the church pence, nor did we attend Mass or seek you out at the shriving pew. I am sorry for that. We are now paying the price for such neglect of both God and man.'

'Helga,' Athelstan replied, 'this is not the time to make reparation.' He turned to Benedicta. 'Thank you, my lady, but let Helga tell her tale.'

Benedicta agreed and returned to the bench. She glared at Pike the Ditcher then sat down between Cecily the Courtesan and Clarice, her sister – two ladies, Athelstan secretly suspected, who lay down in his cemetery more often than the parish coffin. He turned back to Helga.

'Continue,' he said, 'early this morning . . .'

'Horace was taken red-handed,' Helga breathlessly continued, 'breaking into a shop on Cheapside. One of his accomplices – I cannot give his name – escaped and hurried to tell me the news. I in turn hastened across to Newgate. However, Horace had already been arraigned.' She stumbled over the word arraigned, so Athelstan repeated it for her. 'That's right, Father,' she continued. 'Caught red-handed, Horace was placed before a justice who soon established that he had been found guilty of the same crime time and time again. And that's the truth, Father. Horace took to housebreaking as a bird to flying. I knew it would end this way. Anyway, he was condemned to death, sentenced to hang before the week is out.' Helga drew a deep breath. 'He was tried in the court chamber of Newgate. Afterward he was committed to the Abyss, the hell hole, the condemned cell. I asked one of the turnkeys if I could visit my husband. He agreed but only after I let him fondle me.' Helga paused at the muttered curses of those listening to her. 'Never mind,' she continued, 'I met Horace.' She paused, licked her dry lips and brushed her sweaty hands down the front of her gown. 'Horace was in good heart. He admitted he had been caught, but then he confessed he had been here in "The Piebald" yesterday evening. He knew Bardolph was there.'

'And?'

'And, Father, Horace hated Bardolph. Not just because that bastard was a tight-fisted, grubby tax collector who would squeeze blood out of a stone. Oh no, Horace hated Bardolph ever since the Great Revolt.'

Athelstan sensed the deathly silence which seemed to sweep like some harsh breeze through the tap room.

'What about it?'

'Well, Father, Horace joined the Upright Men. He was a captain in the Earthworms, the street warriors who would sweep away the rich and powerful.'

'And?' Athelstan demanded, showing a slight exasperation.

'The truth is,' Watkin bellowed, 'Bardolph was a Judas man. He pretended to be one of us, but in the end, he betrayed our leaders. He not only identified them but informed Master Thibault where they were hiding. When it was all over, Bardolph was rewarded for his treachery by being appointed a chief tax collector here in Southwark. He was truly hated.' Watkin's declaration was confirmed by grunts of agreement.

'And yesterday morning, or indeed that entire day, Horace was definitely here?'

'He certainly was, Father,' Pike rasped, gesturing at Benedicta. 'She will confirm that.'

'But he was gone,' Benedicta declared, 'when the door was forced.' She shrugged. 'Busy with his accomplices, preparing to break into that shop along Cheapside, no doubt.'

'Very well,' Athelstan declared, turning to Helga. 'What did Horace actually tell you, I mean about Bardolph's murder?'

'That he killed the tax collector with a blow to the heart. How he stole the tax money and fled.'

'Did he say when or how he did that?'

'No, Father, he did not.'

Athelstan stared down at the floor. He felt the cloying atmosphere of the tap room where so much mischief was plotted. The air was thick with the fumes of the kitchen, different smells swirled – burnt meat, charcoal, beer, wine as well as the stench from the jakes closet just outside the back door. Athelstan suddenly felt slightly sick. He rubbed his stomach. He heard the scrabble of mice in the far corner and a screech as two of them were seized by the tavern cat.

'Father, are you well?' Benedicta was now standing beside him, face full of concern. He glanced to his right and left. His parishioners were now busy gossiping amongst themselves.

'I need quiet,' Athelstan murmured. 'Benedicta, I will go up to the Avalon Chamber now. Please tell my parishioners to remain here till I return.'

Athelstan walked across to the staircase as Benedicta proclaimed the Friar's message. Joscelyn tried to follow, but Athelstan shook his head and shooed him away. He climbed the stairs and walked along to the Avalon Chamber; its door had now been moved. Athelstan paused to inspect this. He concluded that when the door had been forced, great damage had been caused to the two bolts, one at the top, the other at the bottom, whilst the simple lock had been badly ruptured, the key still inside twisted and bent. He studied all of this and walked back in. The room was now well aired and clean. The floorboards had been recently scrubbed whilst the narrow jakes closet smelled of nothing but some astringent, probably dried herbs, which Joscelyn grew in abundance in his spacious, well-stocked garden at the rear of the tavern. Satisfied, but still suspicious, Athelstan went back to stand in the doorway as he reflected on what he had seen, heard and felt. Bardolph was undoubtedly an unpleasant character, a principal tax collector now and a Judas man during the Great Revolt. Certainly, those who had survived the cruel bloodletting which followed the crushing of the uprising would have dearly loved to see Bardolph killed. Leaders of the Revolt, the Upright Men, or at least those that survived together with their ardent followers, the Earthworms, would murder the likes of Bardolph in the blink of an eye.

'All this,' Athelstan murmured, 'certainly applies to my beloved parishioners. The likes of Watkin and Pike had sat by the fires of the Upright Men. They had taken the oath and vowed to support the Great Cause.' Athelstan breathed out noisily. 'But why,' the Friar mused, 'why here in this tavern at this time when suspicion would certainly weigh heavy against the likes of

Joscelyn and his mischief-loving coven? Bardolph could have been murdered in some other way surely? An arrow or bolt loosed from the mouth of a dark alleyway would have the same result as well as provide the assailant with more protection.'

Athelstan continued to reflect on the possibilities, including the fact that, at least on Bardolph's part, there was no sign of any disturbance. No evidence that Bardolph, a dagger man who had probably seen military service, resisted. He was apparently sitting on that chair when his murderer approached him. Drawing so close the assassin could plunge a dagger hilt-deep into Bardolph's treacherous heart. But was that feasible? Even possible? How could someone draw so close, so swiftly, so surely to do such a dreadful deed? A lover? A trusted companion? And that riddle – who was responsible for it? What message was the author trying to convey about the so-called death of Bardolph? Why not write clearly and tell the truth? What . . .

'Father, Father!' Benedicta shouted from the foot of the stairs. 'Father, you have a visitor.'

'And I can guess who,' Athelstan murmured. 'So let us go down to meet Master Tiptoft.'

'What could it be, Father?'

'I suspect Sir John . . .' Athelstan paused as Tiptoft came up the stairs.

'We are going to Newgate, Father,' he announced. 'You've heard the news about Horace the Housebreaker?'

'I certainly have, my friend.'

'Ah, well, Father, Sir John was summoned to Newgate and, I am informed, so are you. Horace wishes to make a full confession.'

'In which case let us proceed.' Athelstan crossed himself. 'And may Christ have mercy on us all.'

Athelstan braced himself to follow Tiptoft out of the tavern and down the alleyway leading on to the bridge then up into Cheapside. The usual crowd surged, a mass of humanity pushing and shoving their way forward. Priests with censers puffing plumes of incense smoke escorted some coffin being brought to this cemetery or that. Occasionally there was a single priest with a cope around his shoulders preceded by an altar boy holding a capped candle. The priest carried the viaticum he was taking to some sick person who needed the sacrament. Hunters, rich young men on their gaily caparisoned steeds, shouted joyfully as, with hawks on their leather-bound wrists, they made their way up to the hunting runs north of the old city wall. Wedding parties all plumed and garlanded with winter wreaths rode by, horse harness jingling like fairy bells. Troubadours, minstrels and other music men sang different songs or chanted stories about the Great Silk Road stretching across the roof of the world. Once through these, Tiptoft led Athelstan into a different, more macabre world. The brooding, fearsome Newgate Prison, that Hole of Hell, that House of Iron which would chill the bravest soul.

The prison was a grim, grey building which towered over London's great slaughter house and fleshing market. The place constantly stank of blood and gore, which swilled backwards and forwards across the cobbles. The squalid mess of fetid flesh drew in the crows and ravens, which strutted backwards and forwards as they pecked at the offal. These birds of prey were only driven off by the feral dogs and cats also on the hunt whilst they in turn had to resist the blows and curses of the poor who crawled across the ground searching for their next meal. Newgate presided over all this gruesome chaos with its sinister frontage devoid of any windows, its narrow apertures and doors sealed by iron bars or steel studded gates. Here the execution carts, all regaled for the macabre ceremony of a public hanging, gathered to collect the condemned. The great dray horses, caparisoned in black, pulled carts painted a deep blood red. Most of the executioners and hangmen dressed in a macabre fashion. Athelstan glimpsed Giles of Sempringham garbed in his usual black from head to toe. The Hangman sat on the tail of one of the carts. Athelstan caught his eye and raised his hand in blessing then called out asking if the Hangman had recovered from his ailment.

'I am fine, Father,' he called back. 'Just some severe disturbance of the belly.'

Athelstan nodded and followed Tiptoft up through a narrow-gated door into the prison. This certainly was a place of the damned with its constant jarring noise: the shrieks and yells of those imprisoned there or the perpetual clanging of iron against iron as doors were flung open and crashed shut. Tiptoft led Athelstan down a narrow corridor and up to the Keeper's lodge. He rapped on the door, pushed it open and ushered the Friar inside. Cranston and the Keeper were inside sitting at a table with Horace the Housebreaker perched between them. Although, by his own admission, Horace was not a gospel greeter, Athelstan recognized the man as one of those parishioners who occasionally crossed his path. As soon as Athelstan entered, the housebreaker leapt to his feet. The Friar blessed him then sat down in the shabby chair opposite. As the Keeper poured four stoups of ale, Athelstan studied the feckless housebreaker who had brought him here. Horace was a small tub of a man with an impudent face now all bruised and dirty. Horace smiled, gap-toothed, at the Friar. He then slurped the ale, bringing the tankard down hard on the table whilst wiping his mouth on the back of his wrist.

'I am here to hear your confession, Horace. I mean, how you were caught.'

'Oh, easily enough, Brother. I was hanging around "The Piebald", Joscelyn was holding court. Bardolph arrived full of himself. He was joined by his henchman, you know the former troubadour, oh yes, that's it, Scoresby.'

'That's correct,' Cranston declared. 'Bardolph's henchman is Scoresby; definitely a man with a past, but that's true of all us sinners, isn't it?'

'Well said, Sir John. Ah well, I detested Bardolph. I always have. He was really no different from the rest of his kind, grasping and greedy in so many ways. He creamed off what he collected and bullied those unable to pay. There was many a lady who had to raise their skirts to pay their dues. If I hadn't killed him, someone else would have done. He was wicked to the core. He abused and ill-treated many a poor soul.'

'In God's name,' Athelstan whispered. 'What a villain.'

'In God's name what I have said is true, Brother. A hideous man, Bardolph, and I'll tell him the same when I join him in the choir invisible.'

'Horace, what actually happened in "The Piebald"?'

'Brother, I decided to kill him. Simple enough. I went up to his chamber to give him a piece of my mind. He was sitting on that chair just inside the door with a pannier in his lap.'

'He was still cloaked and booted?'

'Yes, Brother, just sitting there sifting the coins. I drew Bardolph's dagger from its sheath; he had tossed this on to the bed, a simple blade and handle.'

'Did Bardolph resist?'

'Sir John, he was as drunk as a sot, Mawmsey with pot after pot of ale. So drunk he couldn't even pick his nose never mind a dagger. Anyway, I had the blade, I approached him, Bardolph glanced up and I struck. I sank that blade deep into his heart. The shock alone kept him still. He slumped. I watched the life light fade in his eyes then he was gone.' Horace swallowed hard. 'All went quiet. I decided to hide my handiwork behind a mystery. I ruptured the door bolts so they would simply snap when the door was forced.'

'And the lock?'

'Easy enough, Brother. Bardolph's money pouch contained strips of coarse parchment.'

'Ah yes,' Cranston intervened. 'They are used to give receipts for monies collected.'

'I took two of them, narrow but thick. I created two wedges which I pushed beneath the door whilst I also twisted the loosened key. It was the best I could do. Once outside, I closed the door and sealed it again. I hoped, and I was right, that when the door was forced, no one would notice two scraps of filthy parchment lying on a dusty floor.'

'I see,' Cranston murmured. 'You killed Bardolph easily enough because he was as drunk as a fiddler. You loosened the bolts on the top and the bottom of the door to his chamber. You twisted the key in the lock, and you left the chamber, pulling the door close so it stuck on those two wedges of coarse parchment. You murdered Bardolph, but you also found a way out. I have heard of similar tricks and devices. Brother Athelstan, it is possible.'

'Anything else, Horace?'

The housebreaker shrugged. 'Brother Athelstan, I can say no more.'

'Oh yes, you can. What about the money?'

'Gone, Brother. I gave some to Helga, which I am sure she must have spent by now. She's not to blame. I claimed I had won it at Hazard. As for the rest I did gamble. I ate, drank and feasted. I rewarded my accomplices who helped me to break into that shop, which,' Horace added mournfully, 'will now lead to my sad demise.'

'A very busy time,' Athelstan declared. 'Busy as a bee or so it seems. You murder Bardolph, you steal the money, you leave some of your ill-gotten gains with Helga. You then hasten into the City where you reward your followers. You feast, you gamble, you break into a house, and you're caught, trapped and brought here. Your good wife Helga visits you. You probably left her instructions about the money,' Athelstan sighed, 'and now it is all over.'

'God save you,' the taciturn keeper grated. 'But, Master Horace, you must soon join the others being loaded into the carts to be hanged at Vespers time.'

'And before Brother Athelstan pleads for you,' Cranston declared, clapping the housebreaker on the shoulder, 'you have been convicted more times than I care to remember.'

'Do you wish to be shrived?'

'Oh yes, Brother.'

Cranston and the Keeper rose and said they would wait outside. Once they had closed the door behind them, Horace knelt before Athelstan and confessed his sins. Nothing more than a litany of self-indulgence and petty thefts. Athelstan heard him out, pronounced absolution, patted Horace on the shoulder and made to leave. Cranston thanked the Keeper then both he and Athelstan hurried out of Newgate.

The Coroner strode as quickly as he could. The clamour, stench and sight of the execution carts was too much for Athelstan, who walked head down though he paused and glanced up as he heard his name being called. He turned around; the Hangman of Rochester stood there.

'You're all ready for the deadly masque?'

'As ever, Father.' He pulled his hood up over his yellow straw-like hair to frame a face as white as that of any corpse. 'I just came to wish you well, Father. You have been to see Horace?'

'Yes, I have, Giles.'

'You always call me that, Father.'

'Of course I do, that is your true name. Anyway, you are correct. I have been to see Horace. He is about to join the heavenly court. For the love of God, Giles, make it quick.'

'Don't worry, Father. I shall drop him as swift and as sure as a raindrop, directly into the hands of God.'

Athelstan thanked him and followed Cranston up into Cheapside. The bulky Coroner pushed himself through the crowds, aiming like a well-loosed shaft for his favourite chapel, the sumptuous tavern 'The Lamb of God'. Cranston went through the door and immediately seized mine hostess, the Coroner's favourite hostess, or so he proclaimed. He gave his flaxen-haired friend a warm hug before being shown up into the Coroner's holy of holies, the tavern solar. Once there, Athelstan slumped down on a cushioned chair whilst Cranston divested himself of his cloak, war belt and beaver hat. Mine hostess bustled in. The Coroner ordered venison pie and a dish of vegetables which, he proclaimed, he would share with his constant companion. The pink-cheeked hostess bustled out, returning a few moments later with two goblets and a flagon of the finest Bordeaux. Once settled, Cranston and Athelstan toasted each other then sipped their wine.

'You do not like going to Newgate, Brother?'

'I don't, Sir John, I hate it.'

'And Horace?'

'Sir John, I am still agitated. My mind is in tumult. I am not thinking clearly at all. But . . .' The Friar paused, lost in his own thoughts.

'But what, Brother?'

'There is something very wrong, Sir John. Something about that murder at "The Piebald" which gnaws at my soul. However, for the very life of me, I cannot discern it.'

'You get like this, Brother, when you are baffled.'

'In which case,' Athelstan lifted his goblet in toast, 'I am now truly baffled. We are deep in the maze of murder, my friend. We have to reach the centre where we will confront the truth though God knows what's lurking there or what's waiting for us along the way.'

Sir Henry Blondin, Keeper of the Royal Manor of Chafford Hundred in Essex, was also concerned. The Keeper, a former commander in the Free Company, the Via Crucis, sat in his carved oak pew in the manor chapel. Blondin often came here to reflect and beg pardon for his many sins. Years ago, when the blood ran hot in his veins, he had joined the Company of the Via Crucis on their chevauchees across Normandy. There were so many memories, or rather nightmares, and none more so than what happened in the village of Lisieux. The Company had crushed any resistance then pillaged and plundered the hamlet to their hearts' content. No one was spared. Men, women and children were put to the sword and their corpses thrust down the village well, so many they crammed it to the brim. Blondin and his comrades had seized treasure, burned down houses, barns, sheds, stables and dovecots. Nothing was left but blackened, smoking ruins. The Company were preparing to leave when an old woman, swift for her age, appeared as if out of nowhere and began to curse them. Grey hair floating out, eyes full of hatred, her mouth like a sewer uttering a litany of filthy curses for this life and the one to come. Blondin just laughed and rode her down. The old woman, probably a witch, had died beneath the iron-shod, razor-edged hooves of his warhorse, her body cut from head to toe, a mass of wounds, the blood flowing freely.

At the time Blondin didn't care. He passed on. He left Lisieux and soon forgot the old witch's curses. Until times changed. English power in Normandy eventually collapsed under a resurgence of opposition by the French led by skilled commanders such as Du Guesclin. English Free Companies were ambushed. Some stood and fought, others retreated to ports such as Boulogne to get home as swiftly as they could. Blondin had begun his trade of war with Sir Oliver Ingham. He wished he had stayed with that cruel warrior. Former comrades in the Via

Crucis had returned very rich men. Blondin had not. Once in England, his treasure greatly depleted, Blondin had to petition the Crown for assistance and was granted the office of keeper of this manor. Blondin settled down into a life of peace until recently when the dreams began. Nightmares from the very heart of the underworld. In the first dream the witch had emerged out of the well, the one in Lisieux crammed with corpses. She had floated like some ill-omened bird hovering above him, repeating the very curses she had uttered decades earlier in Lisieux. Blondin had, time and again, gone to a priest asking to be shrived. He'd crouched in the mercy pew and confessed his sins. The priest would absolve him, but Blondin always caught the look in the priest's eyes, one of piteous desperation, as if he knew who Blondin truly was and what he would be in the future, a soul pursued by the Furies. More fearful were recent reports from the verderers and manor bailiffs. How strangers had been seen around the manor. The occasional horsemen glimpsed on the brow of a hill or along one of those trackways or coffin paths leading to the manor. Blondin crossed himself and leaned down to pick up the small hand-held arbalest which he took everywhere with him. He cradled it as he reflected on the different rumours bubbling in the City. How former members of a certain Free Company were being cruelly slain, their heads severed and poled on London Bridge. These men had one thing in common. They had all fought in France alongside Ingham. But that was years ago . . .?

'So what is this?' he murmured to himself. Still wondering, Blondin rose and left the choir stall. He crossed to the narrow Devil's door in the far transept but then changed his mind and turned back towards the corpse door which led out into the small manor cemetery. Blondin was almost there when three men emerged from the ill-lit transept. Blondin, hands trembling, tried to raise the arbalest, but he was old, weak and the leader of these mysterious visitors lunged forwards, swift as a cat. He knocked the arbalest out of Blondin's hands and let it clatter down on to the hard paving.

'What is this?' Blondin stuttered as two of the intruders grabbed his arms.

'Why, Sir Henry Blondin, it is for you. Today is judgement day.'

The leader then opened the corpse door and Blondin was dragged out into the cemetery, a doleful place with barren stone or wooden crosses and other battered funereal plinths. The weeping willows and ancient yew trees only deepened the sense of loss and mourning which pervaded the place. Three other men were waiting for them, including Mercier, steward of the manor. A little frog-like man, Mercier seemed to be in a state of absolute terror. The steward was seated on a table-tomb closely guarded by two of the intruders. Blondin was made to sit on a stone slab opposite Mercier. The leader of the intruders came and stood in between them, hands clasped like a preacher eager to deliver his homily. Blondin, now shivering as the mist-hung air froze his sweaty body, could only stare at the intruder whose head and face were hidden by a visor and a deep capuchon.

'Sir Henry Blondin,' the leader of the intruders intoned, 'you are guilty of heinous crimes.'

'I have . . .'

'Do not protest your innocence,' the intruder snapped back. 'Plough your memory. You, Sir, are guilty of truly wicked crimes. Do you remember the village of Lisieux? Oh yes,' the accuser continued. 'As the preacher says, Caput Meum, Caput Meum, Doleo – my head hurts when I recall your litany of horrific crimes. Believe me, Sir, you have been weighed in the balance, you have been measured and you have been found wanting. I am here to deliver judgement. The years have passed, but justice has caught up with you, Sir Henry. Always remember, never forget.' The leader seemed to be lost in his own thoughts. 'Never forget that the mills of God may grind slowly but they do grind exceedingly small.'

The leader snapped his fingers and Blondin was seized, his hands tied behind his back, a blindfold fastened across his eyes. The prisoner moaned. Mercier was now sobbing like a child. The leader of these intruders quietly drew his war sword, tiptoeing like a dancer around his intended victim. Blondin stiffened as if trying to listen then the swordman struck, his blade cutting the air to slice Blondin's neck. A truly powerful blow which sent the severed head dancing, the blood spurting angrily from both that and the decapitated torso, before it too collapsed to the ground. The leader ordered the severed head to be shaken, wrapped in a cloth and placed in a coarse-haired sack. The intruders then made to leave. Their leader paused to pat the sobbing Mercier on the shoulder.

'Pax et Bonum, Master Mercier. You are simply a witness. Tell them about this, the execution of a criminal.' He passed the sack to one of his comrades. 'You know what to do with this. Let him be lifted high on London Bridge. We are finished here. Let us be gone.'

Athelstan sat back in his cushioned chair next to the top of the table where Sir John Cranston sat ensconced, staring down at Master Thibault, who had slipped, like the snake he was, into the chamber. Cranston was now coming out of his sleep. He caught Athelstan's eye. The Friar just smiled, lifting a finger to his lips as a sign for the Coroner to be prudent and observe all the courtesies and niceties of the Court. Cranston had ruled that the meeting would begin at Terce. So, as soon as the bells had finished pealing, Athelstan forced himself to relax, murmuring the 'Jesu Miserere' prayer time and time again beneath his breath. As he did so, Athelstan stared around this lavishly furnished council chamber with its polished oak furniture. Turkey rugs and a host of extravagantly embroidered tapestries warmed both walls and floor. All of them carried the same motif: the arms of the Guildhall or some scene from the history of the City, be it the entrance of a queen or the coronation of a king.

'All is ready,' Athelstan whispered to Cranston, pointing to the Coroner's clerk and scrivener, who had taken their seats at the small chancery table close to the door, pens poised, ready to transcribe.

'Athelstan, shall we begin?'

'No, Sir John, not just yet. I am not sure if everyone is here.' Athelstan stared down the table. Ingham had arrived with his comrades, John Montague and Stephen Crossley. The latter two sat on one side of the table facing Ingham and the Fisher of Men, who slouched, eyes half closed, not even acknowledging his former comrades. There was a knock on the door, which was immediately flung open and Henshaw, the Via Crucis's serjeant and squire, hurried into the chamber. A red-haired, pock-faced man, Henshaw's profuse apologies were almost drowned by the fresh ringing of church bells. Cranston waited until the tolling had ceased then gestured at Henshaw to take a seat.

'And Gumblat?' the Coroner added. 'Where is he, Master Henshaw?'

'My Lord Coroner, I think he'll be here very soon.'

'I hope what you think proves to be correct,' Cranston replied ominously. 'A time was given, and that time must be observed. Master Thibault, shall we begin?'

'Of course,' Gaunt's henchman retorted. 'Indeed, the sooner the better.'

'Very well. Very well,' Cranston replied. 'Brother Athelstan has questions to ask.'

'Thank you, Sir John.' Athelstan stared down the table. 'We have a number of killings, but first let me describe and depict the murderous masque we all have a part in. Whether we like it or not, we have been caught up in the gruesome events which have occurred. So,' Athelstan pointed at Ingham, 'we have the mysterious murders of your comrades, former members of your Free Company, the Via Crucis. Sir Philip Kyne, cornered in his Manor at Malroad, then brutally decapitated, his head taken to be poled over London Bridge.'

'Wait there.' Crossley, his weather-beaten face bitter and angry, rubbed his stomach and leaned forward.

'Sir Stephen,' Cranston barked, 'we are waiting.'

'I understand Kyne's head was taken to Robert Burdon, Keeper of the Bridge, Chief Headsman in that ward. Burdon is an official of the Crown. Couldn't he have resisted, tried to seize or trap the felon who brought the head?'

'Burdon is an officer of the Crown,' Thibault asserted, 'but he is not empowered to seize this person or that in the dead of night. Moreover, God bless us all, criminals, felons and outlaws are being decapitated at many execution grounds both across and around this city. Nor must we forget the gruesome offerings coming from such towns as Bristol, Dover and elsewhere. Burdon was not too sure what he was receiving, so why provoke a confrontation which he could so easily lose?' Thibault's words were greeted with murmurs of approval.

'Continue, Brother.'

'Thank you, Sir John. We have no evidence for why this is happening. Nothing can be discerned; no real evidence is available. Nothing except a stark proclamation nailed to the dead man's skull – "Justicia Fiat" – let justice be done. I have mentioned Kyne, but Lord Roger Mortimer was seemingly the first victim. Mortimer's corpse was roughly exhumed, his head severed and the proclamation nailed to it before it was handed over to Burdon for poling.' Athelstan paused, staring down at the memorandum he had drawn up yesterday in preparation for this meeting. 'Sir Hugh Despencer,' Athelstan continued, 'was the next to die. His murder was truly mysterious. Apparently, no cohort invaded his house to seize him and carry out execution. Not a shred of evidence exists to say why Despencer was killed. Unlike Kyne, whose murder was clearly witnessed by members of his household.'

'But Mortimer,' Ingham interrupted. 'He wasn't murdered, just his corpse abused.'

'I agree.' Athelstan nodded his head. 'Nevertheless, Mortimer's untimely exhumation must have been the work of more than one individual. After all, digging up a corpse is hard work. I suspect those who did it wanted to demonstrate that not even death could save their intended victims from disgrace and degradation.' Athelstan stared down the table. 'How did Mortimer die?' he asked.

'He was old and weak,' Ingham replied. 'He died of a fever. Strange, in his last hours Mortimer's mind wandered, his mouth full of chatter about what happened in France. Anyway, he died, and I don't think any of us even attended his funeral.'

'Leave the dead to bury the dead,' Crossley declared. 'I don't give a fig for Mortimer. What concerns me . . .' Crossley's stubby fingers beat against the tabletop.

'What concerns you, Sir Stephen?'

'Well, Brother, this mysterious band of assassins seems very knowledgeable about Kyne, his manor at Malroad, the whereabouts of Mortimer's corpse and Despencer visiting that derelict warehouse.'

'There's more.' Cranston rapped the table for silence. 'Shall I tell them, Master Thibault?'

'As you wish, Sir John.'

'There's been another murder. I have just received a message from Mercier, steward of the King's Manor at Chafford Hundred. Yesterday a cohort of assassins, similar to those at Malroad, seized the Keeper, Henry Blondin, and took him out into the small graveyard next to the church. The leader of these assassins compelled Mercier to act as their witness. He then accused Blondin of crimes perpetrated years ago in Normandy, the village of Lisieux in particular. Once he had finished, he decapitated Blondin. He then placed the severed head in a sack and left the torso for Mercier to take care of. And yes, before you ask, Burdon received another midnight visitor, who brought Blondin's head for poling. Like the other murders but with one significant difference. Blondin was a member of your Free Company, but he also left you, I understand, to join another group: Les Sangliers Sauvages – the fierce or savage boars.'

'Savage they certainly were,' the Fisher of Men grated. 'I've heard about their atrocities.' He paused and crossed himself. 'Worse even than ours.'

'Sir John, why do you mention this?' Ingham demanded.

'I think it's significant because it shows that membership of the Free Company, the Via Crucis, isn't the sole reason for execution. It's more about what these individuals did. Sir Edmund Lacey, now known as the Fisher of Men, has been in this city for years and yet nothing has happened to him!'

'And the same goes for us,' Crossley declared.

'True,' Athelstan conceded. 'Which brings us to a very important question. Why now? What has happened? What has caused the door to the past to be forced open in such a ruthless fashion?'

'It was war!' Ingham shouted.

'It was murder!' the Fisher snapped back.

'And it still is,' Athelstan declared. 'Gentlemen, let us keep to the matter in hand. Three knights, former members of those Free Companies which roamed Normandy years ago, have been killed. In brief, their deaths are linked to atrocities, massacres or whatever you'd like to call them. The slaughter and bloodletting perpetrated across Normandy is now seeking vengeance, retribution, justice.'

'So,' Cranston intervened, 'who wants revenge or justice?'

'Very true, Sir John,' Athelstan murmured. He gestured at Ingham. 'Do you and your comrades have any suspects?'

'Well, him for a start!' Crossley shouted, jabbing a finger towards the Fisher, who immediately lunged across the table, only sitting back when Cranston bellowed at him. The Fisher, chest heaving, sallow face all flushed, slouched, glaring across at Crossley and Montague.

'I understand,' Athelstan declared, 'you left Sir Edmund Lacey, now known as the Fisher of Men, in the burning ruins of Avranches, a village you had ransacked and pillaged. God knows what would have happened if the French had found him.'

'We had to leave him,' Ingham replied, his face all petulant. 'Lacey's warhorse was badly injured and so was he. A phalanx of French pike men, along with swiftly moving horsemen, were fast approaching. We had to go. We had to flee.' He paused. 'Fisher of Men, or whatever you call yourself, I am sorry we left you, but we couldn't take you. That's the past, but now we are here in this room together, I can confidently say you certainly have the motive for vengeance.'

'And so you acknowledge that you did desert me, abandoned me, one of your sworn company?'

Ingham just sighed noisily, shaking his head as if in disbelief.

'Brother Athelstan, Sir John, I concede,' the Fisher spread his hands, 'that I have a very good motive to kill former comrades, but I am innocent. You know my status and my life. Kyne and Blondin were murdered by a coven of armed men, a small battle-group.' The Fisher laughed sharply. 'You've seen my comitatus, those manikins now sheltering out on that lonely quayside. How could such little ones attack a fortified manor and despatch the likes of Kyne, in the way you have described? And what about Blondin in that graveyard? If I and mine had been there, Mercier would have seen through any disguise.'

'I agree,' Athelstan replied.

'You have the wealth,' Crossley jibed. 'You earn good silver for your work along the river. You have the means to hire a band of assassins.'

'Enough,' Athelstan intervened, eager to avoid further clashes. 'To be sure,' he continued, 'we have no evidence of who these assassins could be or why they have decided to act now. So,' Athelstan cleared his throat, 'let us concentrate on the one murder different from the rest, namely that of Sir Hugh Despencer, whipped to death in that derelict warehouse. So why was he there?'

'I believe we have already told you,' Ingham replied.

'Then tell me again.'

'Well,' Ingham scratched the side of his head, 'we invaded the village of Avranches. We plundered its manor house and found a coffer crammed with the finest gold coin. Every quarter – Michaelmas, Christmas, Easter and mid-summer – we each draw a gold coin for our own use.'

'Where is this gold stored?'

'In the most redoubtable arca in London, Sir John. A great solid iron chest in the cellars of Master Walter Plumpton, Master of the Guild of Goldsmiths here in the City.'

'I know him well,' Cranston observed. 'A most honest and well-respected merchant. Anyway, continue.'

'Well,' Ingham replied, 'we have all grown older. We have matured. We now realize and repent about what we did all those years ago. In a word, we want to make atonement. We eventually drew up a plan, hired architects and stonemasons to build London's greatest leper hospice.'

'And so back to Despencer.'

'He went down to inspect the site. He often did. He planned, at least in his mind, the different buildings and how the hospice would look. He was fascinated by it. Ask any of us. Despencer worked on it from first light to Vespers.'

'And he would go down alone? As he did this time?'

'Yes, Brother, as he always did. He loved to be there. I suspect Despencer preferred the silent loneliness of the riverside to the bustle of the City.'

'And the morning he was murdered?'

'He rose early,' Henshaw the tavern master declared, in a ringing voice. 'He broke his fast in one of our butteries, strapped on his war belt, collected his cloak and left.'

'And his clothing?' Athelstan waved a hand. 'Despencer was stripped, so what happened to his clothes?'

'Nothing,' Master Thibault, who had sat strangely silent throughout the proceedings, declared. 'Nothing at all.' Thibault spread his hands. 'As you know, we collected a few of Despencer's personal items, which we despatched to the Guildhall, but not what he had been wearing. Despencer's assassins must have taken his clothing or thrown them into the river.'

'So,' Athelstan mused, 'there is no evidence. Nothing to explain Despencer's murder, the why, the how or the who?'

'We know the how.' Montague scoffed. 'He was whipped to death.'

'But why that way?' Athelstan countered. 'I repeat how? Despencer was a former warrior. A man skilled in sword and dagger play. How was he taken prisoner? His seizure must have involved a number of assassins, yet we know nothing about them, yes?' A chorus of agreement greeted his question. Athelstan then glanced at Sir John, winked and lapsed into silence.

'Let us grasp the nettle!'

'What nettle, Sir Oliver?'

'Oh come, Brother Athelstan, Sir John, you must know the French envoys are in London?'

'French envoys are often in London.'

'No, no, Sir John, these are envoys of a different kind.'

'What kind?'

Ingham again sighed noisily. 'Sir John, you must know. The envoys are led by Dom Antoine, Archdeacon of the Royal French Shrine at St Denis. The most holy of holies in the history of the French Crown.'

'Yes,' Cranston agreed. 'I have heard of Dom Antoine, a most powerful cleric who wields considerable power.'

'Yes, he does, Sir John. He not only cares for the royal shrine, but he also commands the Chambre Noir and its servants, the Luciferi – the Light-bearers. In a word, Sir John, Dom Antoine's retinue includes spies, assassins as well as Clerks of the Secret Royal Chancery who serve the King of France but take orders from their real master, Dom Antoine.' Ingham paused, head down.

Athelstan remained silent. Cranston would know all about the arrival of the French envoys, but the Coroner was being cunning. He probably wanted to establish just how much Ingham knew. Proof that this powerful knight was receiving information from friends and associates very close to the royal council.

'Continue, Sir Oliver.'

'Rumours abound, my Lord Coroner. How Dom Antoine has come to seal a peace treaty between France and England. Godspeed that process.'

'Amen indeed,' Cranston interjected. 'And?'

'Both sides, Sir John, have demands. One of these is that the French have a list of English commanders whom they want arrested and shipped to France. These men are to stand trial on certain charges regarding alleged crimes perpetrated across Normandy and elsewhere.'

'You are one of these?'

'Unfortunately, yes,' Ingham retorted. 'But that was war!'

Athelstan raised a hand to speak and stared down the table.

'Master Thibault,' he demanded. Athelstan's voice was now powerful and carrying. 'Do you have such a list? Surely you must?'

Master Thibault smiled to himself, dug beneath his robe and took out a scroll which one of the Tower Archers guarding the door brought down to Athelstan. The Friar quickly read its contents, calculating that the manuscript listed at least fifteen names though some of these had been ruled out. He handed the scroll to Cranston.

'We can keep this, Master Thibault?'

'Oh yes, Sir John, it is yours, for what is it worth?'

'And will you?' Athelstan asked. 'Will the English Crown hand these men over to the French?'

'That, Brother, is still to be negotiated. The list I have given you is culled from the records. God knows whom the French have listed or what demands they'll make.'

'We are all deeply disturbed and disquieted,' Ingham declared. 'The French have no right to make such a demand. We fought under the English banner. It was war!' Ingham's declaration met with cries of approval from his companions. 'It would be impossible,' Ingham continued. 'There would be uproar in the Commons, the City and throughout the Kingdom.'

'Such issues,' Thibault's voice was like that of a purring cat, 'will be dealt with eventually. Brother Athelstan, you have more questions?'

'Yes, yes, I do. Many. However, for a while let us concentrate on Despencer's murder, which is different from the rest. A sordid, horrid killing in a filthy, lonely warehouse. Despencer was killed not by a clean stroke of a sword but slowly and most cruelly.' Athelstan shook his head. 'Despencer's death is very different from Kyne's and Blondin's. Indeed, so different that I ask myself are there two assassins at work? The first is this cohort of killers who invade a manor house and perpetrate an execution before a host of witnesses. The second must be a lonely assassin but, there again, how could a solitary man overcome a former warrior like Despencer? I don't know. Anyway, let us return to my questions. I realize I have asked this before. Did anyone go with Despencer?'

'No, no,' Ingham declared, 'neither I nor my companions accompanied Hugh though we knew he was going there.' Ingham spread his hands. 'Brother Athelstan, Sir John, we have talked about this amongst ourselves. We can give you no help, no indication, which might help solve poor Hugh's murder.'

'And the Vaucort Brothers?'

'Sir John, Brother Athelstan, I understand you are meeting them later?'

'Yes, we are.'

'Then let them tell you what they know, Sir John,' Ingham

replied. 'They are no longer boys but mailed clerks who have performed meritorious service for the Crown.'

'Of course, we know that,' Cranston retorted, 'but we also know that you and others murdered their mother, family and neighbours.'

Ingham sprang to his feet as did the rest.

'It's best if we leave,' Ingham declared. 'Master Thibault, we are finished here.' Ingham bowed to the Master of Secrets and, followed by the others, he made to leave then abruptly turned. He strode back, drawing as close as he could to Cranston. 'Don't judge me, Fat Jack,' he hissed, 'you were no better in France. I met the Vaucorts in "The Golden Oriole" this morning. They looked prosperous enough. Thanks to us they have been given a life much better than they would have had.'

'We cannot comment on that,' Cranston retorted. 'We cannot ask about what their futures could have been because you and others murdered their mother and all their kin.'

For a few heartbeats Athelstan thought violence would erupt, that all the ancient hatreds, like pus in an old wound, would now break out.

'Gentlemen.' Thibault slowly rose to his feet. He seemed relaxed as if enjoying the confrontation. He flicked his fingers at Ingham. 'Sir Oliver, take your comrades back to "The Golden Oriole" or wherever you wish to go, but go now.' Thibault then pointed to the Fisher. 'And the same for you, Sir.'

Ingham and his companions did so, clattering noisily down the stairs, followed by the Fisher of Men, who nodded at Cranston and Athelstan then slid like a shadow from the council chamber. Once he was satisfied that they had all left, Thibault slammed the door shut and leaned against it for a while. He then pointed at Cranston, who still slouched in his throne-like chair at the top of the table.

'Jack, there was no need for that.'

'Oh yes, there was, Master Thibault. Ingham and his comitatus are assassins, murderers.'

'And you never did the same?'

'No, Master Thibault, I did not. I fought the French. I met

them in battle, but I never took part in the killing, or indeed the maltreatment, of the defenceless. That's why my name will be on no one's list. And—' Cranston fell silent at a pounding on the stairs. The door crashed open and Tiptoft burst into the chamber.

'Sir John, Sir John.' He paused to catch his breath. 'Squire Gumblat,' he gasped, 'he has been found murdered in his chamber at "The Golden Oriole" tavern.'

PART THREE

'Humans fly with two wings.'

'Murdered you certainly were!' Athelstan whispered as he stood beside Cranston in a beautifully furnished chamber which had been transformed into a murder room. For that, Athelstan reflected, is what the place had become: a ghastly, gruesome slaughter house. The source of what Athelstan had called 'a sheer blasphemy' was the hacked, abused corpse of Squire Gumblat. He had been fastened in a chair. Lashed fast and unable to move, the assassin had thrust a leather gag deep into Gumblat's mouth to silence him when the real horrors began.

'Look.' Cranston plucked at Athelstan's sleeve, and gently coaxed him over to the chair. Gumblat's face was almost unrecognizable due to the blood, skin and muscle, all of which had been ruptured by the cruel device hammered into Gumblat's head.

'What is that?' Athelstan asked. 'Oh yes . . .' He walked slowly to the other side of the chair. 'It's a caltrop, yes, Sir John?'

'Yes, it is, Brother. A foot trap used to catch man and beast. A crude, but very cruel device. Look, it's simply a metal mouth with a row of teeth along both top and bottom. The teeth are nothing more than razor-sharp pointed spikes. Our assassin opened this then lowered it on to Gumblat's head. He hammered the teeth at the top close to the forehead, the lower row of teeth he then forced in under the chin, as far back as the caltrop would allow.'

'But why, Sir John? Why inflict such a death on a fellow human being? I mean faugh, what a stench!' Athelstan went across to a side table for the two pomanders Henshaw had given them. He handed one to Cranston. 'Death stinks,' Athelstan murmured, pushing the pomander against his mouth and nose. 'But murder reeks as high as Heaven.'

'Why this?' Cranston echoed Athelstan's words. 'I mean the caltrop almost fits like a crown.'

'A crown of thorns!' Athelstan exclaimed. 'The crowning with thorns . . .' Athelstan broke off and walked over to peer through the mullioned glass window. He stood for a while, lost in thought, ignoring a spate of questions from the Coroner. Once he did pose some order on his tumbling thoughts, Athelstan turned and beckoned Sir John. Cranston, who was still examining the grievous head wound, was only too pleased to join Athelstan in the window embrasure. He had barely sat down when there was a rap on the door and Ingham entered.

'Where is Master Thibault?' he demanded, glaring at Cranston but averting his gaze from Gumblat's corpse.

'Crawled back to wherever he crawled from as must you, Ingham. Tell your coven that I and the good brother here will be pleased to question them when we are ready.'

Ingham muttered something and left the room, slamming the door behind him.

'Good.' Cranston took a generous swig from the miraculous wineskin. He then passed it to Athelstan who, on this occasion, drank heartily and deep. 'Well?' Cranston took the wineskin back, cradling it like a mother would her child. 'Tell me, Little Monk . . .'

'Friar, Sir John!'

'Never mind that. Tell me what you have discovered. You have discovered something, haven't you? What is it? Any loose thread in this tapestry of deceit should be seized and used. So, what have you found, Little Friar?'

'Not much, Sir John, not really, not yet.'

'Tell me?'

'The Via Crucis, Sir John?'

'What about them?'

'No, not them. Not really. The Via Crucis means the Way of the Cross. A fairly new devotion which takes many forms.'

'And?'

'Basically, Sir John, it traces Christ's passion from the moment he is condemned by Pontius Pilate to his death at three o'clock on a Friday afternoon. In essence there are fourteen possible mediations on the different scenes after Christ is condemned by Pilate. Pilate's judgement is the first station, or scene, along the way. Christ's scourging at the pillar is the second. Christ being crowned with thorns, the third. Christ receives his cross, and so on. So,' Athelstan continued, 'we have our gentle knights, our Free Company of comrades who journey to France to pillage and plunder. They used the title of that devotion, the Via Crucis, to name their Free Company.'

'A blasphemy in itself, yes, Brother?'

'Certainly, Sir John. But the wheel turns. Someone is now punishing them in almost the same way Christ was tortured and abused before he was crucified. Of course, the who, the why and how of this mystery are yet to be resolved. We have Roger Mortimer exhumed to face judgement after death, just like Christ was judged by Pilate. Hugh Despencer, scourged to death fastened to a pillar whilst squire Gumblat is crowned with thorns or spikes and dies of his horrific wounds. Both tortures imitate those our Saviour suffered. Then we have Kyne and Blondin, but their deaths are staged as if they were legitimate executions.'

'I agree.'

'Which means, Sir John?'

'You are correct, Brother. There are two killers here, not one.'

'Oh, most learned of coroners, sharp as a hawk on the wing. You accept my hypothesis. There are two killers here, but whether they acknowledge each other I cannot say. Who directs them remains a mystery and why they have chosen this moment in time to perpetrate their crimes is also hidden away. Undoubtedly someone is waging a horrific war against certain members of the Free Company, the Via Crucis. The murders are carried out in a truly blasphemous fashion because they echo the Passion of Christ. Now this could be one individual, as I have said, or a group.' Athelstan shrugged. 'I cannot say. However, the murders of Kyne and Blondin are definitely the work of a sworn coven of killers about whom we know very little. So, Sir John,' Athelstan rubbed his hands, 'let us question our good knights and their entourage.'

Athelstan and Cranston met Ingham, Henshaw, Montague and Crossley in the buttery of 'The Golden Oriole', a comfortable wall-panelled chamber with quilted-cushioned chairs and benches. Ingham, now wary of Cranston, attempted to treat both the Coroner and Friar as honoured guests.

'So.' Athelstan licked the tip of his fingers to clean away the hot biscuit served along with the stoups of ale. 'I can deduce the following about what happened this morning. You all, apart from you, Henshaw, left "The Golden Oriole" fairly early and made your way to the Guildhall where you sat under the sharp eye of Master Thibault, not to forget Sir John and myself, a veritable host of reliable witnesses.'

'I can, we can,' Ingham declared, 'take oaths that when we left "The Golden Oriole", this morning, Master Gumblat was very much alive. I saw him myself.'

'So,' Athelstan scribbled on the page of parchment before him, 'so,' he repeated, 'when you left "The Golden Oriole" Gumblat was hale and hearty?'

'Yes,' they all chorused.

'And you left the tavern and went straight to the Guildhall?'

'Except for me.' Henshaw spoke up. He pulled a face. 'I saw my comrades leave. Gumblat was not with them. A short while later I went up to Gumblat's chamber. The door was locked. I could hear no sound from within, so I thought he'd left, as I did shortly afterwards.'

'We returned from the Guildhall,' Ingham declared. 'By then the tavern was very busy. Naturally I was concerned that Gumblat hadn't joined us, so I went up to the first gallery where Gumblat had his chamber. The door was unlocked. I pushed it open and then . . .' Ingham just put his face in his hands.

'Sir John, Brother Athelstan,' Crossley spoke up, 'we have encountered war in all its horror, but what we found in Gumblat's chamber?' He just shook his head.

Athelstan was about to ask if they had seen any of the Fisher of Men's retinue in or around the tavern when he paused at a knock on the door and Tiptoft entered the chamber.

'Sir John, Brother Athelstan,' he declared, 'Dom Antoine and his retinue have now left Westminster for the Guildhall.

You must be there to greet them.' Cranston and Athelstan agreed. They collected their cloaks and other items and bade the Company farewell. Cranston added that they were not to leave the City on any matter without first obtaining his permission. He then followed Athelstan down, out through the colourful crowds of Cheapside to the Guildhall. They had hardly settled themselves when Flaxwith opened the door and ushered in Cranston's visitors. Dom Antoine immediately took the chair at the end of the table directly facing Cranston, his retinue flanked either side. Athelstan stared at these men. Dom Antoine's retainers were certainly Luciferi. He gently nudged Cranston.

'Dagger boys,' Athelstan whispered.

'Oh yes, Brother,' the Coroner replied, 'I reckon they are all mailed clerks, very skilled in the chancery as well as with the dagger, the mace and the garotte.'

Athelstan watched them take their seats. The French seemed to be unaware of them. Dressed in black from head to toe, heads completely shaven with heavy rings on their fingers. Cranston had once informed Athelstan how to recognize true fighting men. They have no hair to grab or pull and everything they wear, even the rings on their fingers, could be used as a deadly weapon. Athelstan recognized the hidden menace of the Luciferi. They would certainly kill if they had to.

Once the French had entered and settled themselves, Thibault followed them, strolling in as if he hadn't a care in the world. He winked at Cranston and Athelstan then took a chair close to them. Thibault paid no heed to the French. He had no retinue, nothing to show that he regarded this as an important meeting. And the French took the snub. Athelstan could feel the tension gathering and decided to act before anyone else did.

'Sir John,' he whispered to the Coroner, 'please do as I say. Follow me.' The Friar abruptly rose and walked down the length of the table, Cranston the other side. Athelstan then stopped and knelt beside Dom Antoine's chair.

'Monseigneur, I plead for your blessing.'

Athelstan glanced quickly across and relaxed. Sir John was kneeling on the other side of the chair. Dom Antoine, his rich voice echoing surprise, hastily sketched a cross in the air as he hoarsely delivered a benediction. Cranston and Athelstan then rose, kissed the Archdeacon's finger rings and returned to their seats.

'Welcome to England,' Cranston declared merrily. 'Monseigneur, you know who we are whilst you need no introduction. Your fame and your name go before you.' Dom Antoine, quite flustered by all the flattery, simply smiled and nodded. One of his henchmen leaned across and whispered something. Dom Antoine, the smile fading on his clever, saturnine face, nodded and stared back down the table.

'Sir John, Brother Athelstan, I thank you for your welcome.' The Archdeacon's voice was clear and carrying, his English word perfect. 'I understand you wish to question us on a certain issue. Naturally, as I am the most senior envoy, not to mention the leading churchman of his most Christian Majesty's court, I could refuse to meet to be questioned on anything, but,' he spread his hands, 'for the sake of peace I have agreed.'

'You have come to England to treat for peace?'

'No, Sir John, we come to offer peace and end the ceaseless slaughter across Normandy and along the Narrow Seas.'

'And of course, you have a list of demands.'

'Stipulations, Sir John, stipulations.'

'Which are?'

'Sir John, that is a question you must ask Master Thibault.' The Archdeacon bowed towards the Master of Secrets, who just simpered back.

'Very well,' Athelstan declared, 'let me be blunt.'

'Of course, Brother, otherwise we will spend our time chasing shadows and never seize the substance.'

'I agree, Monseigneur. So, you have a list of English manor lords who fought in France?'

'No, not all of them. Brother, we concede that war is terrible in all aspects. We inflict horrors on you and the English reply in kind. We appreciate that women, children and other innocents are swept up in this storm of violence. We regrettably concede this. What we want now are certain English commanders who deliberately, coldly and maliciously, with the full support of their henchmen, attacked, abused and killed innocent women, children, priests and religious of every kind.'

'Such as Kyne's attacks along the Garonne? And Henry Blondin's sacking of Lisieux?'

'They were massacred, Brother, the needless, cruel slaughter of innocents.'

'So, you come to Westminster to demand that those responsible be handed over to French justice?'

'No, Brother, God's justice.'

'Touché.' Athelstan smiled. 'And in this case God's justice is some hideous death at Montfaucon? Or the gallows beyond the gates of St Denis?'

'If the Court finds them guilty, yes, they could face summary execution. We also seek your king's licence to seize the wealth of these criminals so as to make compensation, petty though it may be, to the kin of their victims.'

'So how many names do you have?'

'About a dozen. Maybe a couple more.'

'Well, Monseigneur,' Athelstan chose his words carefully, 'you do know that some of those names, which you must have on your list, have already been killed in the most barbaric way?'

'Brother Athelstan, we have heard about some of these deaths: Kyne, Blondin and Mortimer were certainly on our list but . . .' Dom Antoine grasped the pectoral cross hanging on a chain around his neck whilst he lifted his right hand. 'I, Dom Antoine,' he intoned, 'Archdeacon of the Royal Chapel of St Denis in Paris, swear that the deaths of certain manor lords here in or around London were not the responsibility of me or mine and so I swear.' Dom Antoine smiled at the surprised reaction of both Cranston and Athelstan.

'Is there another delegation?' Cranston asked.

'What do you mean, Sir John?'

'Is there a war band hired by the French or, even worse, acting on its own initiative?'

'No, no, no.' Dom Antoine shook his head. 'Master Thibault?'

'Sir John,' the Master of Secrets, who had maintained a detached silence so far, tapped the table top, shaking his head, 'if some sort of war band,' he declared, 'has been despatched into this kingdom by the French Crown, or any of its minions or allies, that would be viewed as an act of war, which the French do not want and neither do we.'

'So,' Athelstan pressed his sandal against Cranston's boot, a sign for the Coroner to remain silent, 'we have a number of names. Two of these, Kyne and Blondin, have been formally executed because of alleged crimes in France. Then there's another group, the likes of Despencer and Gumblat, who were not formally executed but murdered in a most barbaric way with no reference to alleged crimes in France or that justice has been carried out. These are the victims so far. What we need to know is who the perpetrators could be. Naturally suspicion falls on you, Monseigneur, yet the French, through you, their most senior cleric, have solemnly sworn that the French Court have not, and are not, involved in the deaths which we are now investigating.'

'Master Thibault,' Cranston called out as the Master of Secrets made to rise, 'how go the negotiations with the French on this issue?'

'Not good, Sir John, we have yet to discuss the list of names. Our king has recommended that we just pay financial compensation and that,' Thibault rose, pushing back his chair, 'and that,' he repeated, 'is all I can tell you.'

'And we can say no more,' Dom Antoine declared.

The Master of Secrets and the French envoys then left the chamber. Athelstan rose and went and stood by a window. He watched Thibault, surrounded by his Spanish mercenaries, make his farewells of Dom Antoine's entourage. Athelstan studied these cunning, clever men, wolves in sheep's clothing. The Friar chewed the corner of his lip, wondering what the real truth was behind all this. He waited until Dom Antoine and Thibault had left with their respective bodyguards then returned to his chair. Cranston was dozing, nestling comfortably in his chair as a babe in its cradle. Athelstan decided to join him. He pulled up his hood, gathered his cloak about him and sat in a cushioned chair. The Friar's eyes were growing heavy when he was rudely disturbed by a knock on the door. This was flung open and Flaxwith escorted two men into the room. Athelstan shook Cranston awake then rose to greet their visitors, who introduced themselves as Benjamin and Benedict Vaucort. Athelstan and Cranston clasped hands and exchanged the kiss of peace with the two neatly attired clerks. They looked similar, almost identical with their coiffed hair cleanly cut to delineate clerical tonsures; this accentuated even further their round smooth-shaven faces. Both men were dark-eyed and solemn-looking. They returned Athelstan and Cranston's stare then abruptly broke into smiles, laughing quietly at the astonishment they'd caused.

'You look so alike. Is there anything to distinguish one from the other?'

'Yes, Sir John.' The clerk who introduced himself as Benedict stepped forward. 'I am the taller of the two and there's this.' Benedict traced the outline of a healed scar just beneath his right eye. 'A legacy,' he murmured, his smile fading.

'Of what?'

'Of the night we lost our darling mother.'

'God rest her,' Athelstan replied, sketching a blessing in the air. 'May God give her eternal rest and God save you, my friends. Come.' He gestured to the top of the table, telling them to sit either side of himself and Sir John. 'Oh, by the way, do you want refreshment?'

'No, Brother, we broke our fast in the great refectory at Westminster.'

'We can guess,' Benjamin spoke up, his voice a little harsher than his twin brother, 'we can guess,' he repeated, 'why we are here.'

'Then tell us.' Athelstan smiled, opening his chancery satchel.

'Certain lords, knights, powerful men who led chevauchees through Normandy during the old king's reign,' Benjamin paused, blinking furiously, 'yes, that's it. Some of these have been executed or slaughtered in the most barbaric fashion, their heads severed and poled on London Bridge for the crows to peck at.' Benjamin pulled a face. 'No, Brother, Sir John,' he continued, 'we have not been given special information or knowledge. What I have described is common chatter in the chancery and exchequer chambers.' He shrugged. 'I concede people know our stories. I suppose they'd wonder if men such as ourselves want revenge on those who killed their kin and devastated their lives.'

'And?' Athelstan asked, deeply curious at the calm, measured demeanour of these two men.

'And what, Brother?'

'Well, to put it bluntly, do you want revenge? Either through brutal murder, such as that of Lord Hugh Despencer, or by bringing pressure to bear on our own men of power to send those accused of atrocities in Normandy to stand trial in some French court?'

'I must concede,' the Coroner declared, 'that what Brother Athelstan has just said is also common chatter along the cloisters of Westminster.'

'We recognize that,' Benedict retorted, 'and we thank you for your invitation to meet us. We accepted and have come here to define our position, our attitude on these matters.' He swallowed hard. 'The past is the past. We were babes in arms when Avranches was sacked. When our mother and kin were killed in that fire which ravaged our parish church. We would have also perished there if it had not been for one Englishman.'

'And you know who he is?'

Benedict smiled thinly.

'Oh yes,' he replied, 'the Fisher of Men! Sir Edmund Lacey. He introduced himself just before he assumed the title, task and trade of being the Fisher of Men.'

'And you know his story?'

'Poor man, Brother Athelstan, God bless him.'

'And the rest? Those responsible for the destruction of your family, your kin and of course your parents, all your futures?'

'We do not want revenge. If we did,' Benjamin added swiftly, 'it would be at the Fons et Origo – the fount and source of all these wars and their horror. No, no, Brother Athelstan, we have journeyed far. We have travelled along the passage of the years. Our souls are at peace.' He smiled. 'We do occasionally meet and celebrate with others like ourselves. We have formed a society, a company as you would say. Children who were also caught up in the chevauchees and, like us, brought to England. We call ourselves the Children of Babylon. Like the prophet Daniel and his companions, we have been carried into exile: this place, this building, this city, this kingdom is our Babylon and we the children of France live here.'

'But you are not bitter about your exile?'

'No, Brother Athelstan, we have all settled.'

'All?'

'Yes, as I have said there is more of us. We are very grateful to the English Crown for what they have done for the two of us as well as others. Now,' Benjamin apparently warmed to his theme, 'the Feast of the Epiphany is on the Sixth January next. It is also King Richard's birthday. He now matures, a true man, a prince in his own right.'

'Yes, yes,' Cranston intervened. 'There are to be festivals, feasts and celebrations across both city and kingdom.'

'My own parish are preparing for it,' Athelstan declared. 'I understand royal decree has defined it as a truly "Holy Day" in every sense of the word.'

'And we will do the same,' Benjamin retorted, excitedly clapping his hands as he beamed at Cranston and Athelstan.

'In what way?'

'Why, Brother, a masque on the theme of the Children of Babylon being protected by their host, your king.'

'What you propose,' Athelstan declared, 'is most worthy and proper. His Grace will be deeply pleased. As you must know, Richard of Bordeaux loves all things French.'

'Our masque will certainly please him. However, Brother Athelstan, Sir John, you are not here to discuss masques but murder, correct? We are two young men, mailed clerks who have fought in the royal army. We are, I suppose, as capable of dagger work as anyone else, even more so. I accept we are logical suspects for the murders you've just mentioned. But I tell you this,' Benedict continued, 'we are not in any way involved in these hideous killings. True, we must be suspects, but why should we murder former members of the Via Crucis and indeed others who later left that company for another such as Henry Blondin out at Chafford Hundred.'

'I agree with my brother,' Benjamin declared. 'Why should we become involved in murder after all these years? What profit does it bring us? Arid revenge, nothing else! Why spoil a good life here and, if caught, face the most severe punishment? Moreover, how could we overcome warriors such as Despencer, murdered out along the freezing Thames, or Blondin in that cemetery? Oh yes, we have heard all the gossip.'

Cranston nodded in agreement. Information about the murders was now common knowledge, the source of rich gossip both at Westminster and along Cheapside where the rich and powerful gathered.

'You could have . . .' The Coroner paused at a screeching from further down the chamber where one of the Guildhall cats, ferocious, feral creatures, had cornered and killed a rat. 'You could,' the Coroner repeated, 'have hired killers to do your work or, indeed, other members of your company might have decided to take the law into their own hands. Gentlemen, I hear what you say. I accept your assurances, but you must admit, you are prime suspects in these awful deaths.'

'Sir John,' Benedict's voice was merry and playful, 'really? Perhaps the Children of Babylon's seamstresses or even our fruit merchants.' He laughed sharply. 'Of course, we are all capable of murder but, I assure you, we had no hand in the deaths of these manor lords. Nevertheless, I will be honest. We will not mourn their passing, will we, Benjamin? And we rejoice that they must now face a court where they will be forced to answer for their sins.'

'Thank you.' Cranston smiled. 'Sirs, Brother Athelstan and I appreciate your honesty.' He turned to the Friar. 'We are finished with these two gentlemen?'

'For the moment, yes.'

'For the moment,' Benedict retorted, 'get to know us better. You must seize the opportunity to learn more about us.'

'Meaning?' Athelstan asked.

'Tomorrow evening at the Vespers bell, come to our house in Osprey Lane, Cripplegate. We shall fete you and show you our masque. Now.' Benedict rose and playfully poked Cranston in his large stomach. 'Come,' the clerk repeated laughingly, 'come and revel with us.'

The two clerks left. Cranston followed them out on to the

majestic staircase, fashioned out of the finest elmwood and polished to a shine. Above this, a hundred-candled chandelier bathed the staircase in light. The Coroner watched the two men go and stood for a while listening to the sounds of the Guildhall, a place, Cranston often declared, which never slept.

'Well, Sir John, what do you think?'

'At the moment, Brother, nothing except that my stomach believes my throat has been cut because I am ravished with hunger.'

Both men left the Guildhall, Cranston swinging his cloak about him, a beaver hat protecting his head. He shouted at Flaxwith to take his cohort for refreshments in the Guildhall refectory. He then grasped a shivering Athelstan by the arm and led him through the gateway and across Cheapside. The day had worn on and turned bitterly cold. Puddles were already iced over, and a harsh frost clung to the woodwork of the mansions. The sharpness of the day became more intense as a river mist swirled in, silver sheets twisting and turning in the biting breeze. Athelstan was surprised at how bitter the day had become and he and Cranston almost threw themselves into 'The Lamb of God' to be welcomed like heroes by mine hostess. She promptly showed them up to the solar where a fire roared like a choir from Hell. Chairs were pushed up close to the flames, now rekindled with two pine-scented logs. Wheeled braziers were placed beneath the firmly shuttered windows. Hot posset was quickly served then mine hostess hurried off to prepare Cranston's favourite dish, a rich beef stew which had been slowly cooking since the day before. Only when they were satisfied did the two men turn back to the day's business.

'So, what do we have?' Athelstan began writing, his quill pen racing across the sheet of vellum he had unrolled across the table and kept open with small weights. The Friar pulled the candle spigot closer so the circle of light fell on the parchment.

'We have,' Cranston replied, 'a Free Company, the Via Crucis, who, twenty years ago, probably more, ravaged Normandy, plundering and pillaging to their hearts' content. The Via Crucis were remarkably successful; its members collected a treasure, almost a king's ransom so they say. This money, a coffer full of pure gold coins, has been deposited in the arca of a leading goldsmith, Sir Walter Plumpton. Every quarter Plumpton disperses one coin to each surviving member of the Company.'

'One day,' Athelstan declared, sipping his wine, 'all members of that company will die and what will happen to their treasure? After all there are no pockets on a shroud. What do you think, Sir John?'

'I think the same, Brother. God knows what will happen to the gold when they are dead, but I am more concerned about what is happening before they die. Now look, I have met the likes of the Via Crucis before, knights who robbed and ravaged until the French drove us out. They all came home and turned virtuous. They must wonder about what they did as they sit in their parish church and stare at the paintings on the wall, especially those describing the horrors of Hell. It's like water seeping from a cracked bowl, Brother, the drip, drip, drip over the years. The realization that gold does not necessarily bring happiness. Then, at night, when the sun has set and the light gives way to the dark, they lie in their beds and wait for the ghosts to cluster. Except . . .'

'Except what, Sir John?'

'What I am describing, Brother, are men with a conscience.'

'I know what you are going to say, Sir John. There are some who have no conscience at all. They kill with all the speed of a lunging snake. They never reflect. They feel no contrition and, I suspect, Sir John, these are the men whom we now have to deal with.' Athelstan repressed a shiver. 'It's only a matter of time before we confront these killers.'

'Are you talking about all the murders, Brother?'

'No, Sir John, Kyne and Blondin were executed with all the formality of a court. I am referring to the savage, bloodthirsty killing of Despencer and Gumblat. Anyway, Sir John, let us return to what we know. The members of the Via Crucis want to atone for their sins by building a great lazar hospital along the mud flats of Southwark.'

'Till murder intervened.'

'True, Sir John. Some of what we are now discussing has already been mentioned. I truly believe we are dealing with two sets of killers represented by their last two victims, Blondin out at Chafford Hundred and Gumblat crowned with thorns at "The Golden Oriole".' Athelstan put his hands to his face. 'Sir John . . .' he whispered, getting to his feet.

'Brother?'

'Crowned with thorns, that's what I said. Look, I have mentioned this before as a possibility, but now I believe it to be a fact, a truly important one. We have talked about the Stations of the Cross, the Sorrowful Mysteries of Christ. They began with Jesus being condemned by Pilate, scourged at the pillar . . .'

'And crowned with thorns?'

'Precisely, my learned scholar, and these occasions have been mirrored in the murders we are investigating. Don't you see, the Company is called the Via Crucis, which, in itself, is made up of the different occasions of Christ's suffering. Such occasions are now being blasphemously mirrored in these murders.'

'So?' Cranston demanded.

'So, are the members of the Company being punished for something? We have no evidence for any of this. However, I am forming an idea about the perpetrator. I believe he is someone who hates the Church, despises religion and mocks Christ. He certainly has no scruple about what he does, what he is guilty of. Blasphemous, sacrilegious murder!'

'I agree, Brother. We know this killer has taken at least two lives in a most heinous fashion. But why? Revenge for what happened in the past, be it here or in Normandy?'

'You are correct, Sir John, but who? And how did they commit their crimes and why now? Sir John, we must also bear in mind that there might be more than one individual involved, which might explain how former warriors like Despencer and Gumblat were overcome with such relative ease. As for the motive for such killings, it must be revenge. Vengeance for sins of the past.'

'And why now?'

'That's even more difficult to answer, Sir John, but I had a thought. French envoys have come to Westminster to demand the extradition of certain manor lords to stand trial in Paris for their crimes. No sooner had the envoys arrived than some of the very men they wanted to arrest and drag back to France are seized and executed in a mock judicial way.' Athelstan paused.

'What is it, Little Friar?'

'Nothing but a guess, Sir John. Did the assassin, or the assassins, responsible for the savage murder of Despencer and Gumblat hope that their killings could merge amongst those who seized and executed Kyne and Blondin?'

'Perhaps,' Cranston sighed noisily, 'but it offers no solution. All we have established, Brother, is that there are two sets of killings, but the reason for them remains a true mystery. I mean why were Kyne and Blondin executed at the very time the French are demanding that both these manor lords, and others on Dom Antoine's blessed list, be sent back to Paris?'

'That's the point I was trying to make before. This question of timing, Sir John. We are dealing with one exhumation – Mortimer – and four murders, but we haven't established who could be responsible, why they acted as they did, why now and what do they plan next?' Athelstan crossed himself. 'And so it is and so it goes,' he murmured. 'Time moves on, Sir John. Oh, talking of mysteries.' Athelstan dug into a side pocket of his robe and brought out what he now called 'The Riddle Manuscript'. He handed this to Cranston, who unrolled it, read the message then repeated his recitation of the riddle a number of times before handing the parchment back to Athelstan.

'Brother, what is this?'

'Sir John, it was left for me. A riddle, which, in some way or other, might lead me to resolving the death or murder of Bardolph the Tax Collector. I have read it time and time again. I have given it to Benedicta to read. But so far, no solution.'

'And you can include me in that, Brother. What else?'

'Well, of course, the four murders we have talked about before. Now Dom Antoine, and I believe him, claims to have nothing to do with the murders, either directly or indirectly. He has not despatched assassins to kill them nor paid others to carry out such murderous work.'

'I agree, Brother. So, let's move from the who to the why. Who hates this group of knights if not the French? Who else could be described as bearing a grudge, eh?' Cranston drained his goblet and slammed it down on the table. 'Someone,' he continued, 'who has good cause, not to mention the means. Our good friend, our comrade, the Fisher of Men. He certainly has the motive, Brother.'

'Although I am reluctant to agree,' Athelstan declared, 'I follow your logic, Sir John.'

'Think, Brother! The Fisher of Men was abandoned, left wounded and extremely vulnerable in Avranches. God knows what pain he had to endure. From being a proud English knight, he became a wounded vagabond, a stricken beggar, a cursed Englishman. If the Fisher had been discovered by the French, he would have been skinned alive, his flesh flayed worse than the punishment inflicted on Despencer. Oh yes, Brother, our Fisher may have had a hand in all of this.'

'But?'

'No, Brother, I doubt very much if the Fisher would use those poor unfortunates, Ichthus, Hackum and the rest, but he could hire killers. Oh yes, and there is only one way we are going to find out!' Cranston sprang to his feet, knocking a stool aside.

'Sir John, why the haste?'

'Because, Brother, I want you to meet the Shadow Master. Now look, Little Friar, you stay and enjoy the warmth.' Then, grabbing his hat, cloak and sword belt, Cranston left the solar. Athelstan heard mine hostess give a shriek as Cranston undoubtedly kissed her on the way out then the tavern door opened and slammed shut. Athelstan returned to toasting himself before the roaring fire. He relaxed as he felt the warmth of its flames and the seeping glow of the Bordeaux nourish and relax his tired mind and body. He glanced quickly at the hour candle on its bronze stand in the corner. The flame was almost at the end of the seventh red ring and, when Cranston awoke him, the flame was approaching the ninth. Athelstan, rubbing his eyes, peered up at Cranston bending over him.

'My Lord Coroner, it is usual for this to be the other way around. Me rousing you from a lovely sleep.'

'Well, Little Friar, there's always a first time and more than a first time. So,' Cranston stood back, 'let me introduce the Shadow Master.'

Athelstan blinked in astonishment. He thought Cranston was by himself but then a figure seemed to just merge out of the shady doorway behind the Coroner. A small thin man, his head completely bald, face all sharp and attentive. He was garbed in dark robes like a Benedictine monk, but the war belts strapped around his waist carried well-sheathed daggers. He smiled as Athelstan extended his hand for him to grasp. He did so then knelt to receive a blessing. Athelstan got to his feet and sketched a benediction in the air.

'Thank you, Brother. Sir John, you have business with me?'

'We certainly do. That's why I came to coax you from your castle, the tavern you call "The Mists of Time", into here, my little chapel "The Lamb of God". Now, my cunning friend, first some wine then down to business.'

Athelstan stifled a yawn as he studied the Shadow Master whilst Cranston ensured everyone was comfortable. Once he had finished, the Coroner sat in his throne-like chair before the fire. He toasted his two companions then stretched over and patted the Shadow Master on the shoulder.

'John Stacpoole, professional spy, skilled scout, a man who can move through the shadows and not be glimpsed. A professional eavesdropper who flits like a shadow against the wall. Here, there and then be gone.'

'What is it you want, Sir John?'

'I want you to spy on the Fisher of Men.'

'A dangerous task, Sir John.'

'But at this moment in time a very necessary one,' Cranston replied. 'You must have heard of him?'

'I know he lodges on that deserted, desolate quayside just past "La Reole". I also know that at least twice a day he takes his majestic war barge "Thanatos" to reap the river and recover corpses. He is assisted and supported by a legion of grotesques.'

'So, you know him and his habits,' Cranston replied. 'What I want, indeed what we want, is something else. You must bring him under the closest scrutiny, especially at night. Try and establish if the Fisher leaves his river dwellings and goes to other places to meet whoever he might be in league with. You, Shadow Master, can achieve that. I am hiring you because I have hired you before and you did not disappoint me. You truly are a shifting shadow, a form glimpsed only to vanish. Above all, you keep a still tongue in that clever head of yours. Anyway, do you have questions?'

'None, Sir John, except I will be paid?'

'You know full well the Guildhall will meet all reasonable expenses. You are true to your word, and I am true to mine. Don't worry, Shadow Master, you will be paid even more if you prove successful.'

'In which case . . .' The Shadow Master made to rise. Athelstan stretched out and seized his arm.

'Brother?'

'Skilled as you are, Shadow Master, could you enter a tavern tap room and blend in with all the other shadows?'

'Of course, Brother. You are referring, I am sure, to that sin shop "The Piebald Tavern" which lies at the very heart of your parish.'

'Very shrewd,' Athelstan declared. 'I certainly am. Not so much a sin shop, more mischief's own workplace. A tax collector, Bardolph, was murdered there.'

'So I have heard.'

'I would like you to go there, be whatever you wish. However, you must become a shadow on the wall and learn as much as you can about that murder.' Athelstan gestured at the Coroner. 'Sir John, will you pay the stipend?'

'I certainly shall but, for now, my bed awaits and more importantly so does the Lady Maude and my two prize poppets. Shadow Master, be about your business. Brother Athelstan, I shall be busy for the next few days, but we shall meet very soon.'

Gilbert Henshaw, mine host and tavern-manager of 'The Golden Oriole', was certainly frightened. He had served as a serjeant, a battle squire in the King's array as well as in the Free Company of the Via Crucis. He had raped, ravished and ravaged across Normandy and returned to England a very wealthy man. 'The Golden Oriole' was indeed a manifestation of his magnificence and that of his comrades. A proud man, Henshaw loved nothing better than to strut up and down Cheapside displaying his wealth. But that had all changed. Life had lurched, taking a sharp turn, and the past had broken through. Lords Mortimer, Kyne, Despencer, Blondin as well as his fellow squire Gumblat had all been despatched into the dark. But who was responsible and why now? All of it was shrouded in mystery. In truth, Henshaw felt that the past had caught up with him. He and his surviving comrades were being cruelly punished for their past misdeeds. Henshaw drew a deep breath as he sat on a high stool near the great buttery table in the tap room of 'The Golden Oriole'. Despite the late hour the tavern was still frenetically busy and would remain so until the bell for Compline tolled and the curfew proclaimed. The beacon fires would be lit in church steeples, a sure sign that the day was done and the City and its citizens were for the dark. The revellers in 'The Golden Oriole' thought different. They would bribe the watch and carouse well into the early hours, long past the chimes of midnight. Henshaw, however, wanted to end the day peacefully, quietly. He did not wish to mingle with the late-night revellers whilst, if he went back to his chamber, they would only follow him up, knocking on the door, begging him to join them.

'No,' Henshaw whispered to himself. 'I'll go to the Nest.'

He rose, strapped on his war belt and left the tap room, going along a gloomy passageway to an iron-studded door leading down to the sprawling tavern cellars. He unlocked the door, primed a lantern horn and carefully made his way down the steep steps. He reached the bottom and stared around. The cellars were a labyrinth of narrow passageways: nothing more than needle-thin runnels which made their way around barrels, tuns, baskets, coffers, chests and caskets, all neatly stacked against the walls or pushed into enclosures. Fixed lantern horns provided the occasional pool of light whilst narrow vents in the ceiling allowed in some fresh air. According to local lore, the site of 'The Golden Oriole' had been a secret catacomb for the early Christian church during the Roman persecutions. A place where Christians could hide. Nevertheless, now and again the Roman authorities would find their way in. Again, local lore maintained that these sombre, shadow-filled galleries were a thoroughfare

for a multitude of ghosts of those slaughtered there. Henshaw
tried to ignore such stories as he made his way deeper into the
cellar until he reached what he called his nest: a small recess
or chamber which Henshaw had furnished to suit both his comfort
and need. The chamber contained a soft paillasse, capped
braziers, lanterns and a coffer containing small goblets and a
flask of wine.

Henshaw lit the candles, fired the braziers and pulled up a
thick woollen blanket around his shoulders. Soon, the Nest
would be very warm, not just because of the braziers but because
it lay directly beneath the huge majestic fireplace in the tap
room above stairs. Once comfortable, Henshaw filled a goblet
with the richest red wine, specially imported from the vines
belonging to the popes at Avignon in Southern France. Henshaw
closed his eyes and clenched his teeth. France! The ghosts of
Avranches were gathering, breaking through the invisible curtain
of time. Years had passed, but the memories remained. Henshaw
recalled the manor lord's house where the gold had been found.
A time of horrid sinning. Henshaw had cut down one young
woman then thoroughly enjoyed another, riding her as he would
a horse. Once he had finished, he had slit her throat. Henshaw
opened his eyes and startled at a sound which echoed along the
dark gallery. He stretched out and pulled his war belt closer.
Surely, he was safe? He was certain he had locked the cellar
door and left the key in the lock and that was the only entrance
to this cellar. Or had he? What was that sound? A rat? Had his
coming down to the cellar disturbed the vermin? Henshaw stood
up, staring into the darkness. No more sound. He went back to
sit on his bed. He drank some wine as he reflected on the brutal
change in fortune. So much had happened! The Via Crucis had
returned home like conquering heroes. They had amassed a
fortune, enough gold to see them through to the grave and
beyond. Nobody had dared challenge them. The notion of retribution for what they'd done had never occurred to Henshaw.
He had gone to France. He had killed. He had ravaged and
ravished and then he had come home. That was the end of the
matter surely? Why had it changed? He'd heard about the
demands of the French envoys, but Sir Oliver had assured him

that nothing would come of that. The likes of Cranston and Athelstan could intervene, but what could they really do? Of course, these were only comforting thoughts. The truth remained. A vengeful wraith had emerged from the dark and men who had served in France were now facing the prospect of a gruesome death.

Henshaw closed his eyes and murmured an 'ave'. He didn't really believe, but prayer was the only thing he could do to ease the tension. Like his masters, Ingham, Crossley and Montague, Henshaw did not care much for preaching on life after death, about reparation for sin or the need for repentance. He turned as he heard the sound again, that shuffling as if someone was in the cellar and moving cautiously towards him. Henshaw drew his dagger and walked down the runnel. He heard the sound once again and half turned just as a black-garbed figure sprang out of the murk swinging a club to smash Henshaw's skull. The former mercenary staggered towards his assailant. Again, the club was swung. Its cracking blow sent Henshaw crashing to the ground. The former mercenary lay moaning, the blood from the two grievous wounds seeping out. The assailant roughly turned Henshaw's body over then, bestriding the fallen man, he twisted Henshaw's head so he could thrust the leather gag into the victim's mouth. He then drew his long Welsh stabbing dirk. Using it like a cleaver, the assassin began to dig a jagged gash down the fallen man's back. Once he had, he dug another across from shoulder blade to shoulder blade, a bloody furrow of a wound.

Late the following day, Athelstan celebrated his Jesus Mass following the ordo of the day, which stipulated that it was still Christmas. The season would last until 6th January, the Feast of the Epiphany, when Christ was made manifest to the world through the visit of the Wise Men. Athelstan stumbled over the words as he recalled his own parish celebrations for the Epiphany. Already animosity had been stirred. The parish was beginning to divide. Athelstan sensed a battle was about to break as debate raged over the coming celebrations and the masque they would present. Who would act as the Wise Men?

Who would be the Virgin Mary? Who would be St Joseph and, above all, who would be the blood-soaked Herod, the villain of the piece? Athelstan, troubled in thought, finished his Mass and divested in the sacristy. Once ready, he went out to sit in his sanctuary chair to meet his parishioners. They had all assembled, not just the parish council but all those who worshipped either at St Erconwald's or 'The Piebald Tavern'. He knew the reason a parish masque was a parish masque. It was a story in their lives and Athelstan's parishioners loved stories. They also wanted to take part in every sense of the word whilst the different roles to be played excited a great deal of attention and considerable negotiation.

Athelstan crossed himself, a sign that he was ready to begin. The parishioners ceased their gossiping and stared at their little parish priest. Mauger took his seat beside Athelstan and laid out the parish documents, including the Blood Book and the parish council ledger. All prepared, he nodded at the Friar to recite the 'Veni Creator Spiritus'. Once he had, Mauger declared the meeting to be in session and Watkin immediately sprang to his feet to harangue the rest about staging their masque. Others objected. Judith the Mummer and Masque Master joined in along with the Hangman of Rochester, who had his own ideas about painting a suitable canvas so as to serve as a fitting backdrop. Athelstan had spoken to the Hangman before Mass. He had assured his parish priest that Horace the Housebreaker had joined the choir invisible in the twinkling of an eye. He also offered to help others bury Horace in the iron-hard earth of St Erconwald's cemetery. Athelstan closed his eyes. He murmured a requiem for Horace, whose corpse now lay sheeted in the House of Abode, the parish mortuary. Athelstan glanced quickly at Helga, the recently made widow, and noticed she was garbed in a smart wool linen coat and a bonnet of similar material. Next to her stood Pike the Ditcher, ever ready to help his close friend and ally, Watkin. The clamour and noise intensified. Matters were brought to an end by an insistent knocking on the corpse door. Athelstan nodded at Mauger, who hurried to answer. He did so and ushered in two visitors, hooded and visored against the bitter cold. Athelstan tensed as these pulled back their cowls. The

Vaucort twins smiled their apology, bowed towards the Friar and genuflected to the sacrament. Once they'd done this, they crossed to Athelstan, who rose to greet them.

'Welcome,' Athelstan declared in a carrying voice. 'Master Benjamin Vaucort and your brother Benedict, you are both welcome. But why are you here?'

'Brother Athelstan, we have come to beg the use of your church.' Benedict's voice rang like a trumpet down the hallowed nave, stilling all noise. The parishioners, dumbstruck by the arrival of these two unexpected visitors and their startling request, milled about like clucking chickens. Athelstan decided to take control.

'Master Benedict, Master Benjamin, do stay!' Athelstan retook his seat and gestured at his parish council. 'My dearest flock, let us hear what our visitors have to say. Let us not make judgement or do anything rash. I discern we have a petition here. We have to decide what we must do with that.' Everyone hastily retook their seats. Athelstan turned to the Vaucort Brothers. 'Do begin.'

'Brothers and sisters in Christ, this is our situation,' Benedict declared. 'My brother Benjamin and I, rightly or wrongly, belong to a community which calls itself the Children of Babylon. We are casualties of the great and horrid war in Normandy, during which our parents were killed whilst we children were brought to England.'

'You French did the same,' Watkin bellowed to a chorus of agreement. 'When your galleys raided the Cinque Ports and all the harbour towns along the Narrow Seas.' Athelstan tensed as he recalled how many of his parishioners had been summoned to serve in the royal array: troops for the old king's forays into France.

'True, true,' Benedict replied, his voice all friendly. 'For the love of God, let me make it very clear. We are not here to debate war but peace. We, the Children of Babylon, have been very well treated here.'

'Very much so,' Benjamin spoke up. 'Look at us, we are well heeled, suitably attired royal clerks, greatly favoured by King and Court. We are here to beg a simple favour.'

'The Children of Babylon,' Benedict now resumed his speech, 'strive to keep alive the song, poetry and dance of Normandy. We have prepared a masque to honour your king on his name day to be celebrated at St Paul's, which, in fact, is January the sixth, the Feast of the Epiphany. We wish to honour that as well as confirm our devotion to your king.'

'A brief but beautiful ceremony,' Benjamin intervened. 'We dance and sing in honour of your king at the same time we celebrate our Norman heritage. God be thanked, your king has graciously consented to our petition to perform before him. Now our number is about sixteen, yes, ten men, six ladies. We have met, as we often do, at our house in Osprey Lane, Cripplegate, but now we would like to rehearse in the nave of a church.' Benjamin spread his hands. 'And what better place than this magnificent, glorious nave.'

Athelstan repressed a smile even as he sensed that his parishioners were much taken with the request. The two clerks bowed towards him and his parishioners before sitting down on the two stools Mauger had fetched from the transept. Athelstan rose to his feet to make a formal reply to what the two clerks had requested. He was about to speak when a thought struck him. He would recommend that the Children of Babylon could use the nave for their rehearsal. However, the proposal might also provide Athelstan with a path out of the tangle confronting him over his own parish's celebration of the Epiphany. The Friar abruptly sat down as the two clerks leaned forward to discuss matters further.

'Brother,' Benjamin murmured, 'your flock seems much taken with our proposal.'

'As am I.'

'Brother Athelstan, tomorrow evening could we have a rehearsal in your nave? We would leave money to buy wine, ale and a range of victuals?'

'Oh yes, on one condition, but let me first put your proposal to my little flock.'

Athelstan rose and moved to the podium. He nodded at Mauger, who began to toll his hand bell as a call for absolute silence. The hushed conversation died away, broken only by Bonaventure, who sped out of the dark in hot pursuit of some vermin hiding in the shadows. Athelstan let the sound die away as he crossed himself and drew a deep breath. He then proposed that the parish allow the Children of Babylon the use of the church to stage their masque. How the rehearsal would take place tomorrow evening as the Vesper bell tolled. By then, Athelstan declared, the day's work was done. This was greeted by a chorus of agreement. Athelstan then went on to propose that they make a true festival of the occasion. Indeed, Athelstan added, their visitors would supply good coin to purchase a variety of refreshments. Athelstan paused as Mauger raised his hand to speak.

'Is that wise?' the bell clerk demanded. 'I mean here in church, a most sacred place?'

Mauger's words were drowned by cries and calls from his fellow parishioners. Athelstan crossed to the bell clerk's table, picked up the hand bell and rang it until he had silence.

'According to Canon Law,' Athelstan declared, 'the Codex Iuris Canonici.' Athelstan deliberately used the Latin, which he knew would impress Mauger and the rest. 'Yes, according to the Code of Canon Law, the nave of the church belongs to the people. The sanctuary is sacred and is reserved only for the use by the priest.' Athelstan's declaration was greeted with cheers, which echoed away as the Friar held up his hands. 'On one condition,' Athelstan's voice exuded authority, 'we are preparing our own masque for the great Feast of the Epiphany. I propose that we have the rehearsal tomorrow evening, a joyous festival of light, then another on the eve of the Epiphany. Again, it will be a solemn but joyful occasion. Such a festival will replace our own masque. Yes, my friends?' Athelstan turned to the two clerks.

'By all means,' Benedict replied. 'It will be a gesture of profound thanks to you and our final rehearsal for what we plan the following day when we celebrate in St Paul's.'

Benedict's declaration was greeted with cheers and loud hand-clapping. Athelstan relaxed. He had managed to escape from the vexed question of the parish masque. At the same time, it also provided him with the opportunity of studying the Children of Babylon more closely. A cohort of able-bodied men and women who certainly had the motive as well as the means to execute certain manor lords who had devastated their early lives in France.

'But we'll see,' Athelstan murmured to himself.

'What was that, Brother?'

Athelstan smiled at Benjamin. 'Just thinking aloud, my friend. The hour grows late. It will soon be time for us to go our separate ways.'

The parish council meeting then broke up. The brothers made their farewells amidst mutual back-slapping, cries of thanks as well as sharp observation about how identical the two brothers were. The Vaucorts took this in good heart. They promised Athelstan that they would be back early the following afternoon so that they would be all ready by the time the Vespers bell rang. Athelstan thanked them and asked Benedicta to escort their visitors out. She did so and returned to manage the excited parishioners. Trestle tables were being brought in whilst Benedicta, at Athelstan's request, was already negotiating with Joscelyn and Merrylegs over the drink and food to be supplied. Athelstan decided to slip away. He was making his way through the corpse door when he almost collided with Tiptoft, garbed in the thickest of green robes.

'Brother Athelstan,' the Coroner's messenger intoned lugubriously, 'Sir John needs you at "The Golden Oriole". Murder, Brother,' he breathed, 'hideous murder!'

Athelstan arrived to find 'The Golden Oriole' closed, its doors guarded by Flaxwith, who let Athelstan and Tiptoft in through a side entrance. They crossed the tap room along to where the cellar door, now taken from its hinges, rested against the wall. Tiptoft helped the Friar on to the steps then made his farewell. Athelstan thanked him and went down to where the Coroner was waiting, standing over a corpse almost floating in a puddle of its own blood. Cranston turned to greet Athelstan. They exchanged the Pax et Bonum. The Coroner then stepped aside, picking up a lantern horn so Athelstan could view the corpse sprawled before them.

'The mortal remains,' Cranston declared, 'of Gilbert Henshaw.'

'Where are his comrades?' Athelstan asked, almost gagging at the horrid, rancid stench from the corpse.

'They're in the buttery, Brother, drinking as if there's no tomorrow.'

'Good,' the Friar breathed, 'they can stay there until we are finished.' Athelstan knelt down, trying not to retch as he glimpsed Henshaw's face, frozen in sudden, violent death. Blood and mucus had drained from the blows to his head, but these two wounds were nothing compared to the deep furrows dug across the dead man's back with another cut sliced from the nape of his neck to the small of his back.

'And Christ carried his cross!' Athelstan murmured.

'What was that, Brother?'

'One of the Sorrowful Mysteries, Sir John, which this assassin is parodying. God help us, my friend, the next will be crucifixion! So,' Athelstan continued, 'Henshaw lies dead. I suspect he came down here and was struck on the back of his head, stunning blows which laid him prostrate. Once accomplished, the assassin then carried out this foul abuse of his victim's body. Sir John, do you agree?'

'I do, Brother. Ingham informed me that Henshaw went missing. He could not be traced. A search was organized. Ingham recalled Henshaw's custom of going down to some place in the cellar he called the Nest.' Cranston shrugged. 'This is behind me in an enclave which also contains a paillasse, a table, a stool, goblet and jug for Henshaw to drink when he wished to be by himself.'

'And?' Athelstan demanded.

'Brother, I agree with you. He was attacked from behind. Savage blows to the head. But here is the problem. Henshaw left the key in the door to the cellar. He locked himself in, so how did the assassin enter? And, before you ask, there is no other secret entrance. Nothing but a hatch for barrels and tuns to be brought down here, but that is firmly padlocked. I have examined the same and I can confidently say the hatch has not been opened for some time.'

'So,' Athelstan murmured, 'Henshaw comes down here. He goes to his nest, a place of comfort. He is alone. He can relax and ponder the macabre occurrences happening all around him.' Athelstan walked around the corpse, going deeper into the darkness to view the enclave, the Nest, with all its comforts prepared. 'Oh yes,' Athelstan declared, 'Henshaw left his bed and moved back along the way he'd come. Unbeknown to him the assassin had slipped in, lurking in the shadows between the barrels or cleverly concealed in one of these enclaves. Henshaw was disturbed, alarmed. Perhaps he'd heard a sound. He is searching for the source, but the assassin is now behind him. The assassin strikes. Henshaw falls and then his body is mutilated. Is there anything else?'

'No.'

'So, we must now talk to the others.'

'They are gathered in the tavern's main buttery,' Cranston replied. 'As I said, drinking fit to burst.'

'Then let's question them before they do.'

They found the knights of the Via Crucis in the warm, luxuriously furnished main buttery with its row of polished tables, soft cushioned chairs and stools. Athelstan could see the knights had all been drinking heavily, their rugged, coarse faces flushed to red. Athelstan recognized them all. Ingham and either side of him Montague and Crossley. Montague was busy lecturing them on the origin of certain names, such as Oriole. They made no attempt to rise when Cranston entered. For a short while they totally ignored the Coroner and his companion as if deeply absorbed with Montague's drunken, slurred lecture. Cranston drew his sword and brought the blade crashing down on the table. All conversation died. The three knights made no attempt to salute their visitors except to raise their goblets and shout at the servants milling around to bring fresh jugs of wine. One face Athelstan did not recognize, a scrawny-haired individual, angry-eyed like that of a frightened horse; his hairy hands clutching a goblet were the colour of mouldering brick. A wealthy man, swathed in a dark crimson cloak edged with the costliest fur. He eventually rose to greet Cranston, clasping hands and ushering both the Coroner and Athelstan to seats around the table.

'Sir Walter Plumpton,' Cranston declared, loosening both his cloak and war belt. 'Sir Walter Plumpton,' he repeated. 'Goldsmith par excellence. A powerful figure both at Court and in our

Guildhall.' Cranston paused to sniff at the goblet of wine a servitor thrust into his hand. 'Brother Athelstan, Sir Walter is master of our Guild of Goldsmiths, a man to be reckoned with.'

Cranston raised his goblet to Plumpton, who greeted the Coroner's declaration with a greasy smirk.

'Well, well, well.' Cranston clapped his hands and gestured at the servants to leave. 'So,' he continued once the room was clear, 'we have another murder, gentlemen. Squire Henshaw, Serjeant at Arms in the Free Company of the Via Crucis. Now, tell me what you might know about his untimely death?'

'Nothing,' Ingham slurred. 'Henshaw went missing. We searched for him but couldn't discover where he could be. Then I remembered him talking about his nest deep in the cellars of this tavern. I tried the door leading down, but the key was firmly embedded in the lock. I raised the alarm, and the door was forced.'

'And the key was still in the lock?'

'Yes, Brother, as I said, it was almost embedded in the lock. Anyway, I went down immediately.'

'As did I,' Crossley added. 'A little while later.'

'We knew something was wrong,' Ingham declared. 'That awful stench. Anyway, we found Henshaw as you did, dead as a nail: his skull pounded in and those horrible cuts both across and down his back.'

'Christ carrying his cross!' Athelstan declared.

'What was that, Brother?'

'It's part of the Via Crucis, Sir Stephen. The real Via Crucis, not the title of your Free Company. Let me make it clear if I haven't already. Each of these heinous murders, blasphemous and sacrilegious, mocks one of the mysteries of Christ's Passion. Mortimer was the judgement by Pilate, Despencer was Christ being scourged at the pillar, Gumblat was Christ being crowned with thorns and Henshaw's is Christ carrying his cross.'

'And the next?'

'Why, Sir Oliver, the crucifixion!' Athelstan ignored Plumpton's gasp of horror. 'I tell you this, gentlemen,' Athelstan brushed the front of his robe, 'all of you should be most vigilant, on your guard. A demon is hunting each and every one of you, fully

intent on inflicting the most horrible death known to man.'
Athelstan's words created an ominous silence broken only by
mice scrabbling in the corner and the echoing sounds from the
streets outside.

'Perhaps,' Ingham grated, 'we should flee the realm for a
while?'

'Not so, not so,' Cranston retorted. 'Sir Oliver and all of you,
on your allegiance to the King, you must stay here until this
business is completed.'

'I must have words with Master Thibault about that,' Ingham
retorted.

'You will not be any safer abroad, Sir Oliver,' Athelstan
declared. 'Indeed, once you leave this kingdom, you become
more vulnerable to seizure by the French.' Athelstan's declaration
was greeted with murmurs of agreement from the rest, though
Ingham still looked doubtful.

'So,' Cranston shuffled his booted feet, 'I ask you on your
oath of loyalty to the Crown. Do any of you know anything more
about the murder of your comrade Henshaw?' Cranston's question was greeted with much shaking of the head and whispered
denials. 'Ah well.' Sir John pointed at the Goldsmith, who had
sat in silence, clearly shocked at what he was witnessing. 'Master
Plumpton,' Cranston declared, 'why are you here on this most
dire of days?'

'I come, Sir John, to discuss the account I hold for these
gentlemen. I am also involved in their plans to erect and develop
a great hospice for lepers along the Southwark side of the Thames.
A most worthy project but very costly.'

'And?'

'We hope to begin building in the spring, Sir John, and complete
by this time next year.'

'Tell me,' Athelstan placed his goblet back on the table, 'none
of you, indeed none of us, are getting younger. What happens if
you all die before the project is finished?'

'Then the responsibility falls to me,' Plumpton declared, 'and
my guild. We would try to finish the project as best we could.
However, we would have to account to the Crown, who would
seize the gold in the name of the King.'

'And until then, what will happen to the remaining gold?'

'It is all held by the members of the Via Crucis.'

'Even if it eventually goes to just one man?'

'That's the agreement made,' Montague declared. 'The last man will be very rich.' He waved a hand. 'It's all drawn up in an indenture, signed, sealed and witnessed.'

'Is there anything more you can tell us?' Cranston insisted. 'I mean about Henshaw's death or, indeed, the others.'

'Nothing, Sir John,' Ingham replied.

'In which case,' Cranston got to his feet, 'I will leave you to your drinking. However, take care, all of you, and keep yourselves available for further questioning.'

PART FOUR

'The right wing is the knowledge of good.'

The following day, St Erconwald's Parish became as busy as any beehive. After his early morning Mass, Athelstan stayed closeted in his house, only leaving late in the afternoon to return to the church. Thankfully, Benedicta and Mauger were in charge, supervising the parishioners as they prepared for the evening festivities. Joscelyn and Merrylegs, despite the freezing cold, had set up a makeshift cooking area with mobile stoves and ovens, together with a roasting spit, all situated close to the cavernous corpse door. Trestle tables, benches, stools and overturned barrels had been brought in. The pillars and walls of the nave were decorated with evergreen, holly, laurel, ivy and the rest. Braziers crammed with fiery charcoal provided gusts of warmth as well as turning the air sweet with the crushed herbs liberally sprinkled across the crackling coals. Children, led by the altar boy Crim, raced up and down the nave whilst Mauger yelled at them to stay clear of the sanctuary. Athelstan had a few words with Benedicta, who looked absolutely resplendent wearing a snow-white apron which covered her from head to toe.

'Don't worry, Father,' she whispered, patting his arm, 'all will be well. All is calm here, though yesterday, whilst you were away, we had a visit from an Exchequer clerk.'

'Oh, what did he want?'

'They accept that Horace committed both the murder and robbery. The Exchequer wants to know if anything has been done to discover where he hid the stolen money.'

'One thing I have learned, Benedicta,' Athelstan retorted, 'is you don't allow the likes of an official to make their problem your problem. Most of that tax money was filched from the hands of the poor, so I pray that it will be found by someone who really needs it.'

'I gave him short shrift, Father. I don't think he'll be back.'

'Anything else, my lady?'

'Oh yes, that strange creature who claims to be a travelling chapman. He comes and goes like a shadow across the wall.'

'Oh yes, him.' Athelstan smiled. 'Keep it secret, but he is someone employed by the Lord High Coroner. Let him remain a shadow deeper than the rest. So, Benedicta the Blessed, until I return, keep a sharp eye on matters.'

She promised she would. Athelstan promptly slipped out of the church and returned to his house. He first checked on Philomel, but the old warhorse looked content enough in his cradle of straw. Hubert the Hedgehog was rolled up in a tight ball whilst Bonaventure, who had followed Athelstan from the church, waited for the Friar to open the door and, swift as an arrow, sped towards the hearth to bask before the flames. Athelstan followed him in, pleased as ever at how warm and welcoming his 'little paradise' was. He built up the fire, gave Bonaventure a bowl of milk and poured a tankard of light ale. He sat and supped for a while before taking out the contents of his chancery satchel. He then crossed to the small side table and quickly studied the parish accounts Mauger had drawn up, listing monies in and monies out. He then checked the Blood Book. This delineated the different families in the parish and the relationship between kin so as to prevent any marriage within the forbidden degrees of consanguinity and affinity. Mauger always kept this in good order whilst Athelstan insisted on inspecting it regularly. He had once served in a village parish where he had seen the effects of marriages between first cousins and the offspring such marriages produced.

Satisfied that all was well, Athelstan signed the Blood Book and dated it. He then returned to studying the murders. Athelstan was convinced he was hunting two assassins and he needed to trap and capture both to establish the truth. Athelstan sat, eyes closed, as he tried to enter the mind of the slayer of Despencer, Gumblat and Henshaw. 'Why did you,' Athelstan murmured, 'torture and kill the way you did? Why? What kind of damned soul are you? Why the torture? Why the sacrilege? Why the blasphemy? And how did you,' Athelstan continued speaking to the silence, 'overcome your victims who, in themselves, were professional killers, veteran soldiers?' Athelstan opened his eyes. He found it difficult to believe that the leading suspect must be Edmund Lacey, the Fisher of Men, yet he certainly had the motive and the means. The Fisher was a skilled warrior who could have hired others to overcome his victims, yet . . . Athelstan sighed and took another sip from his tankard. Then there were the other killings. Kyne and Blondin, not to forget the desecration of Mortimer's corpse. Kyne and Blondin had been tried and executed in their own homes before members of their family or retinue. Over all these hung an air of formal judgement, sentence and death. Certainly, more than one person was involved. Some cohort of professional killers surely? Were they acting on their own? If they had been hired, who had the motive and the means? Dom Antoine and his cohort? The Children of Babylon? Or were those murders the work of other sinners hidden even deeper in the shadows? If so, whoever they were, how did this cohort of killers know where their victims resided and the layout of their manor houses? And, when they left, where did these assassins go? Where did they hide? Athelstan got to his feet, stretched and went to kneel on the narrow prie-dieu pushed away in a gap at the bottom of the bed loft. He pulled the prie-dieu out and knelt down. He recollected, crossed himself and murmured the opening words of a psalm.

'The Lord is my light and my refuge, whom shall I fear . . .'

Athelstan paused as he heard a sound from outside. The slither of footfall. Someone was there! Athelstan rose to his feet. He was certain that someone was lurking in the gathering dark, going around the house like some predator searching for a way in. Athelstan stood, straining his hearing. He could catch faint sounds from those still busy in and around the church. He then tensed as the shutter to the side of the door rattled ominously. Again, the sound of footfall, a slithering sly sound as the predator continued his circling. Athelstan crossed to a small coffer pushed beneath the bed loft. He opened this and took out the small arbalest. He was carefully priming this when he heard louder sounds from outside then Benedicta calling.

'Father, Father, Brother Athelstan!'

Holding the arbalest down by his side, Athelstan moved to the door. Benedicta knocked loudly again, calling his name. He opened the door and Benedicta swept in.

'Good evening,' Athelstan declared, holding up the arbalest. 'Benedicta, I thought you were someone else.'

'No, Father, I called your name to alert you to who I was. I did wonder if you might be asleep. You looked tired.'

'I am fine, Benedicta.' Athelstan plucked the bolt from the groove of the arbalest and placed both back in the coffer. 'Benedicta, is there anything wrong?'

'Nothing, Father.' She approached him and clasped his hands, studying him carefully.

'So why are you here?'

'Father, the great Feast of the Epiphany is fast approaching, the manifestation of the Divine Boy, the Christ child. Father, I need to be shriven. I would like to confess and receive absolution. I want to purge myself and so be ready for the great feast.'

'Benedicta . . .' Athelstan squeezed her fingers then gently released them.

'No, Father, I want confession. Please don't tell me that I don't need it. I do.'

'Very well.' Athelstan pointed at the prie-dieu. 'If you would prepare yourself.'

Benedicta clapped her hands like a child. She helped Athelstan bring his chair closer to the prie-dieu then knelt down, crossing herself. Athelstan waited a while before taking a stole from a wall peg. He placed this round his neck and sat down on the chair. He was relieved at Benedicta's arrival. He had no doubt at what was happening before she did. He was certain that some soul bent on wickedness had prowled out of the darkness to inflict a mischief.

'Father, I am ready.'

'Very well.' Athelstan sketched a cross over her head then listened as Benedicta poured out her heart. No real sin, just the turbulence of everyday life and its constant demands. When she had finished, she raised her head and smiled.

'That is all, Father. There is nothing else except,' she shrugged,

'I cannot make any sense of that riddle you gave me. So, Father, what is my penance?'

'Your penance, Benedicta, is to continue to do what you are doing and God will be with you. As for the riddle, don't worry. I am as puzzled as you are. So, I absolve you from your sins, in the name of the Father, the Son and the Holy Spirit.'

Once he had finished, Benedicta made to leave, breathlessly describing what was happening in and around the church and her need to return to ensure all was well. Once she had gone, Athelstan sat back down in the chair and shook his head. 'Never mind that riddle,' he whispered to Bonaventure, 'let us visit that chamber in "The Piebald". Let us go through that mystery once again. The door was bolted and locked. The victim sat sprawled in a chair with a dagger thrust deep in his heart. No sign of resistance or struggle. No other entrance except that door which had been forced. No tainted wine or food. Nothing malignant which might cause sudden death except that dagger thrust.' Athelstan took off the stole and kissed the cross embroidered in the centre. He was about to place it on the peg when he stopped recalling Benedicta's confession. 'Horace!' he exclaimed. 'Horace!' he repeated. He repeated this so loudly Bonaventure sprang up.

'Bonaventure, my friend, go back to sleep. Brother Athelstan is now realizing that he is not as sharp as he thinks. However, at last I have found one very loose thread in the saga of Horace the Housebreaker's death and, more importantly, his confession.'

Athelstan opened his satchel and took out the riddle: 'Bardolph's death. Resolve this riddle and you will deduce the truth of it all. The riddle is as follows: John is a prisoner held fast and under the constant careful vigilance of three jailors. Matthias, Bernard and Conrad. At least one of these three men were to be on duty at all times. If Matthias was off duty and Bernard was off duty, Conrad would be on duty. However, any time Bernard was off duty Conrad would also be off duty. Quaestio? Could Matthias ever be off duty? Resolve this and you will resolve Bardolph's death.

'It's about movement,' Athelstan murmured, 'who could be where and when? Shape shifting through the shadows?' Athelstan stared at the hour candle. 'Soon I'll pray, think and reflect,' he declared to the now sleeping Bonaventure, 'but for now I will become very, very busy.'

Athelstan left the house with Bonaventure in attendance. The church was now bathed in the light of lantern horns with sconce torches licking the darkness. The nave had been transformed with wreaths, scented braziers, drapes, ribbons and tapestries fastened against both pillar and wall. The Vaucort Brothers and their entourage had arrived in three carts, sixteen people in all: ten men and six ladies. Most of these carried a flute, rebec or viol along with cymbals, a drum and other musical instruments. They had changed into what Benjamin called 'Norman Dress'. This included thick, leather-soled sandals which slapped against the hard paving stone of the nave. Others arrived, including Cranston, who strode into the nave wrapped in a thick military cloak, a beaver hat pulled firmly down on his head. He was accompanied by Giles Argentine, the Royal Physician, similarly dressed. Both coroner and doctor had, as was their wont, drunk deep of the best Bordeaux.

Athelstan greeted these and other guests who milled about the buttery table, which was almost covered by platters of bread, bowls of stewed vegetables and generous cuts of cooked meats: venison, beef, chicken along with duck and fish and trays of sweetmeats. The air was rich with a multitude of savoury cooking odours. These mingled with the scent of the greenery and the perfumed smoke from thuribles crammed with charcoal and incense. Someone shouted that the Vespers bell had rung. Athelstan agreed and nodded at Mauger, who lifted the parish horn and blew three powerful blasts. Silence ensued. Athelstan took his seat on his throne-like chair placed firmly before the entrance through the rood screen. The spectators, now quietly excited at the prospect of the masque beginning, sat on benches facing each other across a well-decorated avenue which swept up the nave to the sanctuary steps. Athelstan had been informed that they were trying to re-create what would happen in St Paul's, where the young king would be enthroned on the top of the steps leading up to the great sanctuary.

All was now ready. Torches spluttered. Candlelight glowed.

Lantern horns shed pools of bobbing light. Crim emerged from the shadows close to the main door. He walked up the avenue between the spectators scattering paper flowers soaked in some type of fragrance. A drum began to beat, echoing through the nave, and the pageant began. The Children of Babylon, as they proclaimed themselves, emerged in pairs out of the darkness which shrouded both the main entrance and the baptistry. They kept their formation, hands clasped above their heads. They paused for a moment then moved towards Athelstan, slightly swaying to the music as they chanted the famous lament: 'By the rivers of Babylon, there we sat and wept when we remembered Zion.' They sang this in a two-voiced choir, now and again pausing to play their instruments. Athelstan and the rest were caught up by this four-fold presentation of dance, song, poetry and music all permeated by a deep-seated longing for home.

The Children of Babylon, led and managed by the Vaucort Brothers, turned and twisted. They approached the sanctuary steps two at a time. They climbed these, bowed to Athelstan and then peeled off to meet their partner. They would then return dancing, singing and chanting to the baptistry. Once assembled, the masque would begin again. A column of lavishly decorated participants moving two at a time towards Athelstan before whom they would bow once again before peeling off to allow the next couple to glide forward in a beautifully organized way. The music, the slap of sandal leather on stone, the melodious constant chant and the swaying, sensual dance of the participants, created a dream-like presentation. At last, with the rattle of a tambourine and the beating of a tambour, the pageant finished. For a few heartbeats there was silence then the spectators, parishioners and guests erupted in a joyous and ringing hand-clapping to shouts of 'God be thanked!' 'Bravo! Bravo!' The Vaucorts and their retinue were flooded with shouts of praise and encouragement. The nave rang with different acclamations. Athelstan singled out the Vaucort Brothers. He congratulated them before moving away as others pressed forward. The evening became one of raucous entertainment. Some of the Children of Babylon then performed individually, or along with one of their colleagues, inviting all the spectators to participate.

Athelstan was pleased. He walked around the nave smiling and praising even though he was distracted by what he had deduced earlier. Eventually he excused himself and went into 'The Piebald', which was virtually deserted except for the occasional servitor. He climbed the stairs to the murder chamber, its door still leaned askew against the wall. Once again, he inspected both locks and bolts. He then went into the chamber and sat down on the chair where Bardolph had been found. Athelstan tried to settle his thoughts. He was fairly certain he had some kind of a possible solution, but it would have to wait, at least for a while.

'Are you joining us, Little Friar? You're not thinking about that murder, are you?' Athelstan glanced to his right. Cranston stood just within the doorway, a massive dark figure against the light. 'You are working, aren't you, Little Friar?'

'Of course, Sir John, you know I never give up.'

'Oh Brother, don't worry about that and, by the way, that riddle means nothing to me. It's arrant nonsense. Anyway, what do you think of the masque?'

'Thought-provoking, Sir John. Fertile ground for all kinds of ideas. By the way, Lord High Coroner, whose idea was it that the Children of Babylon present such a masque before the King at St Paul's?'

'Well, it must be either John of Gaunt or our mutual friend Master Thibault. I mean . . .' Cranston paused at the sound of footsteps. Argentine, the Royal Physician, who had drunk even more than Sir John, lurched into the room, a beatific smile on his face and a deep bowled goblet in his right hand. Argentine raised this in toast and slurped noisily.

'Lovely, lovely evening,' he slurred. 'It's months since I enjoyed myself like that. The music, those lovely young people, not to mention the company. That's why I came looking for you. Ah,' the physician stared around, 'so this is where Bardolph was murdered, yes?'

'Yes,' Athelstan replied. 'Stabbed to the heart.'

'Pardon?'

'Stabbed to the heart, Sir Giles. You saw his corpse in the death house.'

The physician staggered towards Athelstan.

'I tell you this, Brother,' Argentine wiped his mouth on the back of his hand, 'Bardolph may have had a dagger thrust straight to the heart, but that was post mortem, after death. Bardolph was poisoned.'

Athelstan just gaped at Argentine.

'Brother,' the physician declared, 'I may be deep in my cups, but I wasn't when I examined Bardolph's corpse. I saw it today as they were getting ready the shroud. They had removed the dagger. I saw the wound but, as I said, Bardolph the Tax Collector was poisoned. The signs were obvious, probably the work of belladonna or deadly nightshade. Like many such poisons, belladonna only manifests itself after death. Bardolph, either accidentally or not, must have consumed in some form or other this shrub's deadly, dark, shining berries.' The physician smiled and lurched across the chamber to sit on the edge of the bed. 'Strange!' Argentine gulped from his goblet.

'What is strange?' Cranston slurred.

'Belladonna, Sir John. The immediate effects of the poison are very similar to that of a dagger thrust wound: shock, consternation, the urge to flee, but the body is incapable. All of its humours are seriously disturbed as the victim slides towards death. Different poisons have different symptoms. Arsenic, for example, is virtually undetectable except it slows down the process of decomposition in the corpse of its victim.'

'And nightshade?' Athelstan demanded.

'Blue-black streaks emerge on the corpse: the cheeks, the chest and the belly.'

'Well, well, well,' Athelstan exclaimed. 'So, Sir John, we begin again. But that is for tomorrow. Let us rejoin the celebrations.'

Once he had celebrated his dawn Mass, Athelstan gave his excuses to the only two parishioners who joined him, Crim and Benedicta, then made ready to return to his house. Benedicta promised to remain in the church and, when her fellow parishioners emerged from wine-laced slumbers, she would supervise tidying up the nave. Once back in his house Athelstan ate the hot oatmeal Benedicta had prepared along with small manchet loaves smeared with honey. He filled a tankard of morning ale, pronounced himself ready for work and prepared his chancery table.

'First,' he murmured, 'there's that riddle. It's a goad to make me think and reflect. Who is responsible for that? Well, I do recall a morsel of conversation which might be the key to the author of this enigmatic verse. How does it go?' Athelstan crossed to the table and picked up the strip of parchment. 'Bardolph's death. Resolve this riddle and you will deduce the truth of it all. The riddle is as follows: John is a prisoner held fast and under the constant careful vigilance of three jailors. Matthias, Bernard and Conrad. At least one of these three men were to be on duty at all times. If Matthias was off duty and Bernard was off duty, Conrad would be on duty. However, any time Bernard was off duty Conrad would also be off duty. Quaestio? Could Matthias ever be off duty? Resolve this and you will resolve Bardolph's death. Now whoever wrote that,' Athelstan continued, talking to an attentive Bonaventure, 'is advising that I should mark the movements of certain individuals in that tavern and the murder chamber especially. Firstly, who was where and when? Secondly, we have Bardolph poisoned not stabbed. So, why all the pretence that he was attacked suddenly, swiftly, without warning? Thirdly, we have Merrylegs and the Hangman of Rochester falling ill. Were they poisoned as well? If so, by whom, for what reason and how? Fourthly, we have a situation where apparently no one was in that chamber with Bardolph, so if he was poisoned, how? Where is the cup, the jug which might incriminate the guilty party? Apart from Argentine's comment, what evidence is there of poison in the murder chamber? Fifthly, the chamber itself was locked. No one was seen acting suspiciously whilst all our parish worthies, or at least those who might fall under suspicion, were glimpsed here and there around "The Piebald". None of them could be accused of any wrongdoing. Nevertheless, that riddle, that puzzle points to a possible solution which might well include those same parishioners. Sixthly, there's the involvement of our mutual friend, now gone to God, Horace the Housebreaker, and his lovely wife Helga. Was that felon's final confession the truth? Seventhly, there's Helga herself and her breathless journeys to and from Newgate? Oh yes,' Athelstan breathed noisily, 'mischief piled upon mischief. But let me secure more evidence.'

Athelstan went and stood outside. A heavy mist swirled, floating around the tombstones and funeral crosses. It carried the rank stench of the river. Athelstan tapped a sandaled foot. A hard ground frost gripped everything in its vice-like hold.

'Not to worry,' Athelstan murmured. 'Foul weather or not, the truth will out.'

The Friar went back inside. He tightened his sandals and wrapped a heavy cloak about him. He banked the fire, gazed around then left the house. Athelstan crossed God's Acre, taking careful note of all the funereal tablets, stones and crosses he passed. He could detect no disturbance, no sign that the warlocks, wizards and moon worshippers had invaded his cemetery to celebrate their midnight rites. He passed the House of Abode. Thomas the Toad was apparently asleep for all the lights were dimmed. Athelstan quickly visited the church where Benedicta, Crim and Mauger, together with other faithfuls, were busy along the nave. He then hurried on down to 'The Piebald'.

Like the church, the tavern lay under a pall of deep sleep. A slattern answered Athelstan's rap on the door. She assured the Friar that all was well, adding that the revellers were still sleeping off the previous night's indulgence. In turn Athelstan informed her that he was simply continuing his investigation into Bardolph's death. The slattern pulled a face and left him to it. Athelstan went upstairs to the murder chamber. Again, he inspected the room. The floor and the jakes cupboard were freshly scrubbed. Athelstan looked around one last time. Certain that he had not missed anything, he then returned downstairs and walked out into the spacious garden at the rear of the tavern. Joscelyn, like any enterprising purveyor of food and drink, tried to grow as much as he could himself instead of paying the high prices from a market trader. Joscelyn's garden was well and truly laid out and stocked with herbs and spice plots, a carp pond and a wild ramble of grass, fern and bramble. Athelstan had once studied a copy of the 'Pharmacopeia' in the well-endowed library of his

Mother House at Blackfriars. The 'Pharmacopeia' had been a veritable treasure of information about poison and plants of every kind. He soon recalled what he had read and quickly discovered what he was looking for. He did not touch the plant in question as the 'Pharmacopeia' had warned how every aspect of such a plant was, according to the experts, highly dangerous and deeply poisonous.

'So, you are belladonna,' Athelstan murmured, staring at the plant, 'deadly nightshade, the friend and ally of poisoners all over this kingdom and beyond.' Athelstan finished his study then moved over to the rubbish pit, a deep hole hollowed out of the ground where Joscelyn would burn his rubbish. The Friar took a stick and sifted among the most recent deposits. He plucked out, as carefully as he could, the highly polished parts of a wine tun Joscelyn had tossed there. He scrutinized this carefully, using the stick to pluck pieces out and turn them over.

'And so it is,' he whispered, 'and so it was. Truth,' he continued, 'like water, always seeps through.'

Athelstan returned to the tap room, thanked the slattern and walked back to his own house. He completed a few tasks then took out his writing tray and a long sheath of parchment. 'So I begin,' he murmured, 'may the Lord help me with this indictment.'

Benedicta visited him later to declare that the nave was now returned to normal. She put down the food and drink she had brought and left. Athelstan ate and continued to work hard, writing well into the early evening. Now and again, he was disturbed by the occasional visitor eager to discuss the recent pageant and how enraptured they were by the Children of Babylon's presentation. Mauger was ringing the bell for Nones when an unexpected visitor arrived. Cranston, accompanied by a furtive-looking Shadow Master, breezed into the house. Cranston slouched down on a chair opposite Athelstan, telling the Shadow Master to pull up a stool and sit next to him. Both the Coroner and his companion refused Athelstan's offer of refreshment. Instead, the Coroner took a deep slurp from his miraculous wineskin before handing it to the Shadow Master, who took a number of deep gulps before the Coroner snatched it back.

'Well, well,' the Coroner declared, pushing the stopper back into the wineskin.

'Sir John?'

'Brother Athelstan, listen to our friend here.' Cranston gestured at the Shadow Master.

'I missed the festivities last night,' the Shadow Master whined.

'Never mind that,' Cranston snapped. 'So did the Fisher of Men. Tell us why?'

'I took up post in a derelict warehouse which provided a good view of the quayside as well as the two paths. The first leads up to the Fisher's house, an ancient mansion much refurbished. The second takes you to the Chapel of the Drowned Man. Cresset torches lashed to poles provide pools of light. I waited even as I froze.'

'And, my friend, you will be well paid.'

'Thank you, Sir John. I was about to leave when a war barge festooned with pennants, I couldn't make out their insignia, approached to be greeted by the Fisher of Men and his retinue. They helped moor the craft then took their visitors up to the Fisher's mansion.'

'Who were they?'

'Brother Athelstan, I couldn't really say except they were well armed and harnessed for war: helmets on their heads, war belts strapped around their waists. They moved like a well-trained battlegroup.'

'How many?'

'I would say up to twenty in number. They were welcomed and stayed for, oh, it must have been two hours, then they left.' The Shadow Master paused, licking his lips. He glanced mournfully at Cranston. The Coroner sighed and handed across the wineskin. He allowed the Shadow Master a few gulps then snatched it away, face all cross. 'Thank you, Sir John. Please remember the words of St Paul, "take a little wine for the belly's sake".'

'Never mind that,' Cranston barked, gesturing at Athelstan. 'Tell my good friend what you saw and heard.'

'As they were leaving, I heard what must have been their leader saying that they would return this evening as the Compline bell tolled. They then left. As did I, like a hunting fox keeping to the edge of the river bank. A dense mist had rolled in, but then it parted, and I glimpsed two huge war barges, oars dipping, going down river.' He pulled a face. 'I just had a feeling. Well, who else would go along the river at such a late hour? A freezing night when even the birds died on the branches.'

'River pirates?'

'My thoughts exactly, Sir John. I do wonder if they too were interested in that other barge, or the Fisher of Men, or both?'

'Two other matters,' Cranston declared. 'I am not too sure if the first is connected to the Fisher of Men. However, Sir Walter Plumpton . . .'

'The goldsmith?'

'Yes, Brother, the same. Anyway, he presented himself at the Guildhall to report how gold of a strange variety has been offered and traded in the City.'

'You mean the gold from those skeletons found floating in the river just off the Chapel of the Drowned Man?'

'Yes, Brother Athelstan. In the first instance such gold belongs to the King and should be handed over to the Royal Surveyor, Sir Oliver Ingham. God knows, however, the origin of this?'

'You think the pirates were hunting for the source?' Athelstan pointed at the Shadow Master.

'Possibly, Brother. They passed along the river like ghosts, disappearing into the mist boiling around them.'

'This is hard to take,' Cranston murmured. 'I always considered the Fisher a friend, a comrade. But what's he doing with a battle-group of mailed soldiers? Are they the same ones despatched to execute Kyne and Blondin as well as roughly exhume the mortal remains of Sir Roger Mortimer?'

'Hard to believe.'

'In which case, Brother,' Cranston rapped the table, 'we will visit the Fisher tonight just as the Compline bell tolls.'

'Oh Lord,' Athelstan whispered. 'It'll be deathly cold.'

'No, Brother, we won't sit and wait. No. As soon as that bell sounds, we shall move down river and immediately pay our respects to the Fisher of Men.'

'So, we are agreed,' Athelstan replied. He gestured at the

Shadow Master. 'And the task I gave you to pursue at "The Piebald"?'

'At first nothing, Brother, though I was accepted for what I claimed to be. I was allowed to wander the tavern and, on one occasion, I even went up to the murder chamber. Five of your parishioners were sitting around the table. They appeared to be sharing a manchet loaf and drinking wine from the same goblet which they passed from hand to hand.' The Shadow Master shrugged. 'What is the significance of that?'

'Oh, I think I know,' Athelstan replied. 'Who were the five?'

'Why, Pike, Watkin, Crispin, Ranulf and Joscelyn.'

'Brother?'

'Nothing, Sir John. Let me think, let me reflect.'

'Do you want me this evening, Sir John?'

'No, Shadow Master, I don't think so. I will organize two barges. Flaxwith and his beautiful boys in one and a cohort of White Hart archers from the Tower in the other. That will be company enough.'

'And the other business?' the Shadow Master urged. 'Sir John, tell Brother Athelstan what I found.'

'Oh yes.' Cranston opened his belt wallet and brought out a square of parchment. He handed this to Athelstan, who read the script. The letters were bold and black, easy to read. 'To Richard your king,' Athelstan began. 'Mene, Mene, Tekel and Parsin.' Athelstan glanced up. 'I certainly recognize the message. It stirs a memory, but I cannot place it. Anyway, what does it mean?'

'God knows,' Cranston replied. 'But the Shadow Master brought this in whilst I discovered the same proclamation nailed to a side door of the Guildhall. Apparently, this cryptic message has been posted the length and breadth of the City. The Cross, the Standard and the Tun in Cheapside as well as the main door to St Paul's and on the cross in its churchyard.' Cranston shook his head in wonderment. 'Whoever posted this moved swiftly.'

'And undetected!'

'Yes, Brother, he or she certainly did. We recognize that the proclamation is a possible threat to our king. We have summoned in our legion of spies and informers, the street swallows as well as the heralds of the alleyway, but they can tell us nothing worthwhile. Oh, by the way, Brother, talking of making no sense, I cannot understand that riddle. I even gave it to Lady Maude; she is skilled in such matters, but she found it impossible to resolve.'

Athelstan nodded. He murmured his thanks then sat back in his chair and stared at the triptych fastened to the far wall. The painting was a gift from the Hangman of Rochester with his God-given talent as an artist as well as being the dispenser of judicial death. The triptych celebrated the Resurrection of the Dead at the end of time when the very elements would catch fire and melt. The Hangman had depicted long lines of golden light signifying the good whilst the other side of the painting showed the damned experiencing all the horrors of Hell. 'God knows where I will be,' he whispered.

'Brother?'

'Sorry, Sir John, I was daydreaming. Is there anything else?'

'No, my good friend.'

Cranston lumbered to his feet. 'Before I leave your glorious parish, I will hire Moleskin to collect you from here and safely deposit you with me at Queenhithe. So, until then, my little Friar . . .'

They clasped hands. Athelstan blessed the Shadow Master before Cranston dragged the poor unfortunate out of the house into the freezing cold.

Athelstan spent the rest of that day revising his bill of indictment regarding Bardolph's death in 'The Piebald'. He was certain he had the truth of it, but now he must act. He just hoped he could bring the matter to a satisfactory conclusion. He built up the fire, read the psalter for the day and prepared for his journey along the river. Benedicta brought food and drink, a bowl of hot beef stew, fresh manchet bread and a dish of vegetables in a sauce together with a small jug of Bordeaux which, Benedicta insisted, was the very best wine in her buttery: a gift from a sea captain, a close friend of her missing husband. He could savour it here or elsewhere. Athelstan, however, insisted on dining in his own house, knowing what he did now. The Friar quietly promised himself that it would be sometime before he ever dined at 'The Piebald' again.

He ate and slumbered for a while and was woken by Moleskin

knocking on the door. Athelstan grabbed both cloak and satchel and, having prepared himself, locked his house up and followed the bargemaster down to the riverside. Moleskin had no difficulty finding Cranston. He directed his oarsmen to move a little further up river and then the barge, like a well-aimed arrow, headed across to Queenhithe. Athelstan was relieved when they reached the quayside. The Thames was dark, ugly and swollen. Seabirds screeched like a gaggle of ghosts above them whilst rolling clouds of a thick sea mist heightened the danger. Moleskin's sons manned both poop and stern with glowing lanterns whilst the strident bellowing of their hunting horns warned other craft of their approach. Cranston, cloaked and cowled over his battle harness, welcomed Athelstan ashore. He explained how his own war barges were fast approaching. A short while later they did, just as the Compline bells began their pealing and the beacon fires flared in church steeples. The bells were still clanging when Cranston gave the order to cast off and the barges slid away, moving in single file down river, hugging its northern bank. The Thames was still angry, and the barges were buffeted by the strong currents: nevertheless, they managed to make headway and eventually the shadowy outline of the Fisher of Men's dwellings came into view.

Cranston made no attempt at concealment. He loudly proclaimed that the Fisher of Men's other visitors had already arrived, their craft moored along the desolate quayside. Cranston ordered his barges to do likewise and a short while later his war band swiftly disembarked. Of course, there were guards, and the alarm was raised. However, when Cranston bellowed who he was and why he had come, the guards quickly withdrew. Cranston and a group of his cohort followed, climbing the steps, and entered the great hall. This was quite a magnificent building, very similar to the nave of a church only this swept up to a raised dais beneath an ornately carved choir loft. The walls either side of the hall were plastered a bright pink, the floor was expertly paved. Scented braziers and herb pots exuded perfumed smoke whilst a fire blazed in a hearth built into one of the walls, the flames leaping like feverish dancers up a cavernous chimney stack. Trestle tables ranged on either side of the hall and Athelstan soon recognized some of the Fisher of Men's 'faithfuls' as he called them: Ichthus, Hackum, Soulsham and the rest. But there were others, all harnessed for war, and Athelstan thought it strange that they sat hooded and coifed. Cranston tugged Athelstan's sleeve and whispered at the Friar to accompany him up to the dais where the Fisher of Men and his principal guests got to their feet.

'Sir John, you are always welcome.'

'My friend.' Cranston threw back his cloak to reveal his war sword.

'Why this?' the Fisher demanded. 'Why are you here with armoured men in the dead of night?'

'My friend,' Cranston replied, 'I could ask you the same question.'

The Fisher of Men sat down; his eerie-looking guests either side of him did likewise. One of these whispered to the Fisher, who nodded, his eyes never leaving Cranston. Once the whisperer had finished, the Fisher got to his feet.

'Ichthus,' he bellowed, 'look after our unexpected guests both here and the chambers beyond. Let them eat and drink as they wish. They may consort with our other guests, but that is a matter for them to decide.' He then gestured at Cranston and Athelstan. 'My friends, follow me.'

He waited until both men climbed on to the dais then the Fisher led them off through a door at the far end into a comfortable refectory, fully furnished and decorated, with a table running down the centre. The Fisher invited Cranston and Athelstan to sit at one end whilst he and his two companions settled at the other end of the table. Athelstan, intrigued, watched. Soulsham, who followed them in, filled goblets of posset yet these were served in a strange way. One jug for the Coroner and another for the Fisher and his companions. After the manikin had left, the Fisher lifted his goblet. His companions did the same, toasting Athelstan and Cranston, who responded in kind.

'Well.' The Fisher put down his cup. 'Gentlemen,' he gestured at his companions, 'show yourselves to our noble coroner and his most learned companion.' The two men pulled back their coifs and removed the cloth visor which covered most of their faces. Athelstan gasped in surprise. Cranston lifted his goblet and drank noisily.

'Lepers!' Athelstan murmured. He stared at the two ravaged faces with their lesions, cuts and buboes, totally bereft of any eyebrow or eyelid.

'You are shocked?' one of the knights demanded. 'Anyway, now you know who we are and why we sit and drink quite distant from you. Our good friend, the Fisher, has weathered the disease and survived.' He rose and bowed. 'We cannot exchange the kiss of peace or clasp hands with you in friendship, but we do welcome two men of great integrity.'

'Very much so,' the Fisher interjected.

'My name and title,' the knight continued, 'is Lord Tobit of Bethany. My companion is Lord Tobias of Emmaus, both villages in Outremer, two places mentioned in scripture.'

'I accept that, but what are you doing here at such a late hour?' Cranston demanded.

'Sir John . . .'

'One moment. Are you holding gold from those ancient graves?'

'Sir John, let us explain.'

'Do so.'

'We are leper knights of the Order of St Lazarus,' Lord Tobit declared. 'We have done God's work in God's own land. We have left Outremer for a while and returned to England. We have a few hospitals and hospices here, what others call lazar houses. Our company have set up camp further down river in a dilapidated, deserted fishing village. We have makeshift dwellings, but we hope and pray to improve our lot. We keep ourselves to ourselves for obvious reasons. Indeed, when we journey along any road, our bellman goes ahead of us, warning good people of our imminent approach. We have christened the dwelling we now occupy as St Julien's Hospice. We live on alms and the good will of kinfolk.'

'How many are in your company?'

'A cohort of twenty, Sir John.'

'And why are you here tonight?'

'Two reasons,' the Fisher spoke up. 'First they have come to take the gold found on that fresh batch of skeletons.'

'That should be handed over to Sir Oliver Ingham, the King's surveyor. He in turn should pass it on to the Crown, to be stored in the Exchequer vaults at Westminster.'

'Should it really, Sir John?' the Fisher mocked as his two companions laughed: short, sharp barks of derision.

'You do not trust him?'

'No, Sir John, we do not trust him.'

'Do you think he is responsible for the sale of this strange gold in the City?'

'We certainly do, Sir John, but we do not have proof.' The Fisher paused. 'Brother Athelstan, my Lord Coroner. We found this gold. As the good friar informed me, we should receive a portion allocated to the finders. Now, this should be undertaken by Ingham, but he is corrupt. He will not hand it over, even more so now he knows who I truly am. We have only taken what is ours and defined as such by the law. Agreed, Sir John?'

'I would say so,' Athelstan quickly replied. 'Sir John?'

'Very definitely.'

'I am pleased.' The Fisher clapped gauntleted hands whilst his two companions murmured their thanks.

'If he discovers what you are planning, he could pass the blame to you. He could argue that if any of that ancient gold is sold, it is done by you. Have you tried to sell it?'

'Oh no, Sir John,' Lord Tobit murmured through ravaged lips. 'Our good friend the Fisher has handed it over, but we will not trade it here. No, we will take it north for trade in York where we own a hospice under the banner of the Green Cross. Once we have sold the gold, we shall return to build our own hospice.'

'But what about the Via Crucis and their desire to build a fitting lazar house?' Athelstan spoke up.

'Brother, I don't believe any of that. I don't trust any of them, even Despencer. They left me in Avranches. They are not men of honour. Ingham is the worst. He fears neither God nor man. He wouldn't even build a jakes to accommodate anyone let alone an entire hospice.'

'Why do you dislike him so much?'

'I have referred to this before,' the Fisher replied. 'Ingham hates religion and all its accoutrements. He loved to burn churches.' The Fisher raised his right hand as if on oath. 'I don't believe the story about the church burning in Avranches. He informed me that those inside had started it and it got out of hand. All I remember is that when I arrived there, the fire had begun and Ingham did nothing to help control it or rescue those imprisoned inside. I am sure of that.' The Fisher paused. 'Other reasons press hard for my old comrades to be here.' He coughed, clearing his throat. 'Darkness has fallen, but it's a darkness which permeates our souls. I am here, Sir John, exposed to my enemies. Oh Ichthus, Hackum and Soulsham keep faith, but they are little men. Out there the wolves slope through the dark and I ask myself, is there a battlegroup intent on my death? For what purpose? Have I also been marked down for murder? After all I was a member of the Via Crucis Free Company. I was at Avranches and elsewhere.' The Fisher rubbed his face. 'I'd have died there if it had not been for Lord Tobit and his company.'

'There's another reason,' Tobias declared. 'A self-evident truth that the love of money is the route of all evil. News about the gold being found in this desolate place is seeping along the banks of the Thames. Interest has been truly quickened and, as my good friend and comrade has said, the wolves gather, eager to begin the hunt.'

'River pirates?'

'Amongst others, Sir John. Either for themselves or for someone else.'

'So,' Athelstan smiled down at his hosts, 'you will take this gold and use it to found and develop your own hospice?'

'We certainly shall, Brother, and we shall also do our very best to protect our benefactor and former comrade, the Fisher of Men. We may well have to move some of our company here and fortify . . .' He broke off at the pounding on the door, which was flung open, and Flaxwith hurried in.

'Sir John,' he gasped, 'two war barges are fast approaching the quayside. Both are packed with men in battle harness. For the moment they are paused, resting . . .'

Cranston and the rest sprang to their feet and followed Flaxwith out through the hall where others, alarmed by the news, were gathering their weapons, tying on harness and war belts. Flaxwith took Cranston and his table companions up on to a rise which swept down to the quayside and gave a general view of the river. The deep mist had now lifted, and Athelstan could see two war barges facing the quayside rising and falling on the surging tide. Torches glowed at poop and stern, shining on the armour and weapons of what Cranston declared must be a horde of river pirates. A third barge then joined them, and the Coroner pointed out that all three craft boasted a flapping pennant dyed a dark red: the banner of war, threatening imminent attack and a fight to the finish.

'But they don't know, or have not yet realized,' Cranston declared, 'who they are facing. Not just the Fisher of Men and the knights but our comitatus.'

Cranston gestured at Flaxwith to draw close.

'Bring the Tower Archers here. Keep them concealed behind the rise. They are to deploy as if in a battlegroup massed together. Let their leader, the Captain of Archers, be guided by me. He must conceal himself yet ensure he has a clear view of the quayside.'

'And our men?'

'My dear Flaxwith, have them muster behind the archers, but they are only to move on my direction.'

Flaxwith hurried off. Athelstan stared down at the three barges, now fighting the swell as they rose and fell on the surging current. Narrowing his eyes Athelstan could glimpse the captain of each barge all festooned in fearsome war gear, helmets on their heads, grotesque masks covering their faces, garishly decorated cloaks floating in the breeze.

'They are watching,' Cranston murmured. 'They haven't yet seen the barges which brought the leper knights here. They'll attack any moment now.'

As if in reply, war horns brayed, a deep ominous sound full of threat and menace. Voices shouted orders, up came the oars before falling down deep into the surface of the river. All three barges surged forward towards the quayside, turning sharply to moor alongside.

'Ready!' Cranston shouted at the Captain of Archers, who ran to join them. The pirates disembarked. The Captain called out directions. The archers massed then advanced on to the rise. The pirates now fired cresset torches which illuminated the quayside.

'Easy targets,' Tobias murmured. 'Sir John?'

'Now!' Cranston bellowed, his voice echoing out. The pirates paused, staring around, unsure of the voice and what was intended.

'Twenty yards,' the Captain of Archers bellowed. 'Twenty yards and closing fast. Notch! Bend!'

Athelstan watched the bowmen mass together. They swung their war bows up, the staves bent to their fullest extent, shafts all ready with their jagged points and feathered flights.

'Loose!' the Captain screamed. The archers did. The sound of the flight seemed like the fluttering of a flock of birds, then they fell, taking the enemy in so many ways. The pirate line reeled; some ran forwards, others retreated back towards the quayside. The archers had now found their mark. More volleys were loosed, the shafts hissing like striking snakes. Most hit their targets. The line of attackers buckled as the shower of death rained down on them. Men reeled away with shafts piercing face, chest, belly and back. Eventually the enemy broke completely. Some fled back to their barges even as the incessant rain of arrows continued, other hardier souls scrambled to engage. Cranston ordered his bailiffs forward. These streamed down the rise across the quayside and then it was over. The pirate barges, much depleted, pulled away, desperately striving to reach the thick bank of mist which would shroud them against the arrow storm. Others, less fortunate, tried to resist only to be cut down, their corpses joining the rest bobbing along the surface of the river.

At last, a sombre silence descended, broken only by the sound of lapping water, the shriek of hunting gulls and the wretched moans and cries of the injured. Flaxwith came and reported that all of the enemy wounded were beyond human help. Athelstan hurried down to the huddle of injured men: those who could still speak asked to be shrived. Athelstan issued absolution, blessed them and left them to Flaxwith and his bailiffs, who administered the mercy cut: a swift slash which opened their throats. Once the blood had ceased to gush and the chilling choking sounds of the dying had faded to silence, the bailiffs dragged the corpses away. They heaped them in a pile close to the Chapel of the Drowned Man. Both archers and bailiffs ensured that each cadaver was stripped clean of anything of value, be it boots, belts, weapons, armlets and the rest. Cranston ordered that such plunder was lawful booty. He then assured the Fisher of Men that if he had the corpses transferred to the great Death House near St Mary atte Bowe, he would receive generous compensation from the Lords of the Guildhall. Cranston then turned to the prisoners, five in all, including two lads who had served as lantern bearers. Cranston ordered Flaxwith to give each boy a coin and let them go into the City where they could act as street heralds and proclaim, for all to hear. 'How Jack Cranston, Lord High Coroner of the City, dealt with outlaws.' Sir John then moved on to the three other prisoners. He set up court behind the high table on the dais in the Long Hall. The Fisher of Men on his left and Athelstan on his right. The Friar strongly suspected what would happen and his suspicions were soon proved correct. Cranston moved swiftly, proclaiming his status as Coroner and displaying the Royal Seal which reflected his position and power, giving him the authority to try and determine all crimes committed against the Crown. Cranston could act like a Justiciar of Oyer et Terminer and so decide on the cases before him. The process did not last long. The three pirates kneeling before the dais were convicted of assault, attempted murder and, above all, treason for their attack on the King's own coroner.

'The full penalty for that,' Cranston bellowed, 'is to be hanged, drawn and quartered, your head and body parts displayed over the river as a warning to others. However, this court is prepared to be merciful. A simple hanging will suffice if a true confession is made. Now, Master Flaxwith,' Cranston turned to his right where the bailiffs were gathered, 'I understand you have conferred with the prisoners. You believe one of these to be a riffler, a captain in the Company of the Damned as well as the commander of one of those barges?'

'True, Sir John.' Flaxwith, now standing behind the prisoners, clasped one of them by the shoulder. 'Sir John,' he declared, 'this is Ratspain. Ratspain the Great, or so he called himself. A well-known pirate who stands accused of a litany of offences along the river from the bridge to the estuary.'

'Oh yes, I have heard of you.' Cranston pointed at the prisoner whose swarthy face was freshly scarred from the recent struggle. 'Much suspected, though nothing proved, eh?' Cranston continued. 'But now it's different. So, what path do you want to take to the heavenly gates? Master Flaxwith's rope or that long very painful journey from Newgate to Tyburn, lashed to a sledge, dragged across the rutted streets and runnels, the cobbles shredding your back to even worse pain when you reach the scaffold. So, let us decide which path you will take. First the attack. Ratspain, you answer while the others remain tight-lipped unless they have something interesting to add. So, Ratspain, everything depends on you. Now, who organized the attack?'

'I and two others. Leaders of our company. We were approached in "The Tabernacle".'

'I know it well,' Cranston interjected. 'That tavern extends a warm welcome for vermin such as yourself.'

'We were approached,' Ratspain gasped, 'by one man. He was masked and visored. He bought our attention with three silver coins he placed on the table before us. Now we were tempted to attack him and take it, but he promised more whilst he had a bodyguard with him. He described how gold had been found close to the Fisher of Men's manor house along the Thames. He said it was there for the taking.'

'Why didn't he just take it himself?'

'We asked him that. He replied how we would meet again after the assault and determine what to do and how the treasure was to be shared. He added that it was not so much the gold he wanted but the Fisher of Men's death. We could take and keep whatever else we found.'

'And that was it?'

'Yes, Sir John. He assured us that there would be little resistance. We were to kill the Fisher of Men, loot his possessions, take the gold and anything else we found.'

'Do you have any idea who this stranger was?'

'No, Sir John. He talked with an accent as if he may have been French, but he must have known the City for he knew where to find us. Wealthy, I'd say. At first, we thought he'd come alone, but he had taken the precaution of hiring a bodyguard. When he left, so did they. Sir John, we were more interested in the gold and how we were to seize it.'

'So, it was to be a good night's work, eh, Ratspain? All brought to nothing by my good self. Now do you have anything more to say?'

All three mumbled they had not.

'In which case,' Cranston straightened in his chair, 'I sentence you to hang, and may the good Lord have mercy on your souls.'

Athelstan intervened, asking if any of the condemned men wanted to be shriven. All three refused but accepted the general absolution recited by Athelstan as he stood on the edge of the dais. As soon as the Friar had finished, Flaxwith and his henchmen hustled the condemned out of the hall to the derelict gallows on the far end of the quayside.

After they had left, an eerie silence descended, broken by Cranston getting to his feet and informing his hosts that it was time for them to be gone.

'Wait a little while, Sir John,' the Fisher retorted.

'What is it, my friend?'

'Sir John, you do not suspect me or mine are involved in the murderous mischief you are investigating?'

'I shall answer that,' Athelstan cheerfully interrupted. He went round to stand in front of the Fisher and gave him, along with the rest assembled around the trestle table, his most solemn blessing. 'That,' he smiled, 'is our answer.'

Cranston and Athelstan made themselves ready. Flaxwith returned with the executioners and bluntly reported how all three pirates were now facing a higher court. Cranston and Athelstan collected their belongings then left the building, the Fisher of Men and his retinue insisting that they escort them. They reached the quayside and clambered back into the barges and pushed off through the icy mist. Athelstan, sitting in the canopied stern, glimpsed the dangling corpses of the three river pirates twisting in the buffeting breeze. He turned to Cranston.

'Who do you think hired those pirates, or at least urged them to attack the Fisher?'

'Brother, it could be anyone.'

On the following morning Athelstan celebrated his Jesus Mass then broke his fast whilst listening to Benedicta's description of what was happening in the parish.

'Not much,' she concluded. 'Your beloved faithfuls are certainly looking forward to Epiphany eve. Scoresby searches in vain for the stolen tax pouch. I suspect it has probably been found and quickly spent.'

Athelstan agreed though he kept his suspicions to himself.

'Oh,' Benedicta added, 'you also had a visitor. A knight, Sir John Montague. He arrived early in the evening just after you left.'

'What did he want?'

'He talked about the church. He asked, and I informed him, that we had the right of sanctuary. I pressed him on this, but all he would say was that he would return to speak to you, adding, and I think this is what he said . . .'

'What?' Athelstan asked.

'That he is one of us! Father, I know, it doesn't make sense. In fact, I asked him what he meant, but he seemed distracted. He kept insisting that he must speak to you, once again declaring that "he is one of us": that's all I can tell you, Father. Now, you did promise to help me clean the baptismal font?'

Athelstan nodded in agreement.

'Yes, yes,' he murmured, 'we can clean the font and, while we do, I can think and reflect. The humble chores of life, Benedicta, often provoke deeper thoughts, so let us away.'

He and Benedicta left the sacristy and began what Athelstan called 'their labour of love' for the font was where every baby born in the parish was inducted into the retinue of the Lord Jesus. They gave the font a good scrubbing, then cleaned and rubbed its thick oaken stand and heavy lid, polishing both to a shine. They were joined by the Hangman of Rochester, who pushed in his barrow full of brushes, scrapers and all the tools of his artistic profession. Such a sharp contrast to the turbulent, macabre ceremonies around the gibbets of Tyburn and Smithfield. The Hangman leaned his barrow up against one of the drum-like pillars which separated the nave from the transept before coming to greet Athelstan and Benedicta.

'What are you working on, Giles?'

The Hangman's ghostly white face creased into a grin as he tugged at a strand of his strange, straw-like hair.

'You always insist on calling me by . . .'

'Never mind that, what work are you involved in?'

'You remember, Father? We agreed. A small jewel-like painting as if taken from a book of hours.'

'And the theme?'

'The prophet Daniel gazing into the visions of night and seeing one like the Son of Man . . .'

'Yes, yes,' Athelstan sighed, 'Daniel's prophecy about the coming of Christ. You did discuss it with me. You said you wanted the prophet standing at a window and . . .' Athelstan paused as a small postern in the main doorway pushed open and Tiptoft slid, like a shadow, into the church.

'Good morrow, my friend,' Athelstan murmured. 'Sir John must need me?'

'Yes, Brother Athelstan, he certainly does. Lord Montague's corpse.' He paused as both Athelstan and Benedicta exclaimed in surprise. 'He lies stricken, the victim of gruesome murder. A truly horrid sight, Brother.' Tiptoft bowed towards Benedicta. 'I am glad, mistress, you are not coming. It would upset your humours.'

'God have mercy,' Athelstan murmured, 'what else?'

'It would be best if we talked as we walked,' the messenger replied. 'Brother, it is not at all pleasant. Montague has been crucified.'

Athelstan and Tiptoft left St Erconwald's, hurrying down to London Bridge. Athelstan tried to draw the messenger into conversation, but it was nigh impossible. The day was bitterly cold, but the blue sky and winter sun had drawn out the crowds, a noisy colourful throng massing around the entrance to London Bridge. A frenetic place at the best of times, but matters had turned even worse. Two of St Anthony's pigs, with bells fastened around their

necks, had wandered on to the approaches. At the same time a
large brown bear had broken out from its pit where it had been
taken to be baited. The bear had badly mauled its keeper before
it turned on others. Enraged and sore from a previous baiting,
the bear had slaughtered both pigs and then attacked the unfortunate felons imprisoned in the stocks and pillories only a walk
away from the bear pit. The screams of the wounded still rang
through the air. Blood was everywhere, even in the stinging
freezing breeze. Apparently, order had only just been restored
by a party of Genoese bowmen who brought the bear down with
well-aimed crossbow bolts. City bailiffs were also hurrying to
help. Barriers, carts and other defences were being pulled aside.
People stopped to stare, but Tiptoft was determined not to be
hindered. Grasping Athelstan by the arm, Cranston's veteran
messenger skilfully jostled his way through the milling crowds.
Athelstan kept close, following Tiptoft's advice not to be drawn
and so ignore the troupe of mummers dressed as babewyns,
gargoyles and other eerie creatures. The messenger also shoved
aside the street vendors with their shoddy products, the cooks
with their rancid dishes as well as the pardoners and relic sellers
offering portions of skin from a saint allegedly martyred in the
Colosseum so many centuries before. Jongleurs and minstrels
touted for business. These reminded Athelstan about the coming
celebrations at St Erconwald's for the Feast of the Epiphany. The
roar of the water under the bridge, however, together with the
noisome clack of the nearby mills, deeply agitated Athelstan. He
could not think of the future. All he wanted to do was get across
this bridge, a platform which cut through the air above a torrent
of raging waters. At last, they were over, moving through the
different markets and up into Cheapside.

Flaxwith and his bailiffs were guarding the approaches to 'The
Golden Oriole'. They stood back for Athelstan. A servitor led
both Friar and messenger across the tap room into the garden.
A truly rich expanse but now quiet, its glories hidden beneath a
fierce hoar frost. Cranston, together with Ingham and Sir Stephen
Crossley, were gathered close to the high fence which cut the
tavern off from the neighbouring property. Athelstan greeted them
then stared at the great bloodied sheet covering part of the high

perimeter fence. Cranston thanked Tiptoft, who apparently couldn't escape quickly enough, then he pulled the bloodstained canvas sheet to the ground to expose the horrors beneath. Athelstan stared, gagged and walked away. Cranston followed and thrust the miraculous wineskin into his hand. Athelstan took a generous gulp then returned to what he recognized as a truly devilish abomination. Sir John Montague had been stripped, then crucified against the sturdy perimeter fence. Spikes had been driven through his wrists and another through one of his ankles. His head, all bloodied, had tipped back, his ravaged face a mask of horror, eyes popping, mouth all bloodied and gaping.

'Was he dead before this happened? What do you think?'

'Brother, I suspect he was. There is a hideously deep wound at the back of his head, a savage blow which must have killed him.'

Athelstan went closer to the corpse and tipped the dead man's head forward. The wound Montague had received at the back of his head was indeed a deep blow, like that from a hammer.

'He must have been surprised,' Athelstan declared. 'The assassin struck, pounding the back of his head, smashing it as you would a piece of wood. Montague was then pushed up against the fence, alive or dead we don't know, but those spikes were hammered into . . .' Athelstan exposed his right wrist, 'here.' He tapped his wrist just where it met the palm of his hand. 'Contrary to popular belief and art,' Athelstan continued, 'Christ was not nailed to the cross by spikes or nails driven through the palms of his hands; that's a nonsense. The nails would simply be rendered useless as the weight of the body dragged down.' Athelstan flinched at the nasty smell which hung over the corpse. He walked closer to the others. Again, he pulled back the sleeve of his robe and tapped his wrist. 'I have studied the Roman use of crucifixion,' he declared. 'It was a cruel device. They did not hang their victims by their hands but by a small gap in the wrist bones, a hole they exploited as they did for the ankles where the same bone formation can be found. The executioners would find exactly where this was and drive the nail through.' Athelstan paused and sniffed at the pomander Cranston had thrust into his hands.

'What else do we know?' Cranston declared.

Athelstan shook his head. He had already decided not to say anything about Montague's visit to St Erconwald's the previous day.

'Ah well,' Athelstan lowered the pomander, 'this,' he jabbed a finger at the two knights, 'is where the tavern land ends, yes? The fence marks it off from other properties?'

'Yes,' Ingham replied.

'So, is there a rear gate?'

'Yes, Brother, further down.'

'Let's see it,' Athelstan declared.

'It's only a short distance.'

Ingham led them along to a double gate not locked but kept closed by two iron clasps. Athelstan easily moved these back and pushed open one side of the gate. Satisfied, he then crouched down and sifted through the sparse frozen grass, picking at certain spots, especially the dried blood and a few loose threads. He got to his feet and walked back along the path to where the corpse had been nailed. He scrutinized the cadaver again and then gestured at Ingham and Crossley.

'Sir John and I will wait for you in the buttery.'

'Why? What do you want with us?' Crossley demanded petulantly. He had stood in shocked silence since Athelstan had arrived but now seemed to have recovered his poise.

'I want you and Sir Oliver to organize a search along this perimeter fence at least two yards from it on either side.'

'What are we looking for?'

'You'll know when you find it.'

'Flaxwith and his cohort will help you,' Cranston declared, wondering what Athelstan intended.

'Good.' The Friar rubbed his hands then bowed to the knights. 'Come, Sirs, let us begin. We shall be waiting for you in the buttery.'

Once they were back in the tavern, comfortably ensconced before the blazing hearth fire, they ordered goblets of sweet posset. Cranston sipped appreciatively at his then glanced up.

'So, Little Friar?'

'Well, my Lord Coroner, I truly believe Sir John Montague

was intent on leaving, no, fleeing "The Golden Oriole" to seek sanctuary in St Erconwald's.'

'You have proof of this?'

'Oh yes. No less than the testimony of Benedicta the Beautiful. Apparently, Sir Montague visited St Erconwald's yesterday and asked questions about my church having the right of sanctuary. He gave the impression that he would return. He wanted to see me and made the enigmatic remark that "he was one of us" and, before you ask, I don't know what he meant by that. Was he referring to me or someone else? For the moment I cannot decide.' Athelstan sipped at his goblet then sat rolling the cup between his hands. 'Montague must have then returned to "The Golden Oriole" and began his preparations to slip away. He eventually did under the cover of dark. However, his assassin, fully realizing what was happening, began to shadow the unfortunate Montague. He realized Montague would leave through the garden and he was probably lurking near that gate we have just visited. Deep in thought, Montague was an easy victim. The assassin sprang out of the dark. He inflicted a crashing blow to the back of Montague's head and his victim is rendered senseless. The assassin then strips his corpse, takes his clothes and any baggage and throws them away.'

'Which is why Flaxwith and his merry crew are now searching the perimeter?'

'Precisely, Sir John. The assassin would probably throw them into the undergrowth close to the perimeter fence. Once done he turns back to Montague's body. He drags it from the gate to that part of the fence which tilts slightly back, making it easier for him to spread out Montague's naked body. He would position it as he wanted then hammer those spikes through Montague's wrists and ankle.'

'And then?'

'And then, Sir John, let us wait and see.'

A short while later, Flaxwith, Ingham and Crossley came into the buttery rubbing their hands and stamping their feet, complaining loudly about the cold as they squatted on a bench pushed in front of the fire. Once warmed, Flaxwith left the buttery and returned with a set of panniers.

'We found this, Sir John. I left it outside. I just had to warm my hands first.'

Cranston murmured his appreciation for the find. He then opened the panniers and shook its contents out on to the table. A mixed collection of personal items such as a Greek icon, a dagger, coins as well as bits of clothing all rolled up in untidy balls. There was also a psalter, some ave beads and a collection of medals.

'Is that all?'

'Yes, Sir John. Well, we also found his clothing and war belt, but they are outside.'

'Bring them in.'

'There's nothing in them,' Ingham declared. 'But if you insist.'

'I certainly do.'

Ingham nodded at Flaxwith.

'On second thoughts,' Athelstan interposed, 'I'll collect them myself.'

He went out into the buttery entrance and picked up Montague's war belt with its sheaths and wallet. He brought these back into the buttery and first scrutinized the wallet. There was nothing there but a few silver coins, which Athelstan handed to Ingham. He then examined the empty sword sheath, digging his fingers deep into the leather casing. He was about to withdraw his hand when he felt a small scrap of parchment. Athelstan deftly removed this, his fingers hiding what he had found. The others, however, were now in deep discussion about the murder and Crossley's growing panic at what might happen next. The knight clutched his stomach, face all pale and sweaty.

'This does me no good,' he muttered. 'My belly churns and pitches. Sometimes I can hardly breathe.' Ingham tried to soothe him, saying that they would both ask to leave England to shelter abroad.

Athelstan half listened to Cranston's response. The Coroner warned both men that they would not be safe until the assassin responsible for this murder and the others was discovered and hanged.

'Sir John?' Athelstan murmured. 'I agree with you. Gentlemen, watch yourselves. Be on your guard for the Devil, like a roaring lion, seeks your lives if not your souls. So, I give you my blessing and bid you farewell.'

Cranston and Athelstan left 'The Golden Oriole', the Friar diligently following the Coroner as he strode towards 'The Lamb of God'. Once ensconced in its solar, Cranston ordered food to break their fast. Once they had eaten, they both sat relaxing in the warmth of the log fire. Cranston shook himself, murmuring about not wanting to fall asleep.

'Well, Brother,' he declared, nibbling at a honey-smeared crouton, closing his eyes as he savoured its sweet taste, 'what do you make of all that?'

'I am not too sure, Sir John, except . . .' Athelstan opened his wallet and took out the thin, pipelike scroll he had found in Montague's sword sheath. He undid this and peered at the different scrawls.

'Brother?'

'Nothing much, Sir John, just jottings. Montague was very interested in tracing the origin of personal place names and that's what we have here. Mere scrawls. I cannot make out some of the letters, never mind the words. I must sit and study it more carefully.' He glanced up and put the piece of parchment away. 'It can wait, Sir John, for I must be gone. Business, as always, awaits me at St Erconwald's.'

'Trouble? Can I help?'

'No, Sir John, but you will tell me when your couriers return?'

'Of course.'

'In which case, Sir John . . .' They made their farewells of each other, and Athelstan left.

PART FIVE

'The left wing is the knowledge of Evil.'

On his arrival back at St Erconwald's, once he had ensured that both his church and house were in good order, Athelstan despatched Crim to invite Benedicta to join him in his house. He also told him to ask her to arrange for Pike, Watkin, Crispin, Ranulf and Joscelyn, together with Mistress Helga, to meet in 'The Piebald' and wait there until he sent for them. He despatched a similar invitation to Giles of Sempringham and Merrylegs. A short while later, 'Benedicta the Breathless', as Athelstan teasingly described her, arrived. She helped the Friar unstack two wall benches and place them either side of the fireplace whilst Athelstan would take his chair in between, facing the fire with Benedicta seated alongside him. Crim was instructed to take up residence within his stable. Athelstan assured him he would be warm and dry whilst Benedicta would give him a small bowl of sweetmeats.

'You will be my Hermes.'

'Who, Father?'

'The messenger of the Gods in the Greek legends, though I cannot give you winged shoes.'

Crim just stared at the Friar and shrugged, recalling his parents' constant description of the Friar as a 'complete mystery'.

'We are about God's business, Crim,' Athelstan declared, 'the establishment of truth, honesty and, I hope, repentance. So, let's summon the faithful. Master Giles and Merrylegs will begin my masque.'

Swift as a sparrow, Crim left and brought back the Hangman and Merrylegs. These shuffled into the priest's house and sat on a bench staring at their little priest with his strange eccentric ways.

'Father, why are we here?'

'Good man, good man,' Athelstan replied, 'straight to the point. You, Giles, along with Merrylegs here, suffered violent pains on the same day that Bardolph the Tax Collector was found stabbed to death in his chamber. True or false?'

'True, Father.' The Hangman dropped his gaze, staring at the floor as if fascinated by some hidden design there.

'And you, Merrylegs? You suffered the same, didn't you?'

'Yes, Father,' Merrylegs mumbled, his round fat face all flushed as he stared at a point above Athelstan's head.

'Tell me,' the Friar urged, 'exactly what happened.'

The Hangman glanced at Merrylegs, who nodded.

'I'll tell you, Father,' the Hangman replied, 'I'll tell you the truth. On that day late in the evening, God knows the hour, I entered the tap room of "The Piebald". Bardolph slouched there. The bastard was deep in his cups, banging the table and demanding the best wine the tavern had. He specifically asked for Bordeaux.' The Hangman licked his lips. 'Joscelyn went down to the winery in his cellar and brought up what he described as a small tun of the best. I knew Joscelyn had one and couldn't refuse Bardolph. The taxman was a bully, a truly nasty soul. Do you know during the troubles he was a turncoat, a Judas man? He sent a good number of street warriors, the Earthworms, to the gallows. He . . .'

'The wine?' Athelstan interrupted. 'I want to know what happened to the wine, Giles. I know my history; I know what happened. I know Bardolph was a great sinner, God have mercy on him. But I want to talk about the wine.'

'Joscelyn served Bardolph a generous goblet. He called us to have a sip. We did. A short while later I turned truly strange. Pains coursed through my body as if all my humours had been disturbed.'

'I suffered the same,' Merrylegs dolefully echoed. 'My belly strained as if it was going to tear itself apart.'

'Anyway,' the Hangman took up the story, 'we left "The Piebald" and promptly vomited, I mean, Brother Athelstan, truly vomited! We retched and we retched. We lurched back to the tap room to warn Joscelyn that something was very wrong. Bardolph had staggered upstairs. We had further words with Joscelyn about what he had served.' He paused. 'We eventually left "The Piebald". I remember we had a terrible thirst, and we were still retching. So much and so violently I thought my very innards would be expelled. The pain was intense, but the cramps began to recede. We felt weak and staggered off to our homes. Later we heard . . .' The Hangman's voice sank to a mumble.

'I do know what you are thinking,' Athelstan declared. 'I believe you have told the truth. Now, Benedicta.' He gestured at the widow-woman. 'I have changed my mind. We do not need our altar boy any longer. However, I must see Watkin, Pike, Crispin, Ranulf and Joscelyn here and now along with Mistress Helga. Oh, and you two worthies,' Athelstan pointed at the Hangman and Merrylegs, 'you can go. I am sure you will find out later what happened here. You may leave now. Benedicta will see you out.'

Athelstan sat and listened to them go. 'God bless you all,' he murmured to himself. He half dozed for a while and was rudely awoken by a harsh rap on the door as Watkin and his companions, including Mistress Helga, trooped into the house like a line of the condemned. They nodded towards Athelstan and arranged themselves along the benches either side of the hearth, refusing to look directly at their priest who had summoned them here. They knew that he must know something, whatever it was, about the mischief they constantly played. Athelstan delivered a blessing. They all crossed themselves and sat quietly. Athelstan deliberately let the silence deepen until the parishioners began to shuffle their feet in nervous expectation.

'Very well,' he began, 'thank you for coming, thank you for waiting. I think it's worth it. You see, I am going to tell you the truth about Bardolph's death, so I fully expect you to do the same. I have brought you here to listen to your confession, but I cannot force it out of you. Rest assured, Sir John Cranston is not involved in this and, if you speak the truth, he never will be. All of you,' he continued, cutting through the audible sighs of relief from his parishioners. 'All of you,' Athelstan repeated remorselessly, 'are attracted to mischief as birds to flying. God knows how many schemes, stratagems, masques and mayhem you have been involved in since I became your parish priest. The good Lord must really protect you because some of your plots are bizarre whilst others are downright dangerous. So, listen carefully as I describe what happened to Bardolph the Tax Collector in your tavern. No, no, Watkin,' Athelstan held up a hand, 'I know what he was. I have heard time and again what he did during the Great Revolt. I am not bothered about Bardolph's life, but I am deeply interested in his death. Now,' Athelstan drew a deep breath, 'I have questioned Giles of Sempringham and Merrylegs. Undoubtedly, they were given sips of tainted wine which Bardolph also drank, but the good Lord preserved them. They only suffered token signs. They fell ill but, thanks be to God, they vomited and retched the polluted wine. They purged themselves immediately. I have seen it done. One of the standard methods of dealing with poison is to cleanse it from the body as swiftly as possible. That happened to Merrylegs and Giles.' Athelstan glanced at Benedicta, who simply smiled and shook her head in wonderment. Athelstan was about to continue when he paused, gathering his thoughts. He sat in silence for a while then raised his head. 'You now know,' he declared, 'that I now know what you have known all along. So let me hear it from you rather than me tell you.' He forced a smile. 'Joscelyn, finish this turbulent tale. What actually happened in "The Piebald"? And remember, I am not bothered if the wine was smuggled in; that's a matter between you, God and Master Thibault's customs officials. So,' Athelstan spread his hands, 'let me hear the truth.'

'True, Father,' Joscelyn began, 'I smuggle in barrels of the best Bordeaux. Once we have, we broach the casks and pour their contents into smaller tuns or caskets.'

'And?' Athelstan declared. 'What else do you put in?'

Joscelyn cleared his throat. He looked up at the ceiling then down at the floor until nudged by Watkin.

'Tell our priest,' the dung collector grated. 'Tell him the truth.'

'The wine barrels we have, Brother, contain wine but also a healthy measure of some berry juice.'

'So, you not only evade the customs toll, but you also water down your wine. So, what happened this time? What went wrong?'

'I was busy, Father, too busy. I asked my eldest son, God help me, to go into the garden and pull some berries, squeeze the juice and pour it into the barrel. I opened this for that bastard Bardolph. You must know what happened next. I am sure that the Hangman and Merrylegs have told their tale. My stupid son picked and distilled the wrong berries.'

'Belladonna, deadly nightshade,' Athelstan explained. 'One of the most potent poisons to be found in gardens throughout this kingdom.'

'I know that, Father. I just wish my son had.'

'Continue,' Athelstan ordered.

'Well, the Hangman and Merrylegs fell sick. They staggered back into the tavern to warn me. They were vomiting fit to burst. I now realize that saved them, but it was far too late for Bardolph. Our bastard tax collector had taken his goblet up to his chamber. He left the door unlocked in his haste to reach the jakes closet. He too had vomited, but it was a question of too little, too late. Bardolph lay sprawled on the floor. We swiftly tidied everything up.'

'Yes, I noticed that. A slight mistake on your part,' Athelstan observed. 'The chamber was too clean. The jakes closet scrubbed and ready for use. I mean Bardolph was not the most sensitive of men. I suspect he was untidy, dirty in his habits. So, you cleaned the room, what next?'

'We placed Bardolph in that chair,' Joscelyn replied. 'Father, I was terrified.'

'We all were,' Watkin interjected. 'We would be accused of his murder. A royal official. We realized what would have happened then, Father. Bardolph's death could be construed as treason.' Watkin licked his lips. 'We all know the punishment for that, being torn apart by the executioners at Tyburn or Smithfield. What happened next was my decision.' Watkin thumped his chest. 'I took Bardolph's dagger and drove it into the bastard's wicked heart. I did wonder if the symptoms of the poison would manifest themselves. However, I also remembered, from my days of service as a medicus in the King's array, that the shock of sudden death is similar to that caused by a dagger thrust. It has its own peculiar manifestations.'

Athelstan nodded knowingly, more to hide his own surprise at what Watkin had just revealed about his past. In truth, Athelstan was always astonished by the different and varied life histories of his poor parishioners. Watkin could be dismissed as a dirty, dishevelled shit collector but, indeed, he had experienced life in so many ways. Little wonder he was as bright and as sharp as a springtime sparrow. Athelstan glanced along the line of his visitors, his attention caught by Mistress Helga, who was sitting there with a childlike innocence. God knows, Athelstan thought, who the true Helga was beneath that girlish demeanour. Athelstan pointed at her.

'Sometimes, Mistress,' he declared, 'evil circumstances can favour us, yes?'

'If you say so, Father.'

'I do say so. Your husband, Mistress, Horace the Housebreaker, was arrested at midnight on the day Bardolph was killed. You hurried across to Newgate to bid farewell to your beloved. Of course, you needed an escort.'

'That was me,' Watkin spoke up.

'And me,' Pike piped in a nervous screech.

'Of course, of course,' Athelstan declared, 'and I suspect Moleskin loaned his barge for the enterprise. Now let me describe what happened, or what I suspect happened. During the journey, Watkin and Pike began to wonder how they might use Horace's capture and inevitable execution to their own advantage. They made the decision that Horace would confess to the murder of Bardolph. Of course, as you all know, a man's last confession is regarded as sacred. Horace's confession would protect Joscelyn and his fellow parishioners whilst you Watkin and the rest solemnly swore to look after Mistress Helga. Indeed, by the look of her you already have. She seems freshly attired from her head veil down to her very sturdy sandals. Yes, Mistress?' Helga just simpered and glanced coyly at her priest. 'Oh yes, I am sure Watkin, my dearest in Christ, that you used Helga's journey to and from Newgate, not to forget the time you spent there, to tutor Horace and Helga on the details of Bardolph's death. You'd be as zealous as any magister over his horn-book, teaching by rote until both Horace and Helga were word perfect. Not an arduous task, just what to say when and wherever you needed to. A brief pithy tale to convince your listeners. Horace entered "The Piebald", killed Bardolph then fled to fresh mischief along Cheapside.'

'True, true!' Pike whispered.

'I did suspect something was very wrong,' Athelstan continued, 'with the published story proclaimed here, there and everywhere. Horace's last confession to me confirmed my suspicion. You see,' Athelstan crossed himself, 'I cannot reveal what sins a penitent confesses. The seal of the sacrament is absolute. However, I can tell you what a person did not confess to. Canon Law also stipulates that I must not put pressure on a penitent to confess something he was not sure of.' Athelstan paused. 'In a word, Horace did not confess to the murder of Bardolph. Now isn't that strange? I mean a man like Horace was about to step into eternity. He wants to make that fateful step purged of all his sins. He must be fully absolved, ready to meet God with pure heart and hands.' Athelstan pointed at Watkin. 'Just in case, you then tightened this allegedly mysterious murder with another sharp twist. Bardolph's corpse was found in a chamber locked and bolted from within. How was that? I mean the room had no other entrance except that door. How did it all happen?' Athelstan shrugged. 'I'll answer my own question. It's all quite easy if you have a gaggle of conspirators eager to create a masque, a story, a truly tangled tale. You created the pretence of all of you milling about, being seen here and there by other parishioners, in particular by the beautiful Benedicta.'

'True, true,' the widow intervened forcefully. 'I saw all of you that day. Of course now, because of what I have just learned, this was sheer pretence staged for my benefit and others.'

'Including your priest,' Athelstan declared. 'And you nearly did convince me. Anyway, the hour arrives for you to force the door to the Avalon Chamber. One of you was already in that room hiding deep in the shadows, having locked and bolted the door which was about to be forced. You ensure that Benedicta was close by, a witness to all that happened, except for that cunning sleight of hand. The person, whoever it was, hiding in that chamber would mingle with the rest as they surged in once the door was forced. A mere shift in the shadows lasting only a few heartbeats and so the great mystery unfolds.'

'They were all there at Mass?' Benedicta declared.

'Oh yes. I suspect that was the only time this chamber was empty and locked, but from the outside.' Athelstan pointed at Joscelyn. 'Easy enough to arrange. You are the owner. I wager you and one other, possibly Pike or Watkin, were the last to leave the tavern for Mass and the first to return?'

'True again,' Pike murmured.

'And what now, Father?'

'What now, Watkin? Well, the tax money, or whatever is left of it, must be returned now.' He pointed to the wall lantern hanging just near the doorway. 'Take that with you. I suspect that somewhere out in that sprawling God's Acre, you must have secret hiding places. You use them to hide goods smuggled in as you did to conceal weapons before the Great Revolt. I would wager all I have that one of those secret hiding places contains Bardolph's tax pannier, tied at the neck with a strong piece of twine.' Athelstan again pointed at the door. 'Go on, get the money and bring it here without opening and, I repeat, without opening. Well, go on!'

Watkin shuffled to his feet.

'I thought as much,' he muttered. 'I did wonder, Father, whether you'd see through all of this. It is as you say. Bardolph was poisoned. We cleaned the chamber, then we all took turns to stand guard in the room, making sure the door was locked and bolted from within. Pike was the last to take up that post.' He grinned slyly. 'I mean, he's as thin as a rake and so can merge easily with the shadows. We made sure that no one saw the exchange taking place. Indeed, we used the pretence of guarding the chamber to ensure that Benedicta saw each and every one of us sometime during the day.'

'Of course, of course,' Athelstan murmured, 'that's what also concerned me. Forget secret entrances; it's a matter of logic. Bardolph's corpse was in a locked, bolted chamber for hours, the assassin too. Yet, if that's true, who could it be? Benedicta and others saw you all milling about sometime during that day. Nobody could be accused.'

'Ah well, we did our best.' Watkin scratched his head.

'Oh Watkin,' Athelstan replied, 'for the love of God stop getting involved in such tangles. One of these days you will make some dreadful mistake and end up on the gallows hanging from a gibbet for the birds of the air to pick at. Now go! Do not be too long and do not open those money bags!'

Watkin and Pike fled the house. The others sat in silence. Benedicta caught Athelstan's eye and winked. He just smiled and glanced away. A short while later, Watkin and Pike returned, creeping back into the house, the money bags hidden beneath Watkin's mud-smeared cloak. He handed them over to Athelstan, who weighed them in his hands before closely studying the tight twine knots around the clasps. The Friar tapped the twine. 'This shows it was taken and hidden, tied fast to prevent coin slipping out.'

'Too true,' Pike replied. 'We did that.'

'And you've had some of this, haven't you?' Athelstan pointed at Helga, who just stared back all startled.

'We all have, Father,' Pike spoke up, 'I mean except for Benedicta.'

'Well,' Athelstan replied, 'Bardolph probably owed you that and I have no great love for tax collectors.' He shook his head. 'I repeat you took a great risk; that's why you held the mock mass, wasn't it?' Athelstan stared at the accused. In truth, he felt genuinely sorry for them. 'The mock mass,' he repeated quietly, 'I know what it is. You are former soldiers; you have been summoned to the standard for service in the royal array. Soldiers make a compact with each other for mutual care and protection and then confirm this over a ritual meal. They share bread and wine, the same as that used in the Mass, the elements which are to be changed into the body and blood of the risen Christ. You share one bread loaf and wine from the same goblet. You implement the ritual to confirm, as well as to observe, total silence on any matter. I have seen the same done in Italy where they talk about the vow of silence taken between soldiers. Ah yes, that's it, the Omerta! A vow or oath taken over the sacred elements of the Mass. Ah well.' Athelstan placed the money on the floor beneath the table. 'Go now. Keep your vow of silence as I will mine. No one will know the full truth. God alone knows that. Only he understands the human heart and what is intended.' Athelstan sketched a blessing. 'Go now, this business is finished.'

The parishioners left, their relief at the conclusion reached almost tangible. They filed out of the priest's house all silent and solemn. Athelstan closed the door behind them, then he leaned against it until their excited whispers faded away. He grinned at Benedicta perched so prettily on the stool beside his chair.

'A good day's work, Father. I would never have guessed . . .'

'Neither did I until I heard Horace's confession; that confirmed my growing suspicions about what really happened. Anyway, enough of that. Benedicta, of your kindness, slip down to "The Piebald". I need to speak to Scoresby, Bardolph's henchman.'

'You will give him the money?'

'Of course, but first I need to have urgent words with him.'

Benedicta rose. Athelstan opened the door. He stood staring out and abruptly shivered.

'Father, you are well?'

'Oh yes, it's just that the other evening I had a mysterious, and therefore unwelcome, visitor. Someone was roaming around the outside of my house. I also have a feeling of being watched, though that could be my imagination.'

'Take care, Father. I have glimpsed strangers around "The Piebald" and our church. Anyway, go back in, Father, it's getting very cold, and the dark is drawing in.'

Athelstan agreed and stepped back into the house, closing and locking the door behind him. He sat before the fire and warmed himself. He was deep in thought when a knock on the door roused him. He rose, opened it and welcomed both Scoresby and Benedicta into the house, ushering them to seats whilst serving capped goblets of steaming posset which he had prepared in a jug by the fire. Once settled, they sat in silence broken only by the logs cracking under the flames and the haunting hoot of the owls nesting in the old sycamore out in the cemetery.

'Father,' Scoresby cleared his throat, 'you wish to see me?'

'Yes, I certainly do. I also want the truth, whoever you may really be?'

'Meaning?'

'Meaning, Master Scoresby, whether you are a tax collector's henchman or a travelling jongleur or a troubadour or a jester. For that's what you were in a former life. Yes, or no? I have met your type on many occasions,' Athelstan continued, 'frustrated musicians, those who want to create but find it brings them little profit. God have mercy on them all, there's no sin in that. So, am I telling the truth, yes, or no?'

'Yes.'

'Now you can make this easy for yourself. Please accept my assurance you are in no danger whatsoever.'

'None? You swear that?'

Athelstan got up and moved to the Book of the Gospels resting on a narrow lectern. The Friar touched this.

'I so swear,' Athelstan declared, 'on the Book of the Gospels.' Athelstan returned to his chair. Scoresby shuffled his feet and sipped at the posset. 'So,' Athelstan demanded, 'who are you?'

'I was held over the baptismal font at the Abbey Church of Rievaulx. I also attended the cathedral school there in the north transept, a ghostly, holy place. My true name is Ralph Venner, but that's all behind me now. I attended the halls and schools of learning at Oxford, but then I drifted. I served in the royal levy where I became skilled in all games of Hazard, be it the dice or the cards. I also became adept at different sleights of hand.'

'As well as being a master of riddles and puzzles? The kind which delights the rich and powerful as they dine?'

'Yes, Brother, I became very good at creating riddles and puzzles for all sorts of audiences.'

'Very good, Master Scoresby, but let's concentrate solely on the riddle you sent to me. It was you, wasn't it?' Scoresby nodded. 'Why did you send it?'

'Oh, I knew Bardolph was truly hated for so many reasons. I realized his death was cloaked in secrecy. Anyway, when the door to that murder chamber was forced, I saw the same as you did, but I wondered how was it done? I recalled a German riddle about people milling around in and out of a room so you couldn't actually tell who was where and when. It's a matter of logic. Someone must have been in that chamber from the moment Bardolph died to when the door was forced. That's the only acceptable explanation for a murder in a room both locked and bolted from within. The victim was there all the time, and the assassin must have been there as well. Where else could he be in such a chamber with no other outlet except this door, locked and bolted from within? Of course,' Scoresby shrugged, 'I tried to recall whom I didn't see amongst all your parish worthies during that fateful day. I wondered who had been missing but, of course, I saw them all.'

'As did I,' Benedicta spoke up. 'I recalled and I reflected. Yes, fellow parishioners came and went, but I cannot recall anyone being absent all the time.'

'Master Scoresby?'

'Mistress Benedicta has proved my point. Your parishioners came and went. Accordingly, I reached the logical conclusion that there must have been someone hiding in that chamber. Of course, there was, but it wasn't one individual; it was probably three or four, each taking turns. Someone like Watkin or Pike being the last, hiding in the shadows when the door was forced.'

'So why did you send me that riddle?'

'Just in case, Brother. If the mystery began to unravel, I didn't want to fall under suspicion. Brother, if Thibault believed some of your parishioners were involved in Bardolph's death and the theft of those taxes, the torturers in the Tower would become very busy.'

'I agree,' Athelstan replied. 'And?'

'By sending this riddle I was demonstrating that I was not party to any mischief. I also wanted to help you discover the truth without making myself vulnerable.' Scoresby sipped at the posset. 'You must accept that I don't know the full truth of what actually happened. As it is, no specific individual or group of persons falls under suspicion. Matters are helped by the fact that Bardolph's enemies were legion; that was one very good line of defence. Horace the Housebreaker's confession, or whatever that truly was, sealed the matter. Why hunt for Bardolph's murderer when the assassin had been caught for another crime, confessed and duly hanged.' Scoresby smiled wryly. 'Your parishioners, Brother Athelstan, are as cunning as foxes. Bardolph's gone and so are the taxes.'

'No, they're not.' Athelstan leaned down and picked up the bulging money sack from where he had hidden it beneath the table next to the leg of his chair.

'That's it!' Scoresby exclaimed.

'No, that's some of it, my friend,' Athelstan declared. 'I suspect Mistress Helga and our four wise men have taken their due as I am sure you will.'

'Heaven forbid!'

'Heaven forbid indeed, Master Scoresby. Nevertheless, you can now return to the Exchequer as the champion in the lists. You can proclaim how you, the cunning Master Scoresby, searched God's Acre outside. The ground was heavily frosted, but you persisted and found a recent digging, the place where Horace the Housekeeper had hidden his ill-gotten gains.' Athelstan paused. 'You can embellish your story as you see fit. Perhaps you could add how you discovered that Horace's relations, members of his family, were buried in the cemetery at St Erconwald's. You visited the burial mound and, in doing so, made your wonderful discovery. So, my friend, all will be brought to an end. As regards what really happened, you mustn't say anything. Benedicta and I are the same and,' Athelstan laughed sharply, 'I doubt very much whether we will hear anything from "The Piebald".'

'I agree. But, Father, why have you done this?'

'Because, Master Scoresby, I don't want innocents hanged for the likes of Bardolph, who has now gone to God. Secondly, I don't want innocents hanged because of petty taxes forced out of the poor by the wicked and the powerful. So, my friend, take the tax and be out of St Erconwald's and "The Piebald" as swift as a sparrow.'

Solemnly promising that his lips were sealed, Scoresby grabbed the money sack and made his way out into the gathering dark. Athelstan stood in the doorway and watched him go.

'He'll keep silent,' Benedicta called out.

'Too true, my lady, he is committed now, as all of us are.'

Athelstan stared across the cemetery. Here and there a funeral lamp glowed above some tomb in a futile attempt to keep back the dark. Athelstan shivered. He still felt he was being watched carefully and cautiously. But by whom and for what reason? He went back into the house, locking the door behind him. He walked to his chancery satchel and took out a small scroll, which he gave to Benedicta.

'Tomorrow morning,' he urged, 'at first light, can you do me a great favour? After my dawn Mass would you and Crim visit my Mother House at Blackfriars? I want you to seek out Brother Simon, a venerable scholar and chronicler, a man who studies the origin of names. Now, Benedicta, I can't tell you exactly what's happening, but I have studied that scroll. It contains a clear declaration of the true identity of an assassin. But I need to make sure. It is crucially important that I have a reply. Tell Brother Simon how I have formed my own suspicion, but I need his scholarship to confirm it. Stay at Blackfriars. Brother Simon will dictate a reply and give it to you. You will do this for me, please?'

The widow-woman glanced up.

'We have unfinished business, Father?'

'Which is?'

'The riddle, what's its true interpretation?'

Athelstan shrugged. He returned to his chancery satchel, took out a copy of the riddle and laid it on the table, holding the corners of the manuscript down with four small weights.

'Read it, Father, please read it once more for me.'

'Bardolph's death. Resolve this riddle and you will deduce the truth of it all. The riddle is as follows: John is a prisoner held fast and under the constant careful vigilance of three jailors. Matthias, Bernard and Conrad. At least one of these three men were to be on duty at all times. If Matthias was off duty and Bernard was off duty, Conrad would be on duty. However, any time Bernard was off duty Conrad would also be off duty. Quaestio? Could Matthias ever be off duty? Resolve this and you will resolve Bardolph's death.' Athelstan finished reading and glanced at Benedicta. 'The solution is quite simple: if Bernard was on duty, Matthias could go off duty.' He grinned. 'It took some time, but that's the solution.'

'Well?' she insisted. 'Why didn't you ask Scoresby to resolve it for you?'

'Because, my dear Benedicta, I didn't want him knowing too much and the riddle itself is really not important. Scoresby left that riddle to protect himself. Now the whole point of the riddle is to show how the same group of people can mill about so you are not too sure who was where and when, which is exactly what happened regarding Bardolph's death. The riddle is solved by logic. Somebody must have been in that room all the time, but we now know there was not one individual, just a group of conspirators who pretended to act as one and the same person.'

'It could have been a stranger or a visitor.'

'Oh, come, Benedicta. You'd have noticed him, others also. No, no, the riddle is solved by logic and the same logic proves that Bardolph wasn't stabbed to death. He was poisoned and the chamber was locked and bolted from within through a very clever conspiracy. Now, will you take that scroll to Brother Simon tomorrow morning and help me to solve an even more important riddle? One which involves the torture and murder of at least four souls.'

Benedicta said she would and left. Athelstan watched her go down the path towards the church where others had gathered, eager to start the preparations for the festival on Epiphany's eve. Athelstan secured the door, checked the window shutters and moved over to the lectern. He opened the Book of the Gospels and was about to recite the psalm when he heard a knock on the door and Cranston's voice ringing like a trumpet. Athelstan hastened to greet him, and Cranston surged into the house, one hand on his sword hilt and the other grasping the miraculous wineskin. He shrugged off his cloak and sat down at the table.

'Well, Little Friar, I met our two couriers, the messengers I despatched to Malroad Manor and Chafford Hundred. They talked to Kyne's heir Robert and Mercier the steward at Chafford Hundred. My messengers questioned them closely, making them recall every detail. Both Robert and Mercier reported how the leader of the execution cohort quoted scripture fairly often.' Cranston grinned. 'Indeed, as much as any priest delivering his Sunday homily. However, the phrase found on those proclamations to Richard the King: "Mene, Mene, Tekel and Parsin" was not used.' Cranston sighed. 'And that message is still being posted across the City. Anyway, why the interest in assassins who quote scripture?'

'A memory from the past, Sir John. Scripture quotations being uttered during a time of conflict, certainly violence. It jogs my memory. It recalls something from my youth. But, for the love of God, I cannot place it, not yet anyway.'

'So, Brother, you sent for me.'

Athelstan froze, staring in surprise at the Coroner.

'Pardon, Sir John?'

'You sent for me. A message left by Pike the Ditcher at the Guildhall. A verbal message saying you needed to see me urgently, but I was to come alone.' Cranston lumbered to his feet. 'You've done the same before. It's usually Benedicta, but this time,' he breathed, 'it's deceit and deception, so let us arm against it.'

Cranston grabbed his war belt and buckled it on whilst Athelstan pulled out his small hand-held arbalest. He glanced at the door and shutters and breathed a prayer of thanks that they were all tightly sealed. He slipped a bolt into the groove on his arbalest and almost dropped the weapon as the door was rapped and tried.

'Sir John, Brother Athelstan,' a voice called, 'we mean you no harm, but we must speak to you.'

'Who are you?'

'Men who just wish to speak to you then leave in peace. Brother Athelstan, we have met before. I was with you and your brother in Lord Lestrange's array. We fought together in Normandy.' The speaker paused. 'I am Wulfstan Cherdicson,' he continued. 'You remember me, Athelstan?'

'I certainly do. A man who, even in pitch battle, insisted on quoting scripture.'

'A man of God,' the voice replied.

'Not necessarily,' Athelstan retorted. 'Satan can, and has, quoted scripture for his own wicked purposes.'

The speaker outside laughed then rapped on the door. Bonaventure, who had been fast asleep, sprawled in front of the hearth, rose, stretched and meowed. Athelstan stroked the back of the cat's head. 'Hush now,' the Friar whispered. 'Pax et Bonum, Bonaventure.'

'Athelstan, Sir John, I promise you we mean no harm. Permit me, and just one of my companions, to come in. We will explain who we are and why we are here.'

Athelstan glanced at Cranston, who nodded.

'Flaxwith and his cohort,' Cranston hissed, 'are lodged in and around "The Piebald". You have your hunting horn ready?'

'No, but I soon will do.'

'Very good. Listen now,' Cranston raised his voice, 'you and one other, without your war belts or carrying any weapon, may approach the door and knock.'

Athelstan waited. He heard someone approach followed by a sharp rap on the door. Athelstan slid back the bolt and turned the key. Cranston stood behind him, sword and dagger drawn, but their visitors just slipped like ghosts through the half-open door, which Athelstan slammed shut and bolted behind them. The two visitors pulled back their cowls and unfastened their thick military cloaks, allowing them to fall to the floor. Athelstan picked these up and hung them on wall pegs whilst, at Cranston's direction, the two men took seats on a bench before the fire. Athelstan and Cranston took the ones opposite. For a while they just sat in silence studying each other. Athelstan stared at one of them, a man of his own age with closely cropped raven-black hair and a smooth pale face, thin-lipped, sharp-nosed with deep-set eyes. Athelstan now vividly recalled this visitor from his past. He smiled and sketched a blessing which the stranger returned with a grin.

'Athelstan, my friend, Pax et Bonum. You remember me?'

The Friar nodded.

'But not Guido here?'

'No, I certainly don't recognize him.'

'Guido is Spanish, Brother Athelstan: his English is not too good, but he is skilled with the sword, the dagger and the garrotte.'

'I am sure he is,' Athelstan replied, staring at the sallow-faced henchman. 'Well.' Athelstan rubbed his hands together. 'Now we are settled, warming ourselves in front of the fire, let us all go down memory lane. You,' he declared, pointing at his visitor, 'are Wulfstan Cherdicson, the scion of an ancient family with manors and estates along the Welsh march.'

'Correct, Brother. I left there. I entered the Halls of Oxford and Cambridge, residing at the Dominican House in both places. I studied theology and scripture, especially the latter, then I left, as you did, to seek glory and wealth in Normandy. Like you, I joined Lord Lestrange's company.'

'And I remember you well because, even in the fiercest sword and dagger play, you quoted scripture.'

'So very true, Brother, I have a love of the Word of God, which is why I place my trust in him.'

'Even if it means killing another human being?'

'Brother, in the Old Testament the prophet Samuel orders King Saul to put the entire Amalekite tribe to the sword.'

'And you think God has asked you to do the same here in London?'

'I left the royal array,' Wulfstan ignored the veiled insult, 'I left the royal array,' he repeated, 'as I did my studies at Oxford. I decided to form my own select company: the Oxford Clerks. We are a Free Company which pitches its banners in London, Paris, Cologne, Rome, Avignon to name but a few. We are hired for special assignments.'

'Which explains your presence here. Come, come,' Athelstan urged, 'cut to the quick. Time is passing and both Sir John and I have urgent business to deal with.'

'We were hired . . .'

'By whom?'

'I shall reveal that in due time. For the moment, let me repeat. We were hired to carry out judgement on certain manor lords for the hideous crimes they perpetrated in Normandy and elsewhere.'

'Men such as Lord Roger Mortimer?' Athelstan interrupted. 'A man dead and buried, almost rotten to nothing.'

'You probably know why we did that, Athelstan. Just a warning, that not even death and burial could prevent degradation and humiliation. A stark threat to others living on the fruits of their crimes. Men such as Lord Philip Kyne and Henry Blondin at Chafford Hundred. We carried out lawful execution of criminals. However, matters then became complicated.'

'Explain?'

'Well, it became apparent that one cohort of manor lords were already facing punishment and destruction.'

'You mean members of the Free Company, the Via Crucis?'

'The same, Sir John. Lord Despencer, Squires Henshaw and Gumblat and most recently, I understand, Sir John Montague. They were all members of the same company and all executed in a most barbaric fashion.'

'But not by you?'

'No, Sir John, they were not. Now, when the Oxford Clerks accepted the commission, we were assured that we would inflict punishment on certain lords, but in a simple, straightforward fashion.'

'Which became complicated?'

'Yes, it did, Sir John. If these lords were being executed in such a way, why had we been hired? We carried out our task faithfully, confronting the accused in their homes, proclaiming their crimes then carrying out sentence. Hence our very brief but powerful proclamation: Justicia Fiat – let justice be done. Then, as is customary, the severed heads of these criminals were to be poled on London Bridge so that all could see that justice had truly been carried out. However, the killing of individuals such as Despencer and the rest demonstrated that other, quite powerful forces were at work.' Wulfstan paused, shaking his head, murmuring softly to his henchman in a tongue Athelstan could not understand. 'In addition,' Wulfstan continued, 'as Guido just mentioned, we were solemnly promised protection for what we did. We would not be interfered with, pursued or hunted, then trapped.'

'And are you?'

'We certainly are, Brother. By you and Sir John. Your reputation precedes you. I have no doubt that sooner or later you would close with us and that would be disastrous. We felt the sheer injustice of what was happening. We were hired to go hunting, only to discover that we are being hunted for going on that hunt in the first place. I came out here one night to meet you, Brother. I wanted a secret meeting; however, I now realize all I did was alarm you.' Wulfstan coughed. 'To put it bluntly, my friends,' Wulfstan continued, 'we have faithfully carried out our commission. We have done some of what we were hired to do. However, we now feel betrayed, so we wish to leave the field. Our task is finished.'

'Who commissioned you?'

'Sir John, I promise you, Brother Athelstan, I will take the most solemn oath, that I shall answer that question as soon as our safe passage is assured.'

'By whom?'

'By you, Sir John. It's only a matter of time before you came looking for us, which is why we have come looking for you. We have learned how you are making enquiries at Malroad Manor and Chafford Hundred. You will continue to hunt and,' he shrugged, 'we could make a mistake, even be betrayed by those who hired us. We could be declared Utlegatum, put to the horn, condemned as wolfsheads to be killed on sight. I am not saying it would happen, but it is a possibility. In a word, we are finished here, and we wish to go.'

'Then do so.'

'Sir John, there's many a slip between cup and lip. We would like you to provide licences for us to go within the next two days. Letters issued by the Lord High Coroner of London to all port reeves, harbour masters and captains, allowing us safe passage across the Narrow Seas. No one would dare gainsay such permission. Your signature or your seal is our best protection.'

'I am prepared to do that,' Cranston replied, 'but I ask again, who commissioned you?'

'As I have said, we will tell you but only when Guido here, along with one of our companions, collects our licences and letters of permission from you, Sir John, at first light tomorrow morning. They will be at the Guildhall just after the bell for Prime has rung and before the market horn sounds.'

'And if I refuse?'

'Then, Sir John, we will have to resist and fight bravely. But for what? Because we executed criminals? Men who fully deserved the punishment they received for their horrendous crimes? The slaying of innocents, the destruction of homes and churches?'

'He is right, Sir John,' Athelstan interjected. 'Our friend here would have no choice but to fight to get out of this kingdom. Members of his company will die and so will other good men. We now know what happened, but look,' Athelstan pointed at Wulfstan, 'you assured us that you had no part in the other deaths: the gruesome slaying of Despencer, Montague, Henshaw and Gumblat?'

'We had no part in that, I swear,' Wulfstan answered. 'We executed cleanly and swiftly. Whoever is responsible for the other deaths indulged in cruel torture.'

'Master Wulfstan, you quote scripture even when you fight?'

'Of course, the Lord is the light of my life, whom shall I fear?'

'Quite,' Athelstan retorted. 'But, more to the point, are you responsible for the scriptural quotations being posted across this city?'

'Which quotations?'

'To Richard the King: Mene, Mene, Tekel and Parsin.'

'Oh yes, Brother, we have certainly heard of this, a quotation from the book of Daniel. The prophet who gazed into the vision of the night and saw things yet to come.'

'What does it mean?' Athelstan demanded.

'Daniel was a young Jew, a hostage at the Court of King Belshazzar in Babylon. One evening Belshazzar was feasting. He used the sacred goblets, bowls and dishes he had seized from the holy of holies in Jerusalem. Suddenly a disembodied finger appeared sketching a message on the wall of the banqueting chamber. The message was Mene, Mene, Tekel and Parsin.'

'Which means?'

'You have been measured, you have been weighed in the balance, and you have been found wanting. The prophet Daniel then goes on to warn Belshazzar that he would lose his empire to the Persians. So, Sir John, Brother Athelstan, someone is warning your king, threatening his rule, but that is not us. We would have no part in such treasonable activity.' Wulfstan got to his feet. 'Sir John, Brother Athelstan, do we have an agreement? I swear that if we have, I will keep faith.'

Cranston glanced at Athelstan, who shrugged.

'Sir John, we have little choice. Our friend here speaks the truth and simply wishes to be gone. Neither you nor I would hold a candle for the likes of Kyne or Blondin. As I have said, if our visitors want to be gone, then let them be gone.'

Cranston agreed. He and Athelstan clasped hands with Wulfstan and his solemn henchman Guido. Athelstan sketched a blessing in the air then both men left. Once they had, Athelstan and Cranston rearranged the furniture, putting away the wall benches and pulling the two chairs in front of the fire. They sat down in silence, staring into the leaping flames. Eventually Cranston sighed and rose to his feet.

'Yes, I must go. So, until tomorrow, Little Friar!' Cranston gathered his possessions, swinging his cloak around him, pulling over his hood. He and Athelstan clasped hands then Cranston leaned closer. 'Take care, little man,' he warned, 'I shall leave two of Flaxwith's bailiffs on guard outside. The night is cold, but that mad bugger Thomas the Toad can help keep them warm in your mortuary, what do you call it?'

'The House of Abode.'

'So, my friend, you will be protected.' Cranston smiled at Athelstan. 'Take care,' he urged as he released Athelstan, who opened the door. Cranston left, only pausing to ensure that the Friar locked and bolted the door behind him.

The following morning, Athelstan became involved in the frenetic preparations for the entertainment planned that evening and the imminent arrival of the Children of Babylon. Benedicta was absent, but Pike, Watkin and their henchmen, although rather subdued, helped Mauger with the preparations. Benedicta returned just before the Angelus bell. Athelstan thanked Crim, gave him a coin and took Benedicta into the warm and exquisitely furnished chantry chapel: a shrine to St Erconwald and Athelstan's delightful refuge, a sacred space for repose and reflection. More importantly it was secure, a place where Athelstan could talk free of any eavesdropper or busybody. Athelstan asked Benedicta if she wanted some refreshment. She refused as she pulled back her fur-lined hood.

'How was your journey?' he asked.

'Interesting.' She smiled at the little Dominican who occupied her thoughts more than he should.

'Why interesting?'

'Well, Father, your brethren were very keen to have news about you. They've heard rumours, but they wish you would visit them more often.'

'That's good to hear. And Brother Simon?'

'A lovely soul, Father. He showed me up to his carrel in the library, a veritable treasure house of learning. I gave him your piece of parchment and he began immediately. He took down this beautifully bound book, its pages white as snow, the black ink making it so easy to read.'

'And?'

'Father, you were correct. Brother Simon is a scholar, very skilled in the origin of names. Once I had given him your list, he asked me to wait whilst he collected other books and manu-scripts. He assured me he would not take long. He explained how the words you had given him could be easily developed to their present spelling because, in the main, they were the names of noble families who owned those very places.'

'And?' Athelstan smiled at this most beautiful woman who always seemed so eager to help. 'Benedicta,' he murmured, 'you have something for me?'

She nodded, opened her belt wallet and took out a small scroll. Athelstan unrolled this. He read the four short entries and the excitement surged within him.

'Father, you are pleased.'

'More than you realize, Benedicta, but look, many thanks for what you did. Leave me to study what you have brought. I also suspect Mauger sorely needs you in the nave.'

Benedicta, all a bustle, said she would help and left Athelstan sitting in the chair, staring down at what he held in his hand.

'You're the death warrant,' he whispered, 'for one very evil soul.'

He was still sitting there, locked in his thoughts, when Benedicta knocked on the door to the chantry chapel and ushered Tiptoft into the shrine. Athelstan rose to meet and greet him.

'Good morning, Master Tiptoft, and let me guess why you're here.'

'Brother?' Tiptoft flipped his bottle-green cloak and shook off the raindrops.

'Oh yes, let me tell you,' Athelstan continued. 'Sir Stephen Crossley, knight and former member of the Via Crucis, has been found dead in or around "The Golden Oriole" tavern and Sir John Cranston wants me there, yes?'

'Brother Athelstan, you must have second sight.'

'No, my friend, just skill in hunting down and trapping the children of Cain.'

Cranston and Ingham were waiting for them in the small buttery just at the rear of the tavern. Cranston welcomed the Friar whilst Ingham asked for a blessing before leading Cranston and Athelstan into the garden with its herb banks, vegetable plots and ancient oaks. From the branches of one of these hung Crossley's corpse, head slightly askew, hands hanging down. The cadaver turned, buffeted by the breeze, the branches creaking and all around the constant cawing of hunting ravens who sensed dead flesh for the plucking. Ingham drove these away as Athelstan inspected the corpse to ensure there were no ligatures or other signs of binding. He could find none. Athelstan then pulled up the overturned barrel Crossley must have used to tie the rope around the gnarled bough as well as the noose for his neck. He looked at the barrel and the dangling dead feet.

'Yes, yes,' he whispered to himself, 'all possible.' He felt the ice-cold corpse and noticed how the front of the dead man's jerkin was soaked in what Athelstan believed was rich claret. The Friar slowly walked around the corpse then returned to where Cranston and Ingham were standing. He stood there staring across at the gruesome scene. 'Horrid, horrid blasphemy,' he murmured.

'Brother?'

Athelstan gestured at the dangling corpse. 'Crossley has risen high, a hideous mockery of Christ being raised at the Resurrection.'

'Heinous!'

'Yes, Sir John. Please excuse me for a moment.'

Athelstan returned to the corpse and searched the man's purse and wallet but, as expected, there was nothing. He suspected the same to be true of the dead man's chamber. 'All clean,' he whispered to himself, 'all neat and tidy.'

'Brother Athelstan?'

'Yes, Sir Oliver?'

'I have this.' The knight fished in his wallet and handed over a scroll neatly tied with a ribbon of red silk. 'Crossley left it.'

'Did he now?' Athelstan exclaimed.

'A message, Brother, about why Sir Stephen ended his own life.'

Athelstan took the scroll and went and sat on one of the stone garden seats. He carefully undid the scroll. The writing was clear in a clerkly hand.

'I,' Athelstan read it out so the other two could hear, 'Sir Stephen Crossley, Knight, from Battle in Sussex, do dictate this full and final confession to Matthew Hinden, Parson of the Church of the Holy Sepulchre in Farringdon Ward, on the Fifth of January, the year of our Lord 1383. I am, or I was, a member of the Via Crucis battlegroup. I now deeply regret and express contrition for the pain and punishment I and my so-called comrades inflicted on others. I hated that title for there was nothing sacred or holy about us. We were plunderers, robbers and rapists. I came to hate the church and our company, led by Sir Oliver Ingham, a soul more mortally stained than my own. I am now in my winter years. The gold I stole is mine, but the others, now fearful for their immortal souls, wish to hand it over to build a lazar house. Let them do it. I have a sore deep in my bowels. I shit blood and I see the darkness deepening around me. Nevertheless, I still have to listen to my so-called comrades chatter about a lazar house, a hospice for those rotting creatures. They have proved obdurate over this, and I could not tolerate either them or the pain which wracks me. What wealth I have, I needed for myself. I want to keep my treasure. They have ruled differently. They believe they are the Way of the Cross. Well, let them experience what really happened. And so they have. Despencer scourged to death. Gumblat crowned with thorns. Henshaw crushed under the cross. Montague crucified. They have now completed their Via

Crucis and I will join them. They have been punished for their sins. They died horrid deaths and now it is my turn. I prefer oblivion to life. So, alea iacta, the dice is thrown, and I am for the dark. Sir Stephen Crossley, signed, sealed and dated under my own signet.'

Athelstan held the manuscript closer so he could study the imprint on the red wax seal. He recognized Sir Stephen's family arms, a cross in the centre of a lake, next to it the seal of Parson Hinden. Athelstan rolled the scroll up and handed it to Cranston. 'Sir John, you will need this as we also need to question Parson Hinden. You have him here surely?'

'I sent for him,' Ingham replied. 'He is now lodged in a chamber on the first gallery; that's where I placed him. He is all a quiver but ready to confirm all that has happened.'

'Fetch him,' Athelstan demanded.

Ingham hurried off and returned shortly afterwards with the thin, pasty-faced parson, who glanced quickly at the dangling corpse and hurriedly crossed himself.

'You recognize the hanged man?' Cranston demanded. 'Come, my friend, you must have blessed and buried many a corpse. So, go and look hard and well.'

The Parson stumbled across and stood beneath the swinging corpse. He sketched a blessing and returned.

'It is he,' he declared.

'It is who?'

'Why, Brother, Sir Stephen Crossley. He invited me to "The Golden Oriole" yesterday evening. Said he had an important task for me and that he would pay me well.' The Parson coughed and cleared his throat. 'When I arrived, he had parchment, ink pot and quill pen at the ready together with a goblet of the finest wine.'

'Why did he choose you?' Athelstan tapped the Parson on the shoulder. 'You know who we are surely?'

'Sir Oliver informed me as we came down.'

'So, my question. Why did Sir Stephen choose you?'

'Brother, as Sir John will attest, I am an officer of the Crown, an approved scribe for drawing up wills, indentures, charters, writs and whatever.'

'True enough,' Cranston intervened. 'I have seen bills, wills and other documents drawn up by the good parson.'

'So last night, you sat down, and Sir Stephen dictated a document to you, yes? This document.' Cranston handed over the scroll, which the Parson, hands slightly trembling, undid and quickly read the contents.

'Yes,' Hinden declared. 'I transcribed and sealed this document.' He handed it back to Cranston.

'You must have been alarmed by Sir Stephen's references to death, to oblivion, to be gone from this life?'

'Brother Athelstan, I tried to establish what he really meant, what he intended, but he became quite brusque. He told me to mind my own business, to take my fee and go. Which I did. Of course, I was troubled. I intended to return here to make some enquiries but, of course, circumstances have changed.'

'They certainly have,' Athelstan agreed. 'Now, Sir Oliver, Parson Hinden, have you two ever met before?'

'I don't think so,' Ingham replied. 'In fact, I can't recall doing so and why should I? Remember, Brother, I and my comrades lodge in our manors in the shires outside London. We rarely come to London, usually just to discuss a possible site for the new lazar house. As for the management of "The Golden Oriole", we were not city taverners, so we left such matters to our henchmen, Squires Gumblat and Henshaw.'

'I dealt with both,' Parson Hinden declared. 'But again, a rare event. I never met Sir Oliver until now though I have heard of him. I knew his status as I did the others. Now, Sir John, Brother Athelstan, are you finished with me?' The Parson, still agitated, dried his sweaty hands on the front of his quilted jerkin. Athelstan glanced at Cranston, who nodded his head.

'Then go in peace, Parson, and may the Lord be with you.' Athelstan watched Hinden leave then turned to Ingham.

'Sir Oliver, of your goodness. Have Crossley's corpse removed to the death house at St Mary atte Bowe. You must search out the Royal Physician Sir Giles Argentine. Ask him to examine the corpse most carefully and, unless I hear directly from him, Sir John will record Crossley's death as suicide by strangulation.'

The knight promised he would. Plucking at Cranston's sleeve,

Athelstan bade Ingham farewell and led the Coroner back into
Cheapside. Sir John paused and put his hand on Athelstan's
shoulder and gently squeezed.

'What is it, Brother? I can see you are troubled.'

'No, Sir John, I am not troubled, just distracted and determined
to keep hidden what I have discovered and what I intend to do
with it. I have most of the pieces of the puzzle in place. I have
yet to rearrange them in the way I want.'

'In which case . . .' Cranston opened his wallet and took out
a square of the best scrubbed parchment, white as snow with
parts of a red seal still attached. 'Little Friar, you are going to
be very surprised. However, I recall one of your quotations from
scripture. "Put not your trust in princes." Sound advice!'

Athelstan undid the parchment. He read the short blunt message
written in the most clerkly script above a red seal which Athelstan
recognized immediately. He read it twice and exclaimed in
surprise. Athelstan closed his eyes, quietly reciting a short prayer
to the Holy Spirit for guidance.

'Brother?'

Athelstan opened his eyes and smiled. 'Before we act, Sir
John, we must reflect whilst you make certain enquiries.'
Athelstan stamped his feet against the cold. 'You know, Sir John,
I did wonder, I did speculate. But of course, the writ you've just
shown me could be a forgery. Please enquire to prove it isn't.
Anyway, you have issued the licences for the Oxford Clerks?'

'I certainly have, and I am sure that our scholars are, as we
speak, all aboard some war cog heading for Bordeaux, Wissant,'
the Coroner waved a hand, 'or Dordrecht.'

'Very likely, Sir John. I suspect it will be a long time before
they return to these shores. Ah well, such is life. So, my learned
coroner, I look forward to seeing you once the Vespers bell has
chimed. I believe our masque will begin shortly afterwards. Until
then.' Athelstan delivered a blessing and, with two of Flaxwith's
bailiffs either side, the Friar returned across the bridge and into
the frenetic preparations which dominated the parish.

In the end, all went well, and Athelstan was pleasantly surprised.
He was greeted by a crowd of parishioners all eager and excited

about the coming event. Joscelyn, Merrylegs and Benedicta had laid out a repast which Sir John Cranston claimed, shortly after he had arrived, was better than the royal cooks could muster. The Coroner was accompanied by Flaxwith and his bailiffs. At Athelstan's insistence Cranston despatched two of these with warrants to make careful enquiries along Cheapside. The Friar then promised himself that he would stay vigilant and watch how matters progressed.

The Children of Babylon arrived in their colourful costumes: sixteen in all, ten men and six ladies all carefully marshalled by their leaders Benedict and Benjamin. The musicians in the group were placed at the rear of the column which was arranged in pairs. People took their seats. Food and drink were eagerly snatched from the buttery table. Candles were lit, lantern horns positioned and, after a great deal of laughter and teasing, the Children of Babylon presented themselves. Silence descended, broken only by the crackling heat from the capped braziers and the haunting calls of the night birds across God's Acre. The masque was about to begin when further merriment was caused by the late arrival of Thomas the Toad with two boxes of the strange creatures he cared for: toads of every hue and size, all of them noisy. So loud was their croaking Athelstan had no choice but to banish their owner, along with his toads, to the sacristy. The musicians then struck up and the column wound its way slowly but ever so gracefully down the nave with plumes of heady incense pouring from the thuribles which lined their route. As they processed, the Children of Babylon danced and sang their song of exile. 'By the rivers of Babylon, there we sat and wept when we remember Zion.'

Eventually they reached the foot of the steps which led up to where Athelstan sat enthroned in his great ceremonial chair before the entrance through the rood screen and into the sanctuary beyond. Once they had, they circled Athelstan then processed back down the steps to where they had first gathered close to the baptismal font. After the plaudits of all, Benjamin asked if Athelstan thought the masque would be acceptable to the King? Athelstan assured him it most certainly would be, reminding both brothers that King Richard liked all things

French. The pageant was then repeated once again. This time the Children of Babylon invited their audience to participate in both the singing and the dancing. At first, the parishioners were too shy to agree, but eventually they did, and the nave soon rang with laughter, good-natured shouts and the sound of different musical instruments.

PART SIX

'God tears his chosen from the jaws of the Devil.'

At last, Athelstan, tired and heavy-eyed, made his farewells of Sir John and the Vaucort Brothers. Leaving matters in the capable hands of Benedicta, Athelstan returned to the warm, comfortable loneliness of his own house, the music of the pageant trailing around him. Once there he sat staring into the flames, his mind going back over the events of the day. He could still hear the music and he began to hum the verse himself. 'By the rivers of Babylon, there we sat and wept when we remembered Zion.'

'When we remembered Zion,' Athelstan repeated aloud. 'The Children of Babylon sang this lament for their own homeland; in this case France is their Zion.' Athelstan was still reflecting on this when he drifted into a deep sleep. He woke much later when the hour candle had burned two rings. Feeling refreshed and rested, Athelstan rose. He unlocked the door and peered out into the darkness. From what he could see and hear, the festivities in the church were long over. Athelstan stared up at the sky and reckoned it would soon be dawn on this morning of the Epiphany. He went back in, locked the door and poured himself a stoup of morning ale. He then returned to his chair before the fire. Once again, he hummed the words of the hymn sung by the Children of Babylon. He also recalled the ominous warning the prophet Daniel had seen in the visions of the night. A message scrawled on a wall by the finger of God. 'Mene, Mene, Tekel and Parsin – You have been measured, you have been weighed in the balance and you have been found wanting.'

Athelstan abruptly stiffened in the chair. That same warning had been posted across London but by whom and why? The threat was certainly aimed at Richard the King yet where else had he heard similar words? Something like 'Richard your king'. Athelstan went cold as he reflected, his stomach pitching at the sudden shock of what might be crawling out of the darkness. Athelstan's agitation bordered on panic. He hoped that his random thoughts might be mistaken and just prayed that he had it wrong. But what would happen if his fears were justified? The terror he felt about an emerging, deeply menacing threat was tangible. Athelstan got to his feet. He banked the fire and, for a while, walked up and down reflecting on what might be. Eventually he reached a decision. It was best to act rather than ignore, so he prepared to leave. He paused halfway through to take the hunting horn from its casket. He was now determined to resolve matters. He opened the door and, lifting the horn to his lips, he blew three strident blasts which echoed ominously across God's Acre. He waited for a few heartbeats then blew again. He sighed in relief as pinpricks of light appeared across the cemetery. One by one most of the members of his parish council staggered through the dark, rubbing their eyes, complaining about the cold but very keen to discover why their little priest had raised the alarm. They all followed him into the house to be directed by Benedicta and Mauger on where to sit.

'Father?' Watkin got to his feet.

'Not now, my friend. Just bear with me. Ah, good.' Standing on tiptoe Athelstan glimpsed the two bailiffs Cranston had left to keep watch over him. 'My friends,' he called out, 'go to Sir John immediately. You must rouse him and inform him that he must meet me as swiftly as possible outside the house of Benedict and Benjamin Vaucort in Osprey Lane, Cripplegate. He knows where it is. Just make sure he comes.'

'Very good, Father, we will leave now.'

'Godspeed,' Athelstan murmured. 'Now, Benedicta and Mauger, look after the church. There will be no dawn Mass. Giles,' he turned to the Hangman, 'Crispin, Watkin and Pike, make sure you are dressed against the cold. Bring whatever weapons you have and come with me to the same house in Cripplegate.'

Athelstan and his escort, now suitably dressed and armed, left for the house in Osprey Lane within the hour. Athelstan used the special licence given to him by Sir John which granted the Friar the right to walk the streets of London at any hour he pleased. The writ also gave him permission to use Moleskin to take out his barge for whatever reason Athelstan needed. Once they had reached Queenhithe, they swiftly made their way up through the City. The nightwalkers and other creatures of the dark slunk out, then hurriedly withdrew back into the shadows. They had no intention of interfering with a group of well-armed men who were given free passage by the Watch. Athelstan was more than aware of these living shadows: the pimps, prostitutes, wizards, warlocks and other mountebanks who swarmed through the streets of London once darkness had fallen. Different sounds echoed: a baby crying, a man shouting and a woman's pleading reply. The itinerant cooks were busy supplying foul food smothered in cheap spicy sauces. The beggars were also out, grateful for the warmth of the bonfires lit in the mouth of alleyways, their flames hungrily devouring all the rubbish of the day. They eventually reached the house in Osprey Lane. Athelstan and his companions could detect no light whilst the doors and window shutters seemed firmly closed and locked. They found a narrow door to the rear and forced their way through into a small garden stretching up to the house. Watkin broke the shutters over the nearest window and climbed through. Once inside he hacked the lock and bolt on the back door then lit a lantern he'd found to guide Athelstan and the others into a stone-flagged chamber. They then moved through the house using the occasional remains of a candle to light their way.

'Nothing,' Athelstan exclaimed. 'They must have cleared it of all and any ornamentation. No tapestries, no coloured cloths, no crucifix, no triptych. Not one personal item be it a belt or a boot. Nothing but a cold, bare house. I do wonder where they are now?' He paused as he heard Cranston shouting at his bailiffs to stay outside whilst he rapped on the front door. Watkin and Pike wrenched this open, and Cranston swept in like the North Wind.

'Athelstan?' he trumpeted. 'Why the hour? Why the place?'

'Look around you, Sir John, this house has been swept clean. Why?'

'God knows, Brother.' Cranston pulled back his ermine-lined hood. 'They could be planning to return to France or some other place across the Narrow Seas. Athelstan, what is the matter?' Cranston stepped closer, peering down at the little friar. 'Why are you so agitated? Why this search? What wrong have the Children of Babylon done? They can go where they want, do what they want. They are not here because they are probably preparing for the masque later today.' Cranston took a swig from the miraculous wineskin. 'I understand from Master Thibault that the Children of Babylon will be the first in a number of pageants to be staged before our king along the great nave of St Paul's. They have pride of place. They must be almost ready. Remember, Athelstan, they are French, plucked from their homes. They have every right under the sun to return home if they so wish.' Cranston thrust the stopper back into the wineskin. 'Especially now, Brother, with a peace treaty being hammered out between our two countries. Dom Antoine, not to mention our own king, would not be pleased at any hurt being offered to them, be it in thought, word or deed. In fact, their inclusion in the celebrations is supposed to reflect our high regard for them and what they represent.' Cranston took out the miraculous wineskin again. He drank a mouthful and offered it to Athelstan, who refused. 'Come on, Little Friar, what is the matter?'

'Just a feeling, Sir John, that something is very wrong. However, I can only prove this when matters outside my control will make their presence felt. More than that, Sir John, I cannot say.'

'Be careful, Brother. Our king greatly favours Dom Antoine. He does not want the French envoy unsettled in any way. Now, we are attending the Epiphany celebrations and our Lord King's birthdate. Before that happens, you can question our Children of Babylon and ask them any questions you want.'

'Brother Athelstan, Sir John?' The Hangman's voice rang hollow along the passageway, followed by heavy footsteps as the Hangman climbed the steps leading down into the cellar.

'Sir John, Brother Athelstan,' he gasped catching his breath, 'you must see this, but we need sconce torches. You must come down.'

'What is it?'

'Wall paintings, Father. Strange wall paintings.'

Cranston immediately despatched Flaxwith with two of his men to a nearby house. Flaxwith was ordered to show his seal and demanded sconce torches for the King's own High Coroner of London. The master bailiff wasted no time and soon returned. The sconces he brought were fired and they followed the Hangman down into the cellar along a shadowy passageway. The floor was rough though the walls on either side, as well as the ceiling, had been plastered and looked fresh and clean. The Hangman beckoned them on further down the passageway then stopped where the pictures began: a series of crude but eye-catching frescoes. Athelstan raised a torch and followed the colourful story being depicted there. A town was being burned and pillaged, its church nothing more than a mass of leaping flames. Close by this soared a gallows, and from each of its many branches hung a corpse. Around the gibbet, men, women and children were being slaughtered by soldiers wearing the white tabard and red cross of English men at arms. Directing these were horsemen garbed in the colours of the Plantagenets, England's royal family, blue, scarlet and gold.

'English troops sacking a town in France,' Athelstan murmured, 'and there must be more.' He walked further along the passageway, tapping at certain places on the wall where French towns were clearly named. Moyaux, Avranches and Pontigny.

'It's a tableau,' the Hangman declared, 'a tapestry about the violence of the war in France. Look,' the Hangman read aloud a roughly daubed phrase, 'Gerere bellum terra marique, igne gladioque.' The Hangman stumbled over the Latin, but he knew enough to translate. 'To wage war by land and sea,' he declared. 'By fire and sword.'

'It's what the Roman Senate used to decree,' Athelstan declared, 'when it issued their declaration of war.'

'It's thought-provoking,' Cranston declared. 'And eye-catching.'

Athelstan whispered his agreement. What the artist of these paintings lacked in skill was certainly made up with a crude vigour. He had depicted all the horrors of towns being cruelly sacked. Men hung twisting and turning from scaffolds, gibbets or the branches of some tree. Women knelt, clothes all torn, hands raised to Heaven in tearful supplication beside a village well which was crammed with corpses. The wall tapestry, as the Hangman described it, apparently stretched the length of one wall.

'A tableau of terror,' Athelstan murmured. 'I have seen enough.' He stepped back, and as he did, he felt his sandal scrape what felt like small pebbles.

'Surely not stone decay, not here?' Athelstan murmured. He crouched down and ran his hand along the paving stones. In the light of one of the torches he then examined the small blackened grains turned hard as nails by the wet stones. He glanced up at the ceiling, but the roof was expertly plastered with no sign of crumbling.

'Brother Athelstan?'

'Nothing really, Sir John. I just wonder what these hard, thickened grains actually are and where they come from. Ah well, let me wash my hands in one of the rain barrels, then we must be gone.' Once Athelstan had, he and Cranston went into the small solar.

'Brother, I understand your unease.' Cranston shook his head. 'But don't become too suspicious: that fresco is perfectly understandable.'

'I agree with Sir John,' the Hangman offered. 'Paintings often open the doors of your mind, your heart, your soul. It happened to me, Brother. You know it did. My wife and children were murdered by outlaws. For months I thought about what I'd seen and felt. I drew pictures of the horrors they must have gone through. Eventually, I made such paintings real. I hunted down those outlaws and hanged each and every one of them.'

'And that's what worries me,' Athelstan replied. 'The Children of Babylon have expressed their grief, their horror at what happened to their towns: the brutality of English soldiers, their greed, their appetite for destruction. I understand that.

But surely the hatred these events must have caused, the resentment, the deep hostility, could that express itself in more practical ways?'

'Brother, all I can say,' the Hangman shrugged as he tugged at his straw-like hair, 'paintings open the doors of your innermost soul and only God knows what might come crawling through.'

'Very true,' Athelstan declared. 'I must think. I must reflect.' He paused. 'Look, my friends, we are done here. Sir John, will "The Lamb of God" be open?'

'For me it always is, Brother! I've already notified mine hostess that I may come to eat and drink, whatever the hour.'

'Good, then I shall celebrate my Mass in Holy Sepulchre Church. I am sure Parson Hinden will be pleased to see me. Afterwards we can break our fast at "The Lamb of God" then it's down to St Paul's and the day's celebrations.' Athelstan summoned his four parishioners and, courtesy of Sir John, gave each of them a coin as well as an invitation to join him for the Jesus Mass. All four seemed reluctant. However, Athelstan beckoned them closer, assuring them that he still needed them and, once they met at the church, he would tell them why. He and Cranston then left Cripplegate. The Coroner promised Athelstan that Flaxwith and his cohort would not be far behind, once he and the other bailiffs had made the house in Osprey Lane as secure as possible.

The City was now waking up. Bells and horns sounded. Heavily burdened carts and sumpter ponies brought in produce and goods for the stalls now being set up for the day's trade. City bailiffs were marshalling all those found guilty of misdemeanours during the night. These night hawks or nightwalkers were to be locked in the pillories and stocks and would have to remain there until the Angelus bell sounded. They passed the pillories. The clamour and noise shattering the peace of the early morning as felons were clasped tight. Close by, whores caught soliciting outside the boundaries were pulled across a barrel, their skirts pushed back and their buttocks soundly whipped. Funeral parties were also assembling: coffins and sheeted corpses placed across the shoulders of mourners or pushed on a wheelbarrow to some city cemetery.

At last, they reached Holy Sepulchre. Parson Hinden welcomed them with a forced smile though he assured Athelstan that he could celebrate his Mass in one of the shabby chantry chapels along the north transept. The Friar did so with Cranston as his only companion. When the Coroner whispered about the where-abouts of his parishioners, Athelstan just smiled. He then replied that they were also busy on God's work, which he had described to them in brief pithy sentences in the sacristy before Mass. He just prayed Watkin and his companions did not encounter the Parson. When Cranston asked why, Athelstan just shook his head. After the celebration, Athelstan thanked Parson Hinden and promptly left the church. Watkin and the rest were waiting for him at the lychgate. At his invitation, they followed Sir John down to 'The Lamb of God'. On their way, Athelstan listened very carefully to what his parishioners had seen in their wander-ings around Holy Sepulchre, its outbuildings and even Parson Hinden's private quarters. Once they reached 'The Lamb of God' Athelstan thanked all four and watched them go before joining Sir John in the warm opulence of the tavern solar. The buxom blonde-haired hostess was all a quiver at seeing Sir John so early and Cranston had to assure her that all was well. Athelstan gave her a blessing and she hurried off back into the kitchen. They broke their fast on eggs, boiled, peeled and mixed with butter along with thin strips of crisply cooked bacon and freshly baked manchets. They ate in silence. When they had finished, Cranston leaned across and gently patted Athelstan on the shoulder.

'Where to now, Little Friar?'

'What time does the great pageant start?'

'His Grace has ordered that it must begin precisely at twelve noon.'

'Sir John, before we leave for St Paul's, I need to think, reflect, pray and prepare.'

'Then stay here, my good friend. I have business in the Guildhall with a certain city merchant. Oh, and I have not forgotten, Brother, about the other items you asked about.'

Cranston left Athelstan to his thoughts. The Friar made himself comfortable in the chair whilst he assessed the progress he had made. He had certainly discovered the truth about one set of murders and the other simply needed the pieces put in place to reach a lucid, logical conclusion. Athelstan had, to his own satisfaction, resolved the different twists and turns of his quarry. All was ready, but when should he deliver his indictment? Athelstan relaxed, closed his eyes and meditated on his next move. He was roused by Cranston, who swept in, garbed in his best houppelande boasting the royal colours of an important Officer of the Crown. Cranston's moustache, hair and beard had been neatly clipped and his rubicund face oiled with a fragrant nard. He had strapped a war belt around his waist made from the most expensive Cordovan leather.

'You look magnificent, Sir John,' Athelstan teased. 'A true Hector, a warrior prince.'

He and the Coroner embraced. The Coroner then sat down as Athelstan excused himself.

'Mother Nature calls, Sir John. I must ask mine hostess permission to use a lavarium and jakes cupboard in one of the chambers above stairs.'

Cranston grunted his agreement and took a gulp of wine whilst Athelstan hurried away. Once he had finished his ablutions, Athelstan re-joined Sir John. They left 'The Lamb of God' and made their way through the crowds across the City down to St Paul's. In the words of Sir John, 'the world and its wife seemed to be thronging down to the great open door of the ancient cathedral'. Cranston, using his pass, pushed his way up into the cavernous nave. Athelstan followed, then stood staring around. He wanted to remember every single detail he could. He studied the nave, a long broad aisle which stretched from the baptistry up to the sanctuary steps. These were almost dwarfed by the soaring rood screen depicting the crucifixion with life-size figures of the Virgin and St John either side of Christ's blood-encrusted cross. A court squire pointed to the ornate throne on the top sanctuary step, almost blocking the door through the rood screen. The squire explained how Sir John, Athelstan and special guests of Master Thibault would join the other notables in the sanctuary behind the throne where braziers and candles had been lit. A buttery table had also been laid out with platters of food and the best wine of Bordeaux and Alsace. Cranston thanked him and plucked at Athelstan's sleeve, but the Friar pulled away. He pointed across to where the Children of Babylon were gathered beyond the baptismal font deep in the shadows of the north transept.

'Let's visit our friends, Sir John, and they can answer my questions.'

'Be careful, Brother.'

'I just want to question them, Sir John, that's all.'

They crossed the nave and entered the baptistry. Athelstan could almost feel the excitement, a tension that was almost tangible. The Children of Babylon greeted Athelstan and Cranston most joyously, talking about the parish and how they hoped St Erconwald's parishioners would be in the congregation today. Athelstan fended off their good-natured banter and indicated to Benedict and Benjamin that he would appreciate a word in quiet. He met both young men in an enclave built to the right of the main door.

'Brother Athelstan?'

'I went down to your house in Osprey Lane. I found it deserted, cleared of all your personal possessions. I didn't want to be intrusive, but I was alarmed at seeing the house so empty.'

'We understand, Brother Athelstan, but remember we are French by birth and upbringing. Benjamin and I, along with the others, need to return to our own people.'

'The Children of Babylon?'

'Yes, Brother, the Children of Babylon are returning from exile at the Court of King Belshazzar.'

'And you have the necessary licences and passes?'

'All issued by Monsieur Thibault whilst we have also reached an agreement with the captain of a cog bound for Boulogne. Brother, is there anything else?'

'I saw the fresco? On the cellar wall?'

'A fitting memorial, Brother, wouldn't you say? To our past and what has formed us?'

'What do you mean?'

'Sir John, what is painted on that wall is our past as well as the reason for our actions both now and in the future. Talking

of which,' Benedict grasped his brother's wrist, 'Sir John, Brother
Athelstan, we have our pageant. Please excuse us.'

'Oh!' Athelstan exclaimed. 'One further thing?'

'Yes, Brother.'

'Does the phrase Mene, Mene, Tekel and Parsin mean anything
to you?'

'No, Brother, it certainly does not. What does it mean? Should
it mean anything to us?'

'Never mind, just a thought.'

The two brothers bowed and hurried back to join their
companions, who seemed very eager to learn what was
happening.

'Come, Brother,' Cranston murmured, 'no need for disquiet.'

'Oh, there's every need, Sir John, but not yet.'

They walked slowly up the nave which was quickly filling
with people jostling and pushing each other to get the best view.
A loud hum of conversation filled the air, almost drowning the
sound of the bells being prepared, doors being shut and stewards
shouting instructions to keep the crowd in order. Cranston and
Athelstan entered the well-guarded sanctuary where liveried
servants waited to take cloaks and offer refreshment. Sir John
tapped his war belt and reminded the squires that he was one of
the few people allowed to carry a sword in the presence of the
King. The squires agreed and left him alone. Athelstan stared
around. Most of those present were important royal officials and
favourites of the Court. They milled and jostled about, very
conscious of their dignity, calling and status, quick to take offence,
eager to do a rival mischief. Cranston often described them as a
pack of ravenous wolves who, if they had no prey, would eagerly
turn on each other. 'They, we, all wear masks,' Cranston had
once declared 'and when these masks are taken off there are
more beneath.'

Athelstan half smiled at the memory and yet, he mused, there
was a beauty here. Men and woman garbed in precious cloth
and furs, sweetening the air with the fragrances of their bodies
and costly costumes. Athelstan sat down in the shadows with
his back to a pillar. He closed his eyes and prayed all would be
well. He made himself comfortable on the stool then startled at

a bray of trumpets, loud and carrying, repeated time and again until they imposed a silence throughout the church. There was one last further blast and the royal heralds, in their gorgeous tabards, announced the entrance of their lord and master. The King swept out of the darkness shrouding the main doorway. To cries of 'Vivat Rex', Richard made his way along the nave towards his throne. Athelstan, standing on tiptoe, stared at the young king, resplendently handsome with his sun-coloured hair, alabaster skin and icy blue eyes which reflected his ever-changing mood. The King was garbed in the cloth of gold with an exquisitely jewelled coronet clamped on his head. Richard the King looked every inch the powerful prince. Behind him to his right and left walked his uncle, Lord John of Gaunt, and Master Thibault, Keeper of the Royal Secrets. The way both men were dressed, the swagger in their walk, proclaimed their power and status as their prince's principal henchmen. The King reached his throne and sat down, Gaunt likewise on a cushioned stool to his nephew's right with Thibault on the left of the throne. A chamberlain loudly announced how Richard the King wished the pageant to begin on this solemn and holy feast day of the Epiphany. Immediately the music began followed by the first line of the song 'By the rivers of Babylon, there we sat and wept . . .' The Children of Babylon emerged from the baptistry, their voices growing stronger. The congregation, which had fallen silent now, became slightly agitated. Athelstan tensed, grasping Cranston's arm.

'Brother, what is it?'

'Sir John,' Athelstan hissed, 'you heard them. They claim not to know about Belshazzar or that message inscribed on his palace wall. Nonsense! I am sure they know all about the exile to Babylon. They must have come across . . .'

The Children of Babylon were now very close, parting to circle the throne when a voice abruptly shouted.

'My lords, there is a fire in the crypt.' The shout was clear and carrying. Athelstan pushed his way forward. A ripple of unrest echoed through the cavernous church, but the Children of Babylon continued their pageant singing in clear, lucid voices. Athelstan watched as the performers circled the King. Benedict and Benjamin paused just before the throne, a matter of heart-beats, before they pulled daggers from beneath their cloaks. Benjamin held two, but he fumbled, and one slid from his grasp on to the floor.

'Sir John!' Athelstan yelled. 'Treason! Treason!'

Benjamin had already reached the bottom step and was begin-ning to climb. A royal squire, sharper than the rest, had seen what happened. He ran to confront the would-be assassin, who lashed out, cutting the squire's face open. The squire, however, still managed to lunge forward and grab the dagger the assassin had dropped. The squire snatched this up and thrust it deep into Benjamin's chest. All was now in turmoil. Knight Bannerets searched for their weapons, but Cranston was swifter than the rest. Sword drawn, he went to help the squire, slashed badly across his face. He then turned to confront Benedict, who, dagger at the ready, clambered towards the King. The Coroner, however, swiftly charged into him, knocking the would-be assassin away. Cranston then swung his great two-handed war sword, a scything, powerful slash which severed Benedict's head as a gardener would a rose.

The King retreated, leaving his throne. He would have joined the fight now erupting around him, but he was seized by his bodyguard of Knight Bannerets, who quickly formed a shield wall around him. The nave was now a battlefield, a slaughter house. Many fled. Others engaged with the Children of Babylon in violent dagger and sword play. The air was full of shrieking yells and curses. The conflict spilled further down the nave. The Children of Babylon, both male and female, fighting what they knew would be a battle to the finish. The dead lay spilling blood, the living just stood or crouched, sweat-soaked and desperate. The King, sheltered by his shield ring, shouted he would move into the great sacristy. Athelstan stood next to Cranston, who was now directing matters. Master Thibault had stayed, but most of the other officials had disappeared. The fighting ebbed away. The noise of battle faded. Cranston's bailiffs, led by Flaxwith, now marshalled those assassins who had survived the brief but brutal sword play, four men and two women: hands quickly pinioned, they were made to crouch, all bloody and bruised, on the sanctuary floor. The cathedral was cleared. A serjeant at arms appeared and breathlessly announced that the fire in the crypt had been extinguished.

Athelstan sat down on one of the cushioned stools beside the throne. He felt sick at heart at what had happened. The Children of Babylon were assassins, but he felt sorry for them because the violence which had engulfed them as children had now swept back to tear their lives apart. The Friar took his ave beads out and began to recite prayers to the Virgin even as he watched Cranston enforce order. Two of the Children of Babylon were grievously wounded. Athelstan lurched to his feet and gave them a blessing, then Flaxwith cut their throats. The same remedy was applied to any other wounded now reckoned to be beyond all earthly care. For a while the silence of the nave was broken by a hideous gargling as the dying choked on their own blood. Carts arrived at a side door. Those who required a physician or a leech were loaded on to these to be taken to St Bartholomew's hospital. Street scavengers were brought in to sweep, brush and wash away the bloodstains and all the other macabre remains of the violent affray. Of course, news of the disturbance in St Paul's had swept the City and two cohorts of Tower Archers, displaying the King's own insignia, erected barriers to keep the curious away. Archdeacon Tuddenham arrived with his bulla of closure. The Bishop of London's henchman had a few brief words with Sir John then went to stand on the top sanctuary step and read out his sentence in a sombre voice. The message was simple and stark. 'Bloodshed had occurred in God's own house of St Paul's. Accordingly, no further ceremonies, be it the Mass or the Sacraments, could be celebrated in that church until he purged, cleansed and reconsecrated both nave and sanctuary.' The Coroner declared the King had decreed the same. Once Tuddenham had nailed his proclamation to the rood screen door and left, Cranston went and sat on the throne, turning to face Athelstan still slumped on the quilted stool.

'You were right, Little Friar.'

'I was and I wasn't, Sir John. Perhaps I should have probed why this group called themselves the Children of Babylon.

Children is a soft word; it invokes tender memories. We all
know that. Babylon is different. In the Book of Revelation,
which narrates what will happen at the end of time, Babylon
is depicted as representing all the powers of darkness. There's
a verse "the Great Whore of Babylon who shelters Satan and
all the horrors of Hell." Babylon represents God's enemy, the
army of sin.'

'So, my friend, Babylon is not the most healthy or heartening
description for our country.'

'Correct, Sir John. The Children of Babylon were exiles,
plucked cruelly from their own kingdom and forced to live here
in Babylon. The only comforts they had were their memories of
their own country which, by way of contrast, is Zion the Holy
City, the Heavenly Jerusalem. Zion is the opposite of Babylon.
I should have probed such language more deeply, scrutinized it
more carefully. I also overlooked and did not concentrate on one
strand of their deep animosity.'

'Which was?'

'We were once talking about King Richard by the Grace of
God. The Children didn't describe him as "our king" but "your
king". An implicit rebuttal of any allegiance on their part to the
English Crown. They rejected a prince whose father and grand-
father, the Black Prince and Edward III, were ultimately responsible for all the horrors inflicted on them, especially their forced
exile to this country.' Athelstan shook his head. 'Even those
warnings posted all over the City were a sign of things to come.
They were issuing a proclamation of war and I failed to draw
the correct conclusion. I did not realize the significance of what
they'd done till we met Wulfstan and his Oxford Clerks. Only
then did I reach lucid and logical conclusions.' Athelstan wiped
his mouth on the back of his hand, aware of the silence and the
ghosts listening carefully to what he was saying. 'The Children
of Babylon,' he continued, 'were locked in their own world. They
mourned their past. They secretly hated their exile. Richard our
king was not their king; in fact he was the living embodiment
of all they hated. The phrase Mene, Mene, Tekel and Parsin was
used as a threat as well as a warning that retribution was pending,
vengeance was coming.'

'Of course,' Cranston breathed, staring around. Apart from a few men at arms and archers, the sanctuary now lay quiet. The prisoners had been taken down to the crypt now the fire had been extinguished.

'Sir John?'

'I'm thinking about those warnings, Brother. The Children of Babylon were well situated to deliver such proclamations around the City. They were probably written out by those two clerks and the rest of the Company could distribute them swiftly and secretly.'

'Very true, Sir John. This only enhanced the threat emerging in different places all over the City. Our visit to Cripplegate deepened my suspicions whilst their apparent ignorance of the Mene, Mene text was neither logical nor possible. They must have known about the Book of Daniel and his prophecies, especially its most famous, the finger of God writing that warning on a palace wall. In my view, that sealed their guilt. Of course, they also chose a time and place to strike which would bring their actions to the attention of all of Europe. A blow to our king and the Common Good of this realm.' Athelstan shrugged. 'True we could have intervened earlier, but I remembered what you told me, Sir John. How our king was looking forward to their pageant. How Dom Antoine viewed it as a symbol of harmony between our two kingdoms. What if I was wrong?'

'But in the end, you weren't,' Cranston retorted. 'I have questioned the prisoners. They confessed that they have all taken the blood oath to stand and die by what they planned. They hoped some of them would escape and reach that cog at Queenhithe but . . .' Cranston leaned across and patted Athelstan on the shoulder. 'Indeed, some of them would have escaped but for you. Their plot was subtle and cunning. Look around this church, Brother; there is no shortage of doors and windows. Moreover, once they got outside, they could lose themselves in the crowds. The London mob is notorious for its dislike of a highly unpopular court. Indeed, our good citizens are ever ready to interfere with John of Gaunt's soldiers and men at arms! Oh, by the way, the Children of Babylon were also responsible for that fire in the crypt.'

'Igne gladioque – with fire and sword,' Athelstan whispered. 'That's what they wanted. They wanted to wreak damage with that fire in the crypt as well as the swords and daggers they carried concealed. They wanted to inflict on our king and his court what their own families and kin were subjected to. They must have brought a small tun of gunpowder. On reflection, those hardened grains I found in the cellar of their house in Osprey Lane were grains of black powder used to fire a culverin or cannon. How did it happen, Sir John? How could they smuggle in a cask of fire powder?'

'Well, I suspect people were coming and going. The Children of Babylon would have been allowed to wander where they wanted. They'd take a small barrel of fire powder down into the crypt, a place usually cloaked in darkness. They would light a slow fuse and let the Devil do the rest. Remember, Athelstan, both Benedict and Benjamin had served as mailed clerks in the royal array. They would know about fire powder, fuses and the damage that could be caused. They wanted vengeance, didn't they? Revenge for the past. Anyway,' Cranston got to his feet, 'I have to visit Master Thibault. He is also bent on revenge. He is convoking a commission of Oyer et Terminer. He wants the prisoners swiftly tried and just as swiftly punished. He's vowed that.'

'Who will be on the commission?'

'Oh, me, Thibault and one other.'

'Who?'

'I don't know.'

'Sir John, of your goodness, ask that Sir Oliver Ingham be the third.'

'Why him?'

'For my own secret purposes, Sir John. On this matter, what you don't know will not harm you. Please, I need Ingham on that commission.'

'A suitable choice,' Cranston murmured. 'Ingham is a senior royal officer, being the King's own surveyor. Oh,' Cranston grinned down at his companion, 'the trial will be in "Camera sub secreto Sigillo" – away from the public eye under the authority of the King's Secret Seal. You will have to attend as the Crown's own prosecutor. Athelstan, you have no choice about it. You cannot refuse.'

'No, no, Sir John, I half expected I'd be swept up in the aftermath of what has happened.'

'And what an aftermath!'

'Sir John?'

'Well, Thibault's bent on vengeance. Thibault wants justice to be done as swiftly as possible. I've already sent Tiptoft to fetch your parishioner, the Hangman of Rochester. He will certainly be needed here before the end of the day. He has also demanded, or is in the process of doing so, solemn assurances from the French envoys, Dom Antoine in particular, that the Crown of France, its court and above all the Chambre Noir, had nothing to do with this most treasonable affray.'

'And?'

'The French are taking the most solemn oaths that they know nothing about the incident. Master Thibault believes them and so do I.'

'But he'll use that to its best advantage?'

'Of course, my little friar. The wolf doesn't change its ways, well, at least not in my part of the forest. Oh yes, the affray here this morning remains cloaked in its own mystery.'

'What do you mean?'

'Athelstan, questions will be asked. Who gave the Children of Babylon permission to stage their masque? Why were they allowed to begin the celebrations? Why were they not searched? Of course, hindsight makes us all very wise, and questions will proliferate as lice on a dead dog's coat. I have already glimpsed what is coming.'

'Sir John, is there something I should know?'

'Well, there's something you might find interesting. Flaxwith was dealing with the wounded, which included those of the Children of Babylon. One of these, Armande, was sorely wounded, grievously hurt. He was dying, but nevertheless he begged Flaxwith to fetch Lord Thibault. Flaxwith passed this on to Alfonso, captain of Thibault's Spanish mercenaries, who had been in the nave with the rest when the assault took place. The mercenary must have spoken to his master, but the outcome

was rather eerie. Alfonso came into the sanctuary, crouched by
the wounded man, listened to him talking and gasping in a
tongue Flaxwith couldn't understand. The captain did not reply.
He just drew his dagger, gave the wounded man the mercy cut
then left the sanctuary. Strange, yes? Anyway, I must be gone.'
Cranston stomped off, leaving Athelstan to his thoughts. But
then the Coroner returned full of apologies. 'Brother, Brother,
I am sorry, I overlooked you. You cannot go home. You must
stay here. Father Prior has invited you to use the refectory and
buttery in their guest house along with a closet chamber should
you need to rest. So, you can stay in comfort, Little Friar, and
relax.' Cranston then swept away. Athelstan stayed for a while
before taking advantage of the Prior's kind offer. He broke his
fast in the small well-furnished buttery then adjourned to a bed
chamber in the guest house.

The special commission to hear and determine met just as the
bells of the City tolled for Vespers. Athelstan had risen sometime
before this to wash and refresh himself at the lavarium before
going back into the nave. He'd already sent a message to
Cranston that a certain individual be brought to St Paul's but
kept well hidden away. For the rest, Athelstan prepared his
indictment for what would happen once the trial of the Children
of Babylon was finished. Athelstan knew that Thibault would
see the survivors hang. Only then would he be satisfied.
Athelstan stayed in the sacristy watching the practical preparations being carried out. The sanctuary, now out of use thanks
to Archdeacon Tuddenham, was transformed into a judgement
chamber. A large trestle table had been set up and, like King's
Bench in Westminster Hall, this was covered with a green baize
cloth which displayed the usual symbols of justice: a crucifix,
a Book of the Gospels, letters patent from the Crown author-
izing the commission. In the centre of the table lay an unsheathed
sword. Sconce torches flickered and spluttered in their wall
clasps whilst a host of beeswax candles cast circles of fluttering
light.
    The trial began and the prisoners were brought up. Athelstan
took his seat on his chancery chair at one end of the judgement

table. He looked up and exclaimed in surprise. The prisoners, four men and two women, were bound by the wrist, but they were also gagged. Sir Oliver, who had taken his seat to the left of Master Thibault, sprang to his feet, banging the table with his fist.

'Are the prisoners,' he demanded, 'to be gagged throughout?'

'They are, Sir Oliver,' Thibault retorted. 'My Lord of Gaunt has decreed it to be so.'

'But, but,' Ingham stuttered, 'we are supposed to hear and determine.'

Thibault just gestured at Ingham to take his seat.

'The Crown has spoken,' he declared. 'However . . .' Thibault paused as the door opened and the Captain of Archers, who had been setting up a guard, came in with six of his bowmen. These stood behind the line of prisoners. 'Captain,' Thibault declared, 'remove the gag from one of them, that red-haired woman, do so.' The woman's wristbands as well as the gag were removed. 'You can answer for them all,' Thibault declared.

Athelstan caught Cranston's eye and the Coroner leaned closer.

'It's best that way,' Athelstan whispered, as Thibault read out the charges, 'the swifter the better for all concerned. The prisoners are going to die, and this must be torture for them. What can they say in defence? Who will plead for them? No, let's quickly end this murderous masque.'

Nevertheless, what did follow was farcical. Thibault, as the principal justiciar, laid out the charges, accepted a plea of guilty from the woman who'd had the gag removed, then Thibault sentenced each of them to death – punishment to be carried out immediately on the great gallows in St Paul's churchyard close to the famous cross. No time was wasted. The prisoners, all bedraggled, injured and bruised, were hustled across the sanctuary through the Devil's door and out into the great churchyard dominated by soaring four-branched gallows. The Hangman of Rochester, garbed in black, his head and face covered by a hood and mask, moved swiftly to bring the macabre ceremony to an end. He was helped by a cohort of White Hart archers. Athelstan offered to shrive the condemned, but Thibault, standing in the shadow of the Devil's door, closely guarded by his Spanish mercenaries, shook his head.

'If this is to be done, it's best done now,' he declared. 'Give them a blessing and general absolution then they'll be gone.'

Athelstan walked back to stand between the two scaffolds, even as he repressed a cold spasm of deep fear. Night had fallen. The darkness had closed in though the torches carried by the archers bathed the execution ground in an eerie, juddering light. The gibbets, black and forbidding, soared up against the moonlit sky. A malignant silence seemed to have smothered all sound except for the creak of the ladders on which the condemned stood leaning against the gibbet post. The gasps, groans and pleas for mercy from the condemned were like some ghostly evensong. The Hangman now hurried to finish his task, ensuring each prisoner stood at the top of a ladder, hands now free. The Hangman greeted Athelstan and beckoned him closer so he could deliver the blessing and the prayer of absolution.

'Make it swift, Giles,' Athelstan whispered once he'd finished. He glanced over his shoulder to where Ingham stood next to the Coroner. They had to be present as witnesses. 'The business of the night,' Athelstan whispered, 'is not yet finished, so let this be fast.'

'Father, I promise. It will all be as swift as moonbeams falling on a meadow. In a trice, they will be with God.'

'Hangman,' Thibault shouted harshly, 'carry out sentence.'

Athelstan turned and walked away then he stopped and stood with his back to the gallows. He heard the Hangman's footsteps as he moved from one ladder to another. Athelstan heard the scrape of wood against stone then a gasp of breath followed by that horrid sound as the necks of the condemned snapped, neatly broken. This was the Hangman's unique skill. Death as swift as a shadow, not that hideous strangling and gargling. No gruesome dance in the air, just a hasty end, a door quietly closing on a life. Once it was over, Athelstan turned and blessed the six dangling corpses before moving across to Master Thibault.

'Sir,' he whispered, 'I need words with you.'

Thibault pulled a face but beckoned Athelstan closer.

'Sir,' the Friar urged, 'it's in the best interests of you, my Lord of Gaunt and the King, to learn about certain conclusions I have reached which Sir John and I must share with you. Sir Oliver Ingham must also be there. No one else except, if you wish . . .' Athelstan gestured at Thibault's mercenary captain standing in the dark behind his master.

'I agree, Brother Athelstan. You wish to meet, and I appreciate it must be important.' Thibault gestured at the dangling corpses. 'What an unexpected end to a memorable day. Come, Brother. Sir John, Sir Oliver,' he called across the yard, 'let us return to the judgement table.'

They all went back into the sanctuary. Alfonso sheltered deep in the shadows whilst the rest, including Athelstan, took their seats along the table. The Friar stared around and shivered. The sanctuary was no longer a sacred place adorned with greenery, winter flowers, drapes, tapestries and cloths. All of these had been removed. Now it was a hall of the deepest shadow with torchlight dancing over the tombs of those long dead. Corpses entombed close to the high altar as a protection against the demons who came hunting after death.

'Will you be witnesses?' Athelstan whispered to himself.

'Brother Athelstan?' Thibault rapped on the table. 'Do begin, the hour is late.'

'But not too late for the truth.'

'Then let's hear it, Brother.'

'Very well. Master Thibault, you know, as do all of us, that the English Crown waged bitter war across Normandy and beyond. Slaughter, pillage and plunder rode alongside the armies of this kingdom. During the conflict, English lords went beyond the rules of war, if there are any such. Little or no chivalry was shown to the weak and the vulnerable.'

'I am, we are, not responsible for the sins of others.'

'Oh, but we are, Master Thibault, if justice is to be maintained and God's ordinances observed. To be blunt. Several, indeed a goodly number of English lords, revelled in the bloodshed and cruelty they inflicted.'

'Don't preach,' Ingham snarled. 'It was war.'

'Oh yes, the common, useless excuse used to explain away such hideous events. Anyway,' Athelstan continued, 'time passed. We English were forced to withdraw. However, careful note had been made of certain milords, guilty of grievous sins against the people of France, and these included members of the Via Crucis, a Free Company, a battlegroup led by you, Sir Oliver. Memories were kept alive, incidents recorded and, only recently, the Chambre Noir asserted itself. The French Crown despatched Dom Antoine to England with a list of lords to be extradited: they were to be tried in open court for their crimes against the people of France.'

'We know all this,' Ingham snarled, 'for the love of God . . .'

'Watch your tongue.' Cranston, who had sat silent, now leaned against the table. 'What my good friend here said is the truth. To a certain extent anyone who fought in Normandy is tainted. God knows I've prayed for forgiveness for any wrong I did.'

'We all know what happened,' Ingham replied haughtily.

'Oh, I am sure you know all about the massacres in France,' Athelstan declared. 'As well as the anger of the French and their growing determination for justice, but things took a strange turn. Master Thibault.' Athelstan glanced down the table. 'You knew full well that the French insistence that powerful manor lords be extradited to France to face trial for their crimes would never be accepted by the Commons or indeed the Kingdom as a whole.' Thibault didn't reply; he just sat, one hand covering the bottom half of his face. The sanctuary had now fallen deathly quiet. Athelstan repressed a shiver. This was now a chamber of darkness. Here the ghosts of those who'd died earlier that day still thronged, confused, fearful as they awaited the arrival of God's angels to bring them before the final judge of all.

'Brother,' Cranston murmured, 'we wait.'

'Yes, of course, my apologies. To cut to the quick, Master Thibault. You would never agree to an extradition treaty, so what you did was to secretly hire a cohort of professional assassins, the Oxford Clerks. You chose very wisely. You made no attempt to recruit rifflers from this city or any other English towns. No, the Oxford Clerks were a battlegroup who could cross all borders and shelter where they wished. You hired these to carry out sentence on certain manor lords such as Kyne and Blondin. You supplied them with all the information they needed to attack Malroad and Chafford Hundred. You are master of the Royal Chancery – such information is readily available to you. You could then, and you probably did, enter into a secret understanding with Dom Antoine and the Chambre Noir. There would be no extradition, but the French would witness justice being done, not in their own country but here, summary judgement followed by swift execution of the guilty.'

Thibault let his hands fall away from his face.

'And your evidence, Brother?'

'This, Master Thibault.' Athelstan took out the writ Cranston had given him in Cheapside. He undid this and pulled a candle spigot closer so he could read it aloud.

'What the bearer of this writ has done, he has done for the good of the Crown and the welfare of this kingdom. All officials of the realm together with all citizens of good and loyal heart must observe this.'

Athelstan paused and glanced up. He tapped the writ. 'Signed and sealed by you, Master Thibault. You can inspect this if you wish.'

Thibault just flicked his fingers, head down as he smiled to himself.

'What is this?' Ingham protested, all a bluster.

'Sir Oliver,' Athelstan retorted, 'keep silent because we now come to your involvement.'

'In God's name!'

'Oh yes, Sir Oliver, in God's name I will speak. The Oxford Clerks,' Athelstan continued, ignoring Ingham's bluster, 'carried out two assignments. I suspect there would have been more, but, as I have said, matters took a most surprising turn. Other murders occurred. Members of the Via Crucis which, I now know, were certainly not the work of the Oxford Clerks but you, Sir Oliver.'

Ingham made to rise, but Thibault lifted a hand and Alfonso, standing in the darkness, stepped forward, sword drawn. He laid

the blade ever so gently on Ingham's shoulder and the knight
retook his seat, flailing his hands and mumbling his protest.

'Sir Oliver, let me begin with your last murder, Sir Stephen
Crossley. According to the accepted story, Sir Stephen was
certainly not in the best of health. He dictated his last will and
testament to Matthew Hinden of Holy Sepulchre Church in
Farringdon Ward and afterwards hanged himself in the garden
of "The Golden Oriole". Now his last will and testament, if we
can call it that, reads as follows.' Athelstan took out what Hinden
had transcribed.

'I, Sir Stephen Crossley, Knight, from Battle in Sussex, do
dictate this full and final confession to Matthew Hinden, Parson
of the Church of the Holy Sepulchre in Farringdon Ward, on the
Fifth of January, the year of our Lord 1383. I am, or I was, a
member of the Via Crucis battlegroup. I now deeply regret and
express contrition for the pain and punishment I and my so-called
comrades inflicted on others. I hated that title for there was
nothing sacred or holy about us. We were plunderers, robbers
and rapists. I came to hate the church and our company, led by
Sir Oliver Ingham, a soul more mortally stained than my own.
I am now in my winter years. The gold I stole is mine, but the
others, now fearful for their immortal souls, wish to hand it over
to build a lazar house. Let them do it. I have a sore deep in my
bowels. I shit blood and I see the darkness deepening around
me. Nevertheless, I still have to listen to my so-called comrades
chatter about a lazar house, a hospice for those rotting creatures.
They have proved obdurate over this, and I could not tolerate
either them or the pain which wracks me. What wealth I have,
I needed for myself. I want to keep my treasure. They have ruled
differently. They believe they are the Way of the Cross, well, let
them experience what really happened. And so they have.
Despencer scourged to death. Gumblat crowned with thorns.
Henshaw crushed under the cross. Montague crucified. They have
now completed their Via Crucis and I will join them. They
have been punished for their sins. They died horrid deaths and
now it is my turn. I prefer oblivion to life. So, alea iacta, the
dice is thrown, and I am for the dark. Sir Stephen Crossley,
signed, sealed and dated under my own signet.

'But of course, you dictated this, not Crossley, who, by then, was probably hanging from a branch deep in the tavern gardens. In that document, you, Sir Oliver, expressed your own hatred of the church, priests and all aspects of religion. You're the one who loves to see churches burn, priests and others butchered, be it in Avranches or elsewhere. Indeed, I do believe those gossips who claim you crucified a French priest. You also fiercely resented the Free Company of the Via Crucis. I suggest you thought it highly amusing to give a company that name, a cohort of killers and despoilers.'

'What's this about Crossley?' Ingham shouted.

'Oh, everything. You killed Crossley as you did the others, sharing a flagon of wine but one that contained a heavy sleeping philtre. Of course, you made sure you didn't drink. Crossley did, spilling the wine on to his doublet before he sank into the deepest torpor. Once he had, you, under the cover of darkness, dragged his body and hung it from that branch. Poor Crossley would have strangled to death.'

'Nonsense,' Ingham shouted. 'Parson Hinden will testify that I did no wrong. Or are you saying he was party to this too?'

'Oh yes, I certainly am. Sir John, you have the priest, the person I told you to bring here?'

'As you asked, Brother. He's now under lock and key with Flaxwith guarding him.'

'Master Thibault?' Athelstan demanded.

'Bring him in, Brother.'

A short while later Flaxwith and one of his bailiffs dragged the Parson from the sacristy and into the sanctuary. Hinden was now so nervous he had to kneel on the floor before the judgement table, sobbing and pleading. Ingham could only stare in horror at what he knew would prove to be his death sentence. Athelstan held up his hand for silence. He went over and crouched by the Parson, whispering softly to him. He ignored the sharp comments of Master Thibault, who declared he would have the Parson flogged if he didn't compose himself. At last, Hinden calmed down. Athelstan rose and went back to his seat whilst Hinden wiped his tear-drenched cheeks and sat on the stool Alfonso brought for him.

'So,' Athelstan declared, 'Parson Hinden, tell us what happened.'

'I plead benefit of clergy. I demand to be tried in a church court.'

'You are not being tried, just questioned,' Athelstan replied. 'As I whispered to you. You can answer truthfully and be dismissed or your guard, Master Flaxwith, will take you down to the crypt. He and Captain Alfonso will adopt a different type of questioning which you will remember all the days of your life. Now look, Parson Hinden, I, or rather my parishioners, wandered your church. Not much for a parish in one of the more wealthy wards of this city. Your house, however, is truly comfortable, even luxurious. In a word, Parson Hinden, you love wealth. Let me be blunt; you can keep your gold and silver, your tapestries, turkey rugs and elmwood furniture provided you confess the truth. Do so now.'

'One evening,' the Parson scratched his face, wiping the sweat from his brow, 'I forget which one. I am too nervous.'

Athelstan watched him carefully. The Parson was undoubtedly terrified, but he was now beginning to realize that the truth was the safest path forward.

'We are waiting, priest,' Thibault rasped.

'I was summoned to "The Golden Oriole". He,' Hinden pointed at Ingham, 'dictated a confession under the name of Crossley. Of course, I found it strange, but, but he, uh . . .'

'Paid you very well, yes?'

'Yes, Sir John, very well indeed. I could see no harm. True,' he pleaded, 'I thought that would be it. However, once I'd signed and sealed the testament, Ingham took me out into the garden and showed me Crossley's corpse hanging from that branch.' The Parson shook his head in despair. 'I was shocked and frightened. I protested, but Ingham told me not to worry. Crossley had been very sick with a malignancy deep within him. Ingham claimed that's why he committed suicide, to escape the pain. The last will and testament were necessary to expedite certain matters, to help resolve a number of legal anomalies with respect to property and the likes.'

'What anomalies?' Athelstan demanded.

'I don't know. By then I was truly frightened, concerned by what I had seen and heard. He,' the Parson gestured at Ingham, 'he paid me very well. He claimed that I was now party to what had happened, so it was best if I adhered strictly to what he told me. I promised I would and then fled.'

'It's not true what he said,' Ingham shouted. 'Crossley hanged himself after dictating that last will and testament.'

'So, you are claiming Crossley is the author of that document, that final statement, not you?'

'Of course,' Ingham blustered. 'Crossley summoned the Parson to "The Golden Oriole". He dictated that final declaration and then hung himself.'

'So why should the good parson say you dictated the document? Eh?' Athelstan insisted. 'Had you met before? Were you bound to each other by some favour?'

'No, no,' Hinden gabbled, 'I have not seen Ingham or Crossley before this.'

'So, Sir Oliver, why should our good parson be lying? You can see he is highly nervous. I think he is telling the truth. Sir Oliver, you killed Crossley. You drugged him with opiate-laced wine then hanged him from that branch. Once you had, you dictated that so-called last will and testament.'

Ingham just shrugged, rubbing his face with his hands. He stared longingly at the door before sitting back in his chair.

'I know that document, that last will and testament, had nothing to do with Crossley,' Athelstan continued. 'Indeed, the document summarizes your character, your soul. Poor Crossley, his murder was one of a number you perpetrated, and this fictitious document actually provides your motive in committing the murders you are guilty of. You hate religion, Sir Oliver, in all its forms. You plundered Normandy and found a treasure trove which you loved beyond measure. You returned to this kingdom a wealthy man. You rose in prominence, but then the shock occurred. The surviving knights of the Via Crucis decided to make full reparation for the many crimes they had committed. They would devote the entire treasure to building a magnificent lazar house – a hospice for lepers. Whether they did or not is another matter. However, I can only imagine your silent, but raging, fury. You certainly risked losing your treasure, so all the bile of your rotten soul burst out. You would wreak revenge and, in doing so, protect your beloved gold.' Athelstan paused, staring down at the bills written in his own clear hand. 'Gold is your God, Ingham. You wanted the treasure from Avranches for yourself. You also lusted after the ancient gold dug up along the river bank. You have already started to steal it. Seething with anger at the Fisher of Men, you also hoped to settle grudges with him. You would annihilate the Fisher and his company then, as royal surveyor, have the freedom to ransack the entire site. That is why you hired those river pirates.'

'Nonsense!'

'No, no, Sir Oliver, murder is second nature to you, be it to seize the ancient gold or that from Avranches. As regards the latter, it was only a matter, quite a simple one, of removing your remaining comrades in the Via Crucis. You were given further motivation by the rumours trickling in. How certain manor lords, who had participated in the different chevauchees carried out across Normandy so many years ago, were being mysteriously executed. Worse still, you are a senior royal official. You learned about the French Embassy and Dom Antoine's demands for the extradition of certain manor lords to France. Of course, the Crown would never agree to that, would they, Master Thibault?'

Gaunt's henchman just stared bleakly back.

'Continue,' Cranston urged. 'Brother Athelstan, please continue.'

'I certainly shall, Sir John. You, Ingham, decided to act, to seize all the gold you could and eventually disappear across the Narrow Seas. You began murdering your comrades. Lord Hugh Despencer was your first victim. I suggest you joined him at the House of Lonely Souls along that lonely stretch of river bank. No one else would know about this, only you and poor Despencer, who would not be coming back. You arrived in the House of Lonely Souls with a wineskin. What better than a belly full of the best wine on a winter's day in such a bleak, horrid place. Of course, the wine was drugged with a sleeping potion. You had the wine and two goblets. You would

be full of talk about future plans with the hospice. Despencer
drank, but you certainly didn't. Oh, by the way, our Lord High
Coroner's men have questioned most of the apothecaries along
Cheapside, especially those close to "The Golden Oriole". And
yes, Sir Oliver, some of these certainly remember you
purchasing sleeping powder under the pretext of old war
wounds which kept you awake at night. Yes?' Athelstan paused
and stared at Ingham waiting for an answer, but the knight just
clenched his fists, lips moving as if talking to himself.
'Despencer was drugged,' Athelstan continued. 'He was then
stripped and lashed to death. Squire Gumblat was next. You
visited him in his chamber at "The Golden Oriole" on the
morning you were supposed to go down to the Guildhall. Now,
all of you knights are wine lovers. Once again, you offered
your victim a drugged goblet of wine. Gumblat drank heartily
and fell into a deep sleep. You then locked the door and carried
out hideous execution. Gumblat was bound fast, gagged and
that caltrop pushed on to his head. The shock alone would kill
him. You stirred the mystery a little further by saying you
knocked on his chamber door and he seemed hale and hearty.
Whether you did or not, or whether you actually saw him, is
neither here nor there. Gumblat was dead. Henshaw was next;
he was easy enough. Frightened by what was happening, he
went down to shelter in his so-called "nest" in the cellar. He
did not lock himself in or take out the key. You were watching
him, and you followed him down into the cellars. You slipped
through the shadows, lurking in some enclave, waiting for
Henshaw to pass as he prepared to leave the cellar. Eventually
he did and you knocked him senseless then abused the dying
man.' Athelstan paused to take a sip from his stoup of morning
ale. He gazed around the shadow-soaked sanctuary. 'Good,' he
whispered to himself. 'The ghosts do gather to witness justice
being done.'

'Brother Athelstan?'

'My apologies, Sir John. I was just reflecting on Henshaw's
murder. Is it a coincidence that the man who discovered
Gumblat's corpse also found Henshaw's? Isn't it another coincidence that both men were visited, or at least their chamber

was, by Sir Oliver Ingham? A further coincidence is that he
discovered their corpses. Oh, by the way, as I said, Henshaw
did not lock himself into the cellar. You did when you followed
him down. You killed that poor man, then you left, locking the
door behind you, taking the key. You keep it ready for the time
when the door would be forced. Questions would be asked.
How could a man be killed in a locked, sealed cellar? Once
the door was forced, you simply tossed the key you had hidden
away somewhere close to the fallen door. So Gumblat and
Henshaw were despatched into the dark. Crossley I have dealt
with: he was drugged and then hanged. He would have strangled
to death as he struggled to wake from his drunken revelry.'
Athelstan stared and pointed at Hinden still crouching on a
stool, sobbing noisily. 'Master Thibault, for the moment we
have finished with Parson Hinden.'

Thibault nodded, snapping his fingers at his captain of mercenaries and pointing at Hinden. 'Take him away,' the Master of
Secrets ordered in English then Spanish. 'I must talk to you,
Parson Hinden, about your house and your wealth, but that can
wait for now. Take him away. Let your men keep him secure.'

The captain seized Hinden and took him out through the
sacristy. Athelstan waited for him to return.

'As for Sir John Montague's death,' the Friar continued. 'He
knew, or he believed he did, what was happening. He'd reached
the conclusion that the killer was, in his own words, "one of
us". Now Montague, as I have said before, was keener than the
rest. He, like me, reached the conclusion that the killer was
within not without. When I inspected his corpse and went
through his personal belongings, I found a small scroll of parchment hidden in his sword scabbard. Perhaps it got there by
accident or did Montague hide it there deliberately? Anyway,
at first, I thought it wasn't much, mere scribblings. But then I
recalled Montague's love of studying the origin of names and
I began to wonder if what was written on that scrap of parchment was really some sort of code or cipher. You see, there was
a phrase "Meadow of the Cross", and another "Engas Ham". I
decided to despatch a copy of the scribblings to my learned
colleague, Brother Simon, in our Mother House at Blackfriars.

Simon is also a *peritus*, an authority on the origin of names. He soon discerned that the phrases written on that scrap of parchment were in fact the origin of two names. Crossley was the meadow of the cross. Ingham came from "Engas Ham", which is Engas village or hamlet.'

'And?' Thibault demanded.

'And, Master Thibault, I can show you the original. I would do so in a formal indictment. However, beside Engas Ham, Montague had written a quotation from a well-known Latin poet. At first, I thought it was a mere scrawl, almost indecipherable, but Brother Simon also unpicked this, so it reads: "Ille amat occidere amicos, Engas Ham" or Ingham who loves to kill his friends.'

'God have mercy on poor Montague.'

'Amen to that, Sir John,' Athelstan replied. 'The dead do take an interest in the living. I wonder if poor Montague helped me find that scrap of parchment. Sir Oliver, you have been indicted not only by me but also by a member of your own company. Master Thibault, what I describe here is the truth. If you want, I could draw up a bill, "a billa vera" – a true indictment accusing Sir Oliver Ingham of a litany of horrid crimes for which he should pay with his life. I shall place that before the justiciars then let God and the Court decide.'

'Oh sweet Lord,' Ingham cried, 'oh Lord, have mercy on me.' He clutched his chest. 'Brother Athelstan, for the love of God, please help me.' Ingham, still seated, pushed himself away from the table. 'I cannot breathe,' he gasped. 'Brother Athelstan, please.'

The Friar hurried around the table on to the dais. Sir John and Thibault let him pass. Ingham had turned in his chair, still clutching his chest, head down, gasping and spluttering. Athelstan crouched before him. Ingham lifted his head and Athelstan realized he had made a hideous mistake. No injury, no pain. Ingham's eyes were full of hate, mouth all flecked with a frothy spittle.

'You bastard priest! You interfering little shit!' Ingham spat the words out as he seized Athelstan by the front of his robe, drawing him closer as he searched for the dagger beneath his

cloak. Ingham lurched to his feet, still clutching the Friar. He
lifted the dagger he'd concealed. Behind him Athelstan heard
Cranston cursing as he tried to draw his sword from the war belt
he had looped over the post of his chair. Athelstan struggled to
get away from Ingham, shouting prayers as he tried to break free.
Then Ingham abruptly lurched forwards, arms extended. He then
swayed backwards and forwards as a second crossbow bolt shat-
tered the back of his head. He let go of the Friar and slumped
to his knees, sprawling forwards on the floor in a shower of
blood, bone and brain.

Cranston helped Athelstan to his feet. For a while the Friar
stood leaning against the table as he stared at the smiling Alfonso,
his saviour. The mercenary captain lifted his small arbalest in
salute. Athelstan responded with a blessing before Cranston
helped him back to his chair. For a while all was confusion as
Ingham's corpse was dragged from the dais to lie in an ever-
widening pool of blood on the sanctuary floor. Flaxwith and his
bailiffs were quickly summoned. They stripped the corpse.
Thibault shouted at them to pile all the dead man's possessions
in a heap, saying that Flaxwith and Alfonso could share what
they found between themselves. Flaxwith nodded and dragged
the corpse by its ankles along the ground into the sacristy where
he was joined by both the Spanish mercenaries and his own
cohort, eager to share the spoils.

Cranston tried to soothe Athelstan, but the Friar just shook his
head, one hand clutching the arm of his chair, the other a set of
ave beads. For a while he prayed. The business in the sacristy
was finished and both the mercenaries and Flaxwith's bailiffs left
to take up their posts at every door leading into the sanctuary.
At last Athelstan crossed himself, took a deep breath and smiled
at Cranston sitting beside him.

'Are you well, Little Friar? I am so sorry.' Cranston shook his
head to hide the tears welling in his eyes. 'I never thought,' he
murmured, 'I never thought that would happen until it was almost
too late.'

'Sir John,' Athelstan patted the Coroner's tear-stained cheek,
'neither did I, but I suppose you cannot change your habits. For
a few heartbeats, Ingham was no longer a true killer but a sick

man in deep distress. I believed him and, for a mistake like that, I nearly lost my life.'

Both men fell silent as Thibault approached, dragging a chair to sit opposite both coroner and friar. For once, Thibault had lost that cynical smile. He stared long and hard at the Friar then extended his hand for Athelstan to grasp. The Friar did so. Thibault murmured his regrets at what had happened. He then opened his belt wallet and took out three gold coins, which he pressed into Athelstan's hands.

'A small gift,' the Master of Secrets murmured, 'to tide you and your parish over until the twelfth day of this month when you, Sir John, and you, Brother Athelstan, are to be received by the King in his Royal Palace of Sheen. We owe you a great debt. Rest assured; it will be paid.'

Thibault paused as Alfonso brought across a tray and three goblets, which the mercenary filled from a jug of the best Bordeaux. Athelstan insisted that Alfonso join them, and the Spaniard hurried off into the sacristy. He returned with a goblet, which Athelstan insisted on filling. The Friar then lifted his own and toasted the mercenary.

'God give you good cheer, my friend.' The Friar smiled. 'As I do my profound thanks.'

They all sat and drank for a while discussing Ingham's death and why he had done what he had. Alfonso just sat with a smile on his face and Athelstan remembered that Thibault's henchman knew very little English.

'You did well,' the Friar declared, pointing at Alfonso. 'He would have killed me but for you.'

'He saw you as the Church,' Cranston declared, 'and he wished to inflict vengeance, revenge. He also, yes, Master Thibault, wanted a much swifter death?'

'He certainly did,' Thibault replied. 'Ingham would have been lodged in the Tower where he would be closely questioned, indeed most cruelly questioned, on his riches and where they were hidden. A man of wealth and I look forward to seizing it.' Thibault licked his lips as if savouring some sumptuous meal. 'Oh yes, the clink of coin in a coffer is a most delightful one and I will have my coffers ready. Anyway, once we'd finished with him in the Tower, Ingham would have been dragged on a hurdle to Newgate. He would be half hanged then his body hacked open, his heart, entrails and testicles plucked up and fed to the scaffold dogs. Ah well,' Thibault smirked, 'what a pity that will now never happen. So, to return to business. Dom Antoine can go back to Paris all placated and soothed. Yes, Brother Athelstan, you were correct, I hired the Oxford Clerks and, in doing so, helped the cause for peace between our two kingdoms. Criminals, men who inflicted horrors on the innocent, have been punished. Some small solace for our new-found allies. Anyway,' Thibault rose to his feet, 'Brother Athelstan, Sir John, I do look forward to meeting you at Sheen. Till then, my friends.' Spinning on his heel with Alfonso trailing behind, Thibault left the sanctuary.

Cranston and Athelstan sat with their backs to the door, waiting until the sound of footsteps faded. In the silence Cranston promptly refilled the goblets and brought two of the tall capped braziers closer to them.

'You'll feel cold,' the Coroner soothed, 'the shock of battle, of near death, will cause that. I recommend my favourite hospice, "The Lamb of God".'

'Yes, we should leave,' Athelstan murmured.

'Only when your composure has returned.' Cranston paused at a rap on the door and Flaxwith came in. 'What is it, my friend?'

'Sir John, I thought I should inform you and Brother Athelstan. Master Thibault has decreed that Ingham's corpse, completely naked, be exhibited on the steps of St Paul's along with those of the Children of Babylon. Sir John, the approaches to the cathedral are like some battlefield, at least thirteen naked cadavers. As Coroner of the City, you may have a view on that?'

'Yes, yes, I certainly do. Master Thibault is simply using those corpses to frighten his enemies both in the City and the Court. A powerful proclamation of what happens to those who challenge his will.' Cranston tapped the table. 'Master Flaxwith, let Thibault have his way. If I remember the City Ordinance correctly, the corpses of traitors and other such malefactors can be exhibited